KU-753-388

PRAISE FOR THE DCI RYAN MYSTERIES

What newspapers say

"She keeps company with the best mystery writers" – *The Times*

"LJ Ross is the queen of Kindle" – *Sunday Telegraph*

"Holy Island is a blockbuster" – *Daily Express*

"A literary phenomenon" – *Evening Chronicle*

"A pacey, enthralling read" – *Independent*

What readers say

"I couldn't put it down. I think the full series will
cause a divorce, but it will be worth it."

"I gave this book 5 stars because there's no option for 100."

"Thank you, LJ Ross, for the best two hours of my life."

"This book has more twists than a demented corkscrew."

"Another masterpiece in the series. The DCI Ryan
mysteries are superb, with very realistic characters
and wonderful plots. They are a joy to read!"

9510000355108

OTHER BOOKS BY LJ ROSS

THE DCI RYAN MYSTERIES IN ORDER:

1. *Holy Island*
2. *Sycamore Gap*
3. *Heavenfield*
4. *Angel*
5. *High Force*
6. *Cragside*
7. *Dark Skies*
8. *Seven Bridges*
9. *The Hermitage*
10. *Longstone*
11. *The Infirmary (Prequel)*
12. *The Moor*
13. *Penshaw*
14. *Borderlands*
15. *Ryan's Christmas*

THE ALEXANDER GREGORY THRILLERS IN ORDER:

1. *Impostor*
2. *Hysteria*
3. *Bedlam*

CRAGSIDE

A DCI RYAN MYSTERY

CRAGSIDE

A DCI RYAN MYSTERY

LJ ROSS

Copyright © LJ Ross 2020

The right of LJ Ross to be identified as the author
of this work has been asserted in accordance with
the Copyright, Designs and Patents Act 1988.

All rights reserved. No part of this publication may be
reproduced, stored in or transmitted into any retrieval
system, in any form, or by any means (electronic, mechanical,
photocopying, recording or otherwise) without the prior
written permission of the publisher. Any person who does
any unauthorised act in relation to this publication may be
liable to criminal prosecution and civil claims for damages.

This is a work of fiction. Names, characters, businesses,
places, events and incidents are either the products
of the author's imagination or used in a fictitious
manner. Any resemblance to actual persons, living
or dead, or actual events is purely coincidental.

ISBN: 978-1-912310-06-7

First published in 2017 by LJ Ross

This edition published in July 2020 by Dark Skies Publishing

Author photo by Gareth Iwan Jones

Cover layout by Stuart Bache

Cover artwork and map by Andrew Davidson

Typeset by Riverside Publishing Solutions Limited

Printed and bound by CPI Goup (UK) Limited

"*The villainy you teach me I will execute,*
And it shall go hard but I will better the instruction."

—William Shakespeare

"*Everyone is a moon, and has a dark side*
which he never shows to anybody."

—Mark Twain

PROLOGUE

Summer, 1975

Joe Ramshaw had no idea he would be dead within the hour.

Morning had broken much like any other, crisp and cool as summer turned steadily into autumn. Salty mist swept in from the North Sea and curled through the rows of identical terraced houses stacked against the hillside leading from the city to the water's edge, their red bricks blackened by soot and grime. Gulls circled high in the steely grey clouds overhead, letting out their shrill cries before swooping down toward the river that ran like an artery through the city, a life force to the thousands of workers who moved inexorably toward the shipyard.

Joe kissed his wife at the front door of their two-up, two-down before tugging on his cap and walking purposefully toward the docks. The little 'uns scuffed along beside him, their legs struggling to keep up with his longer strides and their bell-bottomed jeans trailing against the dusty pavement.

"Da?"

He cast his eye over the boy.

"When'll the ship be finished, Da? Can I come and see her launch?"

Joe stuck his hand in the pocket of his thick coat and felt around for one of the cigarettes he'd rolled earlier.

"It'll be a few months yet, lad."

"But can I come and see?"

"Me too, Da! I want to come too!"

Joe took a long drag of his cigarette and turned to his daughter, whose pigtails flapped around a small face filled with righteous indignation. The corners of his eyes crinkled in amusement and he reached out to ruffle the top of her head.

"Aye, you can both come when *The Valiant*'s ready. Bring your Ma, n'all."

He imagined his wife standing proudly beside him with roses in her cheeks, as beautiful as the first time she'd strolled past the slipway. God only knew why she'd married him but he'd done his best to make sure she never regretted it. He wasn't a rich man and never would be but he'd always put food on the table and a roof over their heads.

Joe walked on, the children squabbling good-naturedly while he whistled beneath his breath in time to the sharp *click* of his work boots against the cobblestones. They fell into step with crowds of other working men who walked in

2

the same direction, chatting about the match the previous Saturday and the beer they would enjoy at the end of the day.

Suddenly, there she was.

They rounded a corner and the ship rose before them, majestic against the skyline. She wasn't finished but her lines were elegant and clean, dwarfing the people and houses so they appeared little more than dolls in miniature.

Joe cast his gaze upward and felt his throat clog with pride.

He'd built that.

Along with hundreds of others, his plain, scarred hands had built the mountain of carved steel towering above them and it was glorious.

He paused to crush the end of his cigarette underfoot, allowing himself a moment to wave off the children who followed him like small shadows.

"Aye, well, best be getting on," he said, tugging his cap again.

"Will you be home for tea, Da?"

He reached across to flick the girl's nose.

"Same as every night. Run along now." He placed a hand on his son's shoulder and knuckled his cheek in an affectionate gesture. "Mind you get straight to school, lad. No playing by the quays, that's no way to get ahead."

The boy swept his eyes downward and a guilty flush crept over his freckled face but he nodded.

"Off with you, then."

Joe stood with his hands thrust inside the pockets of his coarse work trousers and watched them trundle toward the primary school half a mile further along the quayside. The boy was on the cusp of adolescence, his puppyish face already starting to toughen into the lines of manhood. As for the girl, she was all big eyes and big heart.

He was a lucky man.

Smiling, he turned into the arched entranceway to the shipyard and a few minutes later he was climbing down a ladder toward the bowels of the unfinished ship. The machinery control room was stuffy despite its size and already laden with welders preparing to start work. The men chattered among themselves and, now and then, there was a burst of uproarious laughter.

"Mornin', Joe! Didn't see you down at *The Anchor* last night."

Joe shook his head and watched his friend rummage around his pockets for a cigarette.

"When you've a wife like mine waiting for you, there's no need for a skinful before bed," he said.

The welder struck a match, letting out a bawdy laugh which promptly turned to confusion as his cigarette burned down to the filter tip before he'd had a chance to draw on it.

"Bloody cheap rolls," he muttered and started to light another one.

Joe frowned at the cigarette, watching the little orange glow fizzing down to the tip again.

All at once, it came to him.

Too much oxygen in the air.

He spun around to the other men in the room who were kitted out and ready to strike the first electric arc on their welding rods. Eyes wide and filled with horror, he let out a shout of warning and ran forward but he was already too late.

The children had almost reached the school gates when a fireball exploded into the sky, scattering men and steel against the docks and into the river. Flames snapped at the heels of the welders who tried to clamber and claw their way out the single escape hatch. Thick black smoke filled their lungs, choking the life from their bodies so they remained trapped forever inside the steel walls of *The Valiant*.

CHAPTER 1

Saturday 13th August 2016

Forty-one years later

"That's it—the wedding's off!"

Detective Chief Inspector Maxwell Finley-Ryan stood with his feet planted and his arms folded mutinously across his chest as he surveyed himself in the bedroom mirror. The reflection staring back at him was of a tall man decked out in a navy three-piece Victorian-era suit bearing the label of a local fancy dress outfitter, complete with burgundy silk cravat and matching pocket square. His black hair had been slicked back with a generous dollop of gel and a top hat was balanced precariously on his head.

There came a low chuckle from somewhere behind him, then a pair of slim arms wrapped around his waist and the author of his present misfortune peeped over his shoulder.

"I don't know what you're making such a fuss about," his fiancée said. "You look very handsome. Besides, it's only for a few hours and you promised you would come."

"You caught me at a vulnerable moment," Ryan muttered, thinking back to a very memorable evening the week before.

"I'm sure I don't know what you mean…" Doctor Anna Taylor brushed an invisible speck of dust from his sleeve, then grabbed him by the lapels. "Look, we've been staying on the estate for almost four months, it would be rude not to go to the party."

Following the actions of a murderous madman known as 'the Hacker' the previous spring, Anna's riverside cottage in Durham was now a burnt-out shell and Ryan's apartment was up for sale after a deep clean and extensive redecoration. Unfortunately, no amount of industrial chemicals could remove the lingering trace of violent death. It stood empty while the couple relocated to a long-term holiday cottage for the remainder of the summer within the estate grounds of Cragside house, on the outskirts of the Northumberland National Park. The tranquil setting offered a perfect base where they could recuperate, allowing Anna to complete her latest historical textbook on *Viking Northumberland* before the start of a new academic term, while Ryan oversaw the tying up of numerous loose ends following the Hacker's demise. Over the last four months, they'd become immersed in life on the estate and when a gilded invitation to a murder-mystery-themed party had come through the letterbox, it was clear they had finally been accepted into the fold of Cragside's select community.

"It's the staff summer party," Anna continued. "It's very kind of them to invite us."

"Food, drink and a few laughs is one thing," Ryan said. "Wearing this ridiculous get-up to a murder mystery night is another thing entirely. I have a reputation to uphold."

Anna laughed.

"If you're worried I'll tell Phillips about your little foray into period costume—"

"You wouldn't dare!" Ryan paled as he thought of his sergeant and the banter that would spread like wildfire through the hallways of the Northumbria Criminal Investigation Department once the word got out.

"You should be more worried that I'll make you wear something similar at our wedding..." Anna gave him a guileless smile and walked her fingers up his back. "I think you'd look rather fetching. There's another couple of weeks before the big day, still plenty of time to make a few wardrobe changes."

Ryan let out a sound halfway between a growl and a whimper but he admired the way she'd neatly boxed him into a corner. He turned to look down into her mischievous face.

"You're a foxy woman," he murmured, casually flicking the rim of his hat so he could dip his head to hers for a thorough kiss.

Cragside house stood resplendent against the summer sky, built like a gothic fairy-tale castle against a craggy hillside surrounded by acres of lush woodland. The air was fragrant and heavy as Ryan and Anna made their way along the footpath from their rental cottage toward the main house and a light breeze stirred the avenue of pine trees, providing a welcome balm to their overheated skin. The usual influx of tourists had departed hours ago and the estate was deserted, aside from the people who stayed on to celebrate another year as custodians of a slice of Northumbrian history. Ryan glanced across to where Anna walked beside him, long skirts rustling against the ground, dark hair swept back from her face. He tucked her hand inside his arm, thinking that he might as well embrace his old-world character for the evening.

"You look beautiful," he said quietly. "But doesn't it hurt?"

He lifted a hand vaguely toward the corseted waistline of her pale blue dress.

"Like hell," she said. "I've already decided to take this contraption off before dinner. Nothing's going to stop *me* enjoying a four-course meal."

He grinned and moments later they emerged from the forest canopy, finding themselves at the foot of the hillside looking up at a dramatic house built on various levels into the rock face. Turrets and towers, arches and mock-Tudor beams vied for attention with Rhenish gables and gardens that were any landscape architect's dream.

Ryan let out a slow, appreciative whistle.

"Remind me of the story behind this place?"

Anna gave him a pained look, lamenting the fact he would never share her passion for local history however much she tried to convert him. Then again, she had no desire to solve grisly murders for a living, so it was horses for courses, she supposed.

"The house belonged to William Armstrong, who was one of the world's leading industrialists back in the nineteenth century; he built ships, arms, all kinds of innovative machinery. You might say he built most of Newcastle city centre too."

She continued with her potted history as they slowly made their way up the incline leading to the main entrance.

"He was an inventor, really. Cragside was the first house in the world to be lit by electric bulbs, powered by hydroelectricity using water from the lakes on his estate. It's privately owned by the Gilbert family now but they open it to the public most days."

Ryan frowned, trying to remember if he'd met Lionel and Cassandra Gilbert.

"They've been on holiday," Anna said, deciding to help him out. "They flew back from Barbados last week to throw their annual staff party, as a 'thank you' to everyone who keeps the place ticking over while they're gallivanting around the world."

Ryan grunted.

"How'd they make their millions?"

"No idea," Anna replied. "They're both getting on a bit, though. He's in his eighties and she's somewhere around seventy."

"Children?"

"No. Yes," Anna corrected. "Cassandra has two children from her first marriage but neither of them live on the estate."

Conversation died as they reached the grand portico leading into the house and other figures dressed in lacy finery began to materialise, dispelling the whimsical notion that they had the place to themselves.

"Showtime," Ryan pronounced.

Balmy rays of early evening sunshine trailed across the countryside and turned the windows of Cragside house into a glistening beacon for miles around but when Anna and Ryan stepped inside its thick stone walls, they were engulfed by Victorian décor. There was an abundance of dark panelled wood and fussy wallpaper bearing elaborate Chinese silk prints. Almost every mullioned window boasted a spectacular view but the interior remained oppressively dim, illuminated only by a small number of antiquated lamps dating back over a hundred years. They happened to know that the house was connected to the National Grid but it was a point of conservation that it continued to be powered by hydroelectricity, as it had been in the old days. Fortunately, the atmospheric lighting provided the perfect backdrop for a murder mystery party.

The mistress of the house awaited them inside the hallway, dressed in a long navy-blue taffeta dress. Her grey hair had been arranged in a nest of curls above a fine-boned face bearing a deep tan leftover from a summer spent in the Caribbean. Fat pearls hung from her ears and a matching triple-strand was draped around her neck.

"Welcome!" Cassandra Gilbert greeted them warmly and extended a bejewelled hand. "Mr and Mrs Ryan, isn't it?"

She might have been dressed for Ascot but they were delighted to find that Cassandra Gilbert's voice was pure, unadulterated Geordie. The lilting, unpretentious sound of it made them feel instantly at home despite the grandeur of their surroundings.

"Not yet," Anna smiled. "But we're getting married in a couple of weeks. I'm Anna."

"And you must be Maxwell," Cassandra deduced, casting her discerning eye over the tall man with raven black hair and cool grey eyes.

"Ryan is fine," he said.

"I'm so pleased you could come. I'm sorry we haven't had an opportunity to meet in person before now but I understand you're renting one of our cottages for the summer?"

"We're enjoying it very much," Anna said. "You have a beautiful home, Mrs Gilbert."

"Cassandra. Thank you, dear." She turned to Ryan again with open curiosity. "They tell me you're a detective? I seem to recognise you."

Here it comes, he thought.

"Yes, I'm based out of Northumbria CID."

"Of course!" Cassandra raised a delicate hand to her mouth and her eyes widened dramatically. "All that business with the serial killer…"

"Depends which one you mean," he said lightly. "There have been quite a few, over the years."

"Oh, I mean the one last April, that awful man who broke out of prison and killed that poor young girl—"

Sensing their unease, Cassandra broke off and gave them an apologetic smile.

"Well, if anybody can guess the murderer in tonight's game, it will be you," she said. "I'm so sorry my husband won't be joining us this evening but he's come down with a touch of flu. Probably the long-haul flight, last week," she said, tutting. "It's the air-conditioning on the plane, I'm sure of it."

"Sorry to hear that," Anna said. "I hope he recovers soon."

"Thank you. Now, go on upstairs and help yourself to champagne. Tonight, we're celebrating."

As Cassandra turned to greet some new arrivals, Anna and Ryan followed a series of cardboard placards directing them to the mezzanine level of the house, halfway between the first and second floors. Its layout reminded Ryan of a rabbit warren: higgledy-piggledy, with only a few large reception rooms offset by various smaller interconnecting anterooms, countless staircases and corridors, as well as an old lift shaft currently not in use.

Anna lifted her skirts and hauled them up the main flight of wide oak stairs until they reached a long gallery on the mezzanine level where the party was already well underway. Ryan swept an assessing eye over the crowd and estimated around thirty or forty people had turned out, most of them household or ground staff, conservationists and elderly volunteers working at the tea rooms or as tour guides on days when the house was open to the public.

"Anna, Ryan, glad you could come!"

They turned to greet a man in his mid-fifties who was dressed in a flamboyant green velvet smoking jacket with matching cap and pinstripe trousers. He was brandishing fluted glasses of champagne in his outstretched hands.

"Thanks, Dave."

The conservation manager raised his bushy grey eyebrows.

"Tonight, I am Lord Quibble of Newcastle," he corrected them with exaggerated hauteur. When he wriggled an enormous false moustache, Ryan realised the man was actually enjoying himself.

It took all sorts.

"You should be in your element," Dave continued, scooping up another champagne flute from a passing tray. "Wouldn't it be funny if you guessed the murderer wrong? No hope for the rest of us, eh? Mysteries are your forte!"

He bellowed out a hearty laugh and Ryan cast around for something polite to say but was forestalled by Anna's smooth interruption.

"He's been so excited about the party, haven't you, darling?"

She turned to him with innocent brown eyes and he could happily have throttled her.

"Mmm." Ryan gave her a toothy smile before delivering his coup de grâce. "Not as much as you, *darling*. I know you've been dying to find out about the plans for renovating Armstrong's old electrical room."

He took a fiendish delight in her shocked expression and wriggled his own eyebrows.

"Well, you've come to the right place!" Dave exclaimed, blissfully unaware of any nuance in the conversation. "I can tell you all about the electrics. Why don't I give you a quick tour?"

In short order, Anna found herself being led off in the direction of one of the smaller wings of the house by a velvet-clad enthusiast. Ryan had no time to congratulate himself when, scarcely thirty seconds after her departure, a gaggle of female staff took their chance to strike before he had time to deploy any evasive manoeuvres.

"Hello, dear!"

"Looking *so* handsome this evening—"

"Just like Sherlock Holmes!" came the inevitable commentary.

"Now, girls, don't embarrass the poor man." A woman of around seventy he recognised as Maggie, the housekeeper, rescued him with the natural ease of lifelong experience. "Where's your lovely fiancée, Ryan?"

"Ah, she's looking at the renovations," he replied and thought belatedly that the prospect of being bored to tears by a historical aficionado was looking more attractive by the minute.

"Oh, Maggie, here comes your fancy-man!" one of the women said in a stage whisper.

Victor Swann was in his late seventies but could easily pass for twenty years younger, with a shock of white-grey hair brushed back from a tanned face sporting a designer beard and a pair of bright blue eyes framed by deep laughter lines. Clearly, he was in demand as the estate's resident lothario, which Ryan could only admire.

"Good evening, ladies!" Victor doffed his hat and executed a small bow. "May I say, you all look ravishing."

There ensued a maelstrom of giggles and Ryan gulped his drink, searching the room for any sign of an emergency exit.

Two hours crawled by, during which time Ryan was subjected to a lengthy performance of *The Mysterious Case of the Disappearing Duchess* by a troupe of amateur actors who approached their task in much the same way as a Christmas pantomime at the London Palladium. Amid cries of "Send 'im down!", Ryan found himself enlisted to enact the part of the murdered duchess's wayward lover. After it was all over, Ryan slumped back in his chair at the long dining table and prayed for a real murder to take him away from it all. He checked his mobile phone again but there was no message from the Control Room.

So much for his so-called friends, who had abandoned him in his hour of need.

Returning the phone to the inner pocket of his blazer, Ryan made a leisurely observation of his surroundings. The drawing room was the largest reception room in the house and had originally been built for a royal visit, over a hundred years earlier. The style was opulent, with dark red damask walls and plaster panels on the coved ceiling leading up to a long skylight through which the setting sun had blazed during dinner. Now that darkness had fallen, the room was an odd mixture of shadows, relieved only by a central chandelier and a few scattered side lamps, all of which shone a weak, low-wattage glow. The air smelled of musty furniture and it had grown chilly since there was no roaring fire set beneath the vast chimneypiece dominating the southern wall.

At the head of the table, Cassandra Gilbert was engaged in polite conversation with a small group of staff and, catching his eye, she smiled and raised her glass.

Ryan raised his glass in return.

Small groups of staff huddled together, according to their respective roles on the estate. The horticultural staff occupied a position near the door, whereas the older volunteers were seated comfortably in the mid-section of the long dining table. Conservation staff were the most animated and chattered happily about scientific advances in their respective fields from a seating area at one end of the room. The housekeeper stood chatting to Victor, who Ryan knew to be Lionel Gilbert's personal valet.

There was a polished grand piano sitting lonely in the corner and Ryan was considering tinkling the ivories when he spotted Anna weaving through the crowd in his direction. He smiled at the sight of her, as much at home in elegant silks as she was in scuffed jeans and walking boots.

"Nearly over," she murmured, slipping into the chair beside him. "A few people have already made a run for it. We can head off any time you like."

They were halfway out of their seats when a thin, balding man wearing by far the most glamorous outfit they'd seen all evening joined them. Martin Henderson was the new estate manager, charged with overseeing the smooth running of Cragside's agricultural interests, which were substantial. Soon after he'd arrived in his electric BMW sports car, Henderson had issued a string of demands that had not endeared him to his colleagues. His choice of dress this evening was calculated to reinforce his status and, when Ryan enquired politely as to the red fur cloak and regal-looking sash draped across the man's chest, he was informed that the ensemble had been modelled on Edward VII's coronation robes.

"I had the jacket hand-made," Henderson boasted. "And the fur is real, too. None of that tree-hugging faux stuff." He belched and reached across the table for a decanter of wine to top up his glass. "Well, who d' you think dunnit?"

Henderson addressed his question to Ryan, innate misogyny leading him to assume Anna had no thoughts on the matter.

"It's always the butler," Ryan replied breezily, rising in one fluid movement and holding out a hand to help Anna from her chair. "You'll have to excuse us, Martin, it's been a long day and we must be getting back."

They had almost made their escape when the room was plunged into darkness.

CHAPTER 2

Muffled shrieks and drunken guffaws about the ghost of a murdered duchess echoed around the room. People stumbled into one another, bumping into occasional furniture in their haste to find an alternative light source. Taking matters into his own hands, Ryan made his way to the door using his phone as a torch, intending to feel around the wall for a light switch, and barrelled into somebody.

"Sorry," he muttered.

He found the switch and tried it a few times, to no avail.

His eyes adjusted to the darkness and he realised it was the head gardener he had bumped into. She was standing beside him leaning against a marble-topped side table, breathing a bit unsteadily. Her eyes were wide and frightened in the light of his phone torch and Ryan struggled to remember her name—*Charlotte?*—but guessed she was somewhere around fifty, with short blonde hair topped with a long peacock-feathered fascinator.

"Are you alright?"

"I'll be fine. I just had a bit of a fright," she explained. "I hate dark spaces. I think I might have dropped a glass of wine on the carpet—"

Ryan looked around the floor and picked up the errant glass, setting it back on the table next to a large porcelain lamp.

"They'll clean up the spillage later. Here, sit down on this chair," he offered, drawing her down into one of the antique easy chairs set back against the wall.

"Thank you," she said, a bit embarrassed. "I don't know what came over me."

"It's been a long night," Ryan said, with feeling.

When he was satisfied that the woman was comfortable, he turned back to the room at large and raised his voice above the din.

"Alright, listen up!"

It took a few seconds but eventually its occupants fell silent.

"Does anybody know where to find the fuse box?"

He waited to hear from Dave, the self-confessed electrical expert, but was surprised to find it was the valet, Victor Swann, who made his way forward.

"I know where it is. Down on the ground floor next to the kitchen, near the main entrance."

"I'll come with you," Ryan offered but Victor shook his head.

"No, you stay here and look after my Maggie!" He looked over his shoulder to where she stood beside a group of other staff, his lascivious wink made sinister by the light of Ryan's phone torch.

"Here, take this," he started to hand it over but Victor produced a nifty LED torch from his trouser pocket and flicked it on.

"Always come prepared."

He stepped through the doorway into the murky hallway beyond and threw a final, prophetic request over his shoulder.

"If I'm not back in five minutes, send a search party!"

In the end, Ryan gave him ten minutes. Leaving the remaining crowd of revellers, he made his way through the long, silent corridors of the old house in search of Victor. Although he was not prone to an overactive imagination, it was impossible not to experience a distinct sense of foreboding. Floorboards creaked underfoot as he made swiftly for the main staircase at the end of the gallery and painted images of long-dead aristocrats stared down at him from shadowy portraits. The darkness was complete; thick and black with no friendly moon to guide the way, only the single beam of his phone torch flickering against the walls.

Reaching the staircase, he ran lightly down to the ground floor and emerged into the entrance hallway. There was still no sign of another living person but wind whistled through gaps in the old oak doors, sending them creaking on their hinges.

"Victor?"

Ryan's voice reverberated around the walls and he paused at the foot of the stairs, listening for a response.

There was none.

He struggled to recall a map of the house in his mind's eye, then spotted a rack of guide books sitting on one of the hallway tables. Gratefully, he snatched one up and studied a diagram of the house printed on the inside cover, then headed for a nearby servants' corridor.

He found the fuse box easily enough and fiddled with a few switches until the small bulbs lining the dank corridor beside the kitchen blinked on again. A cheer sounded from upstairs and a smile played around his lips before his face fell once again into focused lines. He shed his playful persona for the evening and was, once again, all cop.

The hairs on the back of Ryan's neck prickled as he walked slowly through the maze of rooms, scanning every corner.

There was still no sign of Victor.

Stepping inside the mammoth kitchen, his polished dress shoes clicked against a stone floor that had been worn smooth by the tread of countless feet. The windows were darkened by the night sky and against the glow of the lamplight he saw his own reflection from every angle; a man whose skin was drawn tightly across the hard planes of his face, eyes darkened to a stormy grey as he stalked around the room. A vintage clock on the wall chimed the quarter hour, its tinny sound magnified by the silence surrounding it.

Quarter-past eleven.

Swinging around again, Ryan spotted a narrow staircase leading down to the basement and he started down into the cellar, setting aside any feelings of natural self-preservation. Before he'd reached the third step, he faltered and was forced to throw a hand out to save himself from a nasty fall.

His heart slammed against his chest in one hard motion as visions of broken legs—or worse—flooded his mind.

"Close shave," he muttered.

Moving more cautiously, Ryan shivered as he entered one of the oldest parts of the house. The basement was another network of small spaces, all decked out for tourists with realistic models of raw meats in the game larder and lifelike waxwork mannequins propped against the wall in the scullery, their eyes staring at him unseeingly. His stomach quivered but Ryan moved past them, spotting the old lift shaft that had once been operational and the information boards explaining its mechanism, now rusting with age.

Eventually, he let out a long sigh and was about to retrace his steps when he spotted a back door leading to a courtyard area. Through its dusty panes, he could see a solar-powered light shining an eerie greenish-white glow onto what appeared to be a heap of old clothes. Narrowing his eyes, Ryan tugged open the door and felt a cold rush of air against his face as he stepped outside.

It wasn't old clothes.

Victor lay crumpled at the bottom of a flight of hard stone steps, his body twisted and broken. His hat had rolled a few feet away to reveal a skull crushed like an eggshell, blood and brain matter spattered against the gravel beside him.

Ryan stopped several feet away from Victor's body and wished fervently for more light. He risked contaminating the scene to check for a pulse but he knew death when he saw it. There was a deep gash on the man's temple and blood seeped in a slow trickle across his chalky face, pooling in the hollows of his eyes and mouth. That was the most likely cause of death, Ryan thought, but it could equally have been a break in the neck bone which jutted against Victor's skin at a sickly, unnatural angle. Ryan used his phone again, this time to take some photographs of the scene in the absence of a forensic team. While there were no obvious signs of attack, it was too dark to determine cause of death without an expert and you never knew what sins remained invisible to the naked eye.

Next, he shone his torch onto the stone staircase and spotted a small clump of matted hair and blood clinging to the edge of one of the steps. Turning back to Victor, he thought of a man who had seemed so vital despite his advancing years. Tripping down a flight of stairs seemed such an ignominious way to die.

Accidents happen every day.

Yet, the staircase was lit by a series of solar-powered exterior lights that would have been unaffected by the power failure inside the house. Together with the little LED torch Victor had used, there should have been sufficient light to move safely downstairs, particularly since weather conditions were dry and mild.

How, then, did Victor fall?

The seed of doubt was planted and Ryan decided to put a call through to Tom Faulkner, the Senior Crime Scene Investigator attached to Northumbria CID. Ordinarily, the services of their most proficient forensic specialist were reserved for priority cases already deemed 'suspicious' but it paid to be sure.

After a brief conversation with Faulkner and the Control Room, he kept to the extreme edge of the staircase and retraced Victor's steps back inside the house, scanning the stonework as he went. Ryan took a further two flights upward using the servants' staircase until he re-entered the house and emerged onto the same floor as the drawing room.

Stepping into the carpeted corridor, he heard muted, angry voices. Ryan remained perfectly still, head cocked to one side until he could determine the direction. At the top of the servants' staircase, the corridor forked. To his right, it led to the closest doorway to the drawing room, which had been used throughout the evening. To his left, it skirted around to a billiards room and, from there, continued toward an alternative entrance to the drawing room at its southern end. To his knowledge, nobody had used that doorway during the evening but now there were voices coming from that direction and possibilities began to roam his mind.

Soundlessly, Ryan took the left fork and padded along the plush hallway until he reached the closed door of the billiards room. A thin strip of light shone beneath and the voices grew louder as he approached.

"You must be out of your mind!"

Ryan frowned, trying to place an unfamiliar female voice.

"Have you forgotten who you're talking to?"

The estate manager's tenor held an unmistakable, obnoxious quality that carried through doors and walls. Ryan craned his neck to hear the rest of the conversation but the voices became distant and he pushed open the door to the billiards room, hoping to surprise whoever was in there.

It was empty.

Ryan stored the information away and turned on his heel to deal with more pressing matters.

As the grandfather clock in the drawing room struck quarter-to-midnight, Ryan addressed the staff and volunteers of Cragside house, many of whom appeared worse for wear and ready to turn in for the night. He was sorry to disappoint them.

"I regret to inform you there has been a serious incident. Victor Swann has died, apparently after taking a fall down the rear servants' staircase. The police have been called, as have the ambulance service."

A mixture of tears and stunned disbelief greeted Ryan's statement. He looked among the faces of the crowd to see who might have been the female voice during the little tête-à-tête he had overheard but nobody stood out and Martin Henderson was now mingling with the crowd as if he had never left them.

"What do you mean, *dead*?"

The man stepped forward to place himself firmly in charge, imperious red robes flapping around his knees.

"I mean precisely what I say," Ryan said mildly.

"I'm going to see for myself." Henderson turned as if to head for the door but Ryan took a subtle step forward.

"The party is over." His tone brooked no argument. "Acting in my capacity as detective chief inspector, I would kindly ask you all to remain seated until we have taken care of Victor through the appropriate channels. Statements will be taken from each of you in turn but, until then—"

"If you think I'm going to sit around here all night, you've got another thing coming."

Ryan was silent for a full ten seconds, allowing the tension to build, then he gave Henderson a smile that didn't quite reach his eyes.

"Do you have something more important to do than assist the police? I wonder if I should draw any inferences from that."

A slow flush spread across Henderson's neck and Ryan thought that, for a glorified pen-pusher, the man certainly had a temper. Tight-lipped, Henderson shrank back into the crowd and began to speak in disgruntled tones to anybody who would listen.

Ignoring him, Ryan turned back to the others.

"I realise you're all tired and ready to go home. We won't keep you any longer than necessary."

"Chief inspector?"

Cassandra Gilbert walked back into the drawing room and looked among the crowd of upset faces.

"Has something happened?"

"Yes, I'm afraid it has. Your husband's valet has been found dead in the exterior courtyard downstairs. The police have been called."

"*Victor*?"

She lost all colour beneath her tan.

"I—I can't believe it. Did he have a heart attack or something?"

"I'm afraid it's too early to say. Is your husband well enough to join us?"

Cassandra shook her head slowly.

"I'm sorry, he's fast asleep upstairs. I've just been to check on him," she explained.

Ryan gave her a steady look.

"I'm sorry to inconvenience either of you but I'll need to speak with Mr Gilbert to confirm his statement about tonight's events."

"Why? He hasn't even been downstairs."

Ryan thought privately that, in a house of this size, it would be easy enough for somebody to sneak downstairs without being seen.

"I would appreciate your cooperation."

If she was bothered by the tone of command, Cassandra didn't show it and began to usher her guests back to their seats.

Just then, Ryan's sharp ears detected the unmistakable tread of heavy footsteps along the gallery, followed by a loud, jaw-cracking yawn which preceded the entrance of his sergeant into the drawing room.

Detective Sergeant Frank Phillips was a short barrel of a man in his mid-fifties with a boxer's physique hidden beneath what he liked to call his 'winter hibernation layer', regardless of the fact it was high summer. His salt-and-pepper hair was thinning on top and framed a pair of button-brown eyes that missed very little. He came to an abrupt halt as he spotted Ryan, who remained dressed like an extra from a Victorian melodrama, and let out a rumbling belly laugh he couldn't have hoped to contain.

"Frank—" Ryan injected a note of warning into his voice but it was waved away with one stubby, workmanlike hand.

"Nobody told us the circus was in town!"

Ryan drew in a long, steadying breath.

"Well, now you've had your money's worth, would it be too much to ask you to take down some statements?"

Still chuckling to himself, Phillips gave Ryan a playful slap on the back.

"Aye, keep your hair on," he said but was already thinking of who he would tell first back at CID and practically rubbed his hands together. "Faulkner's van's parked outside and there's a patrol car on the way. No sign of a doctor, yet, but one's been called."

Ryan nodded.

"Did you see the body?"

Phillips pulled an expressive face.

"Aye, poor old bugger. Took a tumble in the dark, did he?"

Ryan lowered his voice a fraction.

"That's what it looks like, doesn't it?"

Phillips rubbed a hand across the stubble on his jaw and gave Ryan a keen look.

"If you believed that, you wouldn't have bothered calling me all the way out here. It doesn't take two murder detectives to decide whether one old man's death is a matter for CID."

Ryan gave him a knowing smile.

"Let's just say I want a second opinion."

While two bleary-eyed constables set to work taking statements, Ryan and Phillips headed outside. Their feet crunched across the gravel as they rounded the side of the house to the courtyard where they spotted Tom Faulkner, who was already suited up in his polypropylene overalls and struggling to contain his mousy brown hair beneath a white plastic cap. A large spotlight had been erected outside, powered by the mobile generator in Faulkner's nondescript black van. It shone a blazing white light on the area surrounding Victor's body, highlighting the greying pallor of his skin and fixed, bloodshot expression of his eyes as they stared out into the night. "Evening, Tom." Ryan shook the other man's hand before accepting a pair of nitrile gloves. "Thanks for coming out here at short notice."

Faulkner adjusted his thick-rimmed glasses and, not for the first time, Ryan wondered why the man didn't wear contacts and save himself the hassle.

"No problem. I wasn't entertaining a hot date," he laughed self-deprecatingly. "Might as well take a drive out and see the stars."

All three men looked up at the sky, which was awash with stars glistening diamond-bright.

"You ought to find yourself a nice lass and go stargazing," Phillips remarked, in his usual fatherly manner. "Got the observatory up at Kielder, some canny walks and that."

Faulkner fidgeted inside his suit.

"My ex-wife never wanted to," he muttered. "She wasn't much of an outdoorsy type. I don't seem to have much luck finding someone who enjoys the simple things in life."

Ryan and Phillips exchanged a surprised glance. Faulkner had divulged more personal information in the past few moments than he had in the last five years of working together.

Momentarily at a loss, Ryan cleared his throat.

"Well—"

"Let's get started," Faulkner cut him off, feeling awkward. "You told me this man—Victor Swann?—headed out to find the fuse box located through that doorway?"

He pointed a gloved finger toward the door leading to the basement.

"Yes." Ryan was happy to get straight down to business. "That door takes you through the basement and up to the kitchen. The fuse box is in the corridor running beside it."

Faulkner raised his professional camera and took a series of photographs. Lowering it again, he nodded toward the stone staircase cut into the exterior wall.

"You think he took these stairs all the way down from the drawing room on the mezzanine floor, intending to use the back door to the basement and re-enter the house to access the fuse box—isn't that a bit of a circuitous route?"

Ryan had already considered that and shook his head.

"No, I'd say it's just as quick to take either route. Quicker this way, perhaps, because the servants' stairs were designed to connect with this part of the house."

Faulkner scratched the side of his head, joggling the cap he wore.

"What if the doors were locked?"

"Victor was Lionel Gilbert's personal valet, so it's highly likely he had a set of keys. Besides, the door was unlocked when I found his body. I used it myself," Ryan added.

"I can't believe people still have valets, these days," Phillips muttered and both men swung around to look at him. "I'm just saying, it's a bit of an outdated profession."

"Everybody has to earn a crust somehow," Faulkner retorted, hunkering down to tap Victor's pockets with gentle fingers until he heard the jingle of keys. His nose wrinkled at the sight of the dead man's face, which was a bloodied mess of flesh and bone, and he wondered if he would have been better off as a gentleman's valet rather than a crime scene investigator.

"What are your impressions?" Ryan folded his arms across his chest to stave off the cold wind whipping through the archway leading from the courtyard.

"As soon as the ambulance gets here and the doc makes his formal pronouncement of life extinct, we'll transport the body across to the mortuary and see what the pathologist says. But I can't see any obvious signs of interference," Faulkner replied. "No injuries that look to have been caused by a man-made implement. There's no evidence of blood spatter around the body itself indicative of blunt force, only a bit on the stairwell."

"You think he fell all the way down those stairs?"

Phillips cast a sympathetic eye over Victor's shrivelled body and then up at the narrow stone steps.

"It's likely," Faulkner agreed. "The initial impact probably gave him that gash on his head and a secondary impact broke his spinal cord at the base of his neck. He probably had a couple of drinks at the party and lost his footing. Terrible bad luck, I would say."

Ryan waited a beat, then asked the burning question.

"Is it possible he was pushed?"

Faulkner shrugged and the plastic suit rustled across his shoulders.

"Anything's possible."

While two young police constables grappled with a group of over-tired and inebriated party guests, one person stole away from the crowd and moved quickly through the hallways of Cragside house toward the staff room on the ground floor. Ryan or his flat-footed sergeant could re-enter the house at any moment and demand to know what they were doing, which made it a very risky excursion. Unfortunately, needs must.

Pausing every now and then to check they were alone, the figure scurried through to an anteroom just off the main entrance, converted into a common space for the staff to use.

The room was lit well enough thanks to a powerful beam shining through the windows from the courtyard outside. A quick glance confirmed that Ryan and Phillips were deep in conversation with a CSI, who had rigged up a kind of freestanding film light.

There was time.

Heart racing, the figure scurried across the room to the long bank of lockers belonging to Cragside staff members. It took very little force to break into the one at the end of the row and even less time to stuff its contents into a plastic bag. It would take another few minutes to hide it but that was factored into the risk.

The figure slipped away, just as silently as it had come.

CHAPTER 3

While Ryan and Phillips debated whether Victor's death should be classified as 'suspicious', Detective Inspector Denise MacKenzie fought her way through a violent nightmare. Her lungs laboured as she struggled to regain control of her breathing and her eyes darted around the bedroom, her pupils wide and unfocused. She managed to push herself upright and was stupidly grateful to find that Frank had left the bedside light on.

She raised shaking fingers to her forehead and pushed back a tangle of damp red hair, fighting the urge to crumble. Her eyes stung with unshed tears but she bore down, digging instead for the rage that festered in her gut.

No more tears.

She looked down at her hands and was unsurprised to find a line of small purple semi-circles dug into the palms where her nails had formed tight fists.

MacKenzie swung her legs off the bed and felt the familiar tenderness in her ankle. It had been four months and she knew the breakage had fully healed, as had the torn ligaments, but there was a persistent ache she didn't need any psychiatrist to tell her was wholly psychosomatic. Her leg bore an angry pink scar where the Hacker's knife had sliced through the muscle, missing a major artery by millimetres. Two fractured ribs had also healed and she could breathe freely again. All in all, she considered herself fortunate to be alive.

But there were deeper wounds only she could see; wounds that might never heal.

She stumbled toward the en suite bathroom in Phillips' house, smiling lopsidedly at the fluffy pink bath mats and matching towels he'd bought to make her feel at home.

She didn't have the heart to tell him she'd never liked pink.

Her mind skittered back to another bathroom in an abandoned farmhouse, to icy cold showers and ritual humiliation.

Anxiety made her chest tight and she gripped the edge of the sink, willing it to pass. She told herself to concentrate on simply letting the air in and out of her lungs but she was already starting to panic. Nausea followed next and she reached blindly for the bottle of beta-blockers she kept on the bathroom shelf, fumbling with the safety cap until she could stuff a couple of tablets into her mouth.

A few minutes later, the panic receded and she found she could breathe again. The black spots clouding her vision disappeared and she no longer felt like she was going to vomit.

But she didn't feel better.

MacKenzie stared at herself in the mirror, at a once-attractive woman in her mid-forties with lank red hair and shadowed eyes. Her skin was almost translucent and she knew a lack of appetite had made her anaemic. Clothes that used to fit like a second skin now hung limply from her bones. Her lips trembled and all the anger and fear she bottled so carefully during the day erupted from her throat in one long, keening wail.

"Don't lurk in the doorway! Come in, if you're going to!" At the sound of that booming directive, Ryan and Phillips exchanged a meaningful look and stepped inside Cragside's master bedroom to greet its elusive owner, Lionel Horatio Gilbert.

They approached an intricately-carved four-poster bed and were met with a robust-looking man in his early eighties, almost completely bald except for a few strands of wispy hair smoothed across the top of his head in one long comb-over. Gilbert was heavily overweight, his rounded face sagging at the jowls with at least two extra chins that they could see. His small, myopic eyes were red-rimmed and the purple damask bed linen was strewn with crumpled tissues. There was a crystal tumbler of lemon water beside the bed, alongside a packet of cold and flu tablets and some throat lozenges.

"Well?" he demanded, peering between them with obvious disapproval.

"We're sorry to disturb you at this hour," Ryan began, and meant it. There were places he would rather be at one o'clock in the morning than questioning a cantankerous old man in his sickbed.

"Cassandra tells me Victor has finally popped his clogs," Gilbert went on, without any note of sympathy. "Don't know why you're all making such a damned fuss. Comes to all of us in the end, you know."

He reached across for a fresh tissue and blew his nose loudly.

"Blasted woman has been in here blubbering about it," he went on, mercilessly. "She should be more worried about *me*, given the state I'm in."

"We can ask Mrs Gilbert to join us, if you'd like?"

Gilbert sighed gustily.

"No, no. Leave her to play Nurse Nightingale," he said.

"We understand Victor Swann had been employed as your valet for the last fifteen years. Is that correct?"

Gilbert shook his head and the excess skin around his chin wobbled.

"Longer than that. I picked him up back in the eighties, when I was living down in Kent. I bought this place a few years ago as a wedding present to Cassandra and he moved up here with us. So long as he wasn't drooling into his soup, I didn't mind him staying on past retirement. Good laugh, old Victor was," he added, with the air of one recalling a distant memory, although the man had been dead less than two hours.

"And when did you purchase Cragside?"

"Oh, back in '98," Gilbert said gruffly. "Cassandra had a fancy for the place."

Ryan nodded, thinking briefly of his own nuptials and the plans he'd made for Anna's wedding present. Sadly, they weren't quite on the same scale.

"Were you fond of Victor?"

Gilbert blew his nose again and chucked the spent tissue onto the bedspread. Phillips eyed it with distaste, wondering whether his millions couldn't stretch to a waste paper basket.

"Vic was a good, loyal employee, if that's what you mean. Did his duties and wasn't bad company. Had a bit of an eye for the ladies but who doesn't, eh?"

He let out a bellowing laugh which promptly turned into a coughing fit. Phillips took pity and handed him a glass of water, which was snatched up. Gilbert handed the glass back to him without a word of thanks and Ryan asked the next question.

"Turning to this evening, when was the last time you saw Victor?"

"It was at about seven-fifteen. He came in to ask if there was anything I needed before he went down to have a bloody good drink at my expense," Gilbert grumbled.

"Did he seem concerned or out of sorts?"

"Not that I noticed. He looked pleased with himself, all suited up and wearing some ridiculous hat or other."

Ryan couldn't argue with that.

"Can you tell me your own movements this evening?"

Gilbert gave him a pointed look.

"What for? Don't tell me you think somebody pushed the old sod? Well, I suppose it's not outside the realms of possibility. Always the quiet ones to watch, isn't it?"

He let out another nasally guffaw.

"As for my *movements*, I've been cooped up in here all night. Haven't so much as left this bed except to use the bathroom, which is right there," he said, pointing a chubby finger at a connecting doorway on the other side of the room. "Hardly seen a soul except for Cassandra, who came in a few times."

"The last time being around quarter-to-midnight?" Ryan offered.

"Haven't the foggiest," Gilbert replied, reaching for another tissue. "I keep dozing off."

Ryan looked at the man's streaming nose and acknowledged that he probably wasn't feigning illness.

"Once again, thank you for your time. We apologise for having disturbed you."

Gilbert grunted, his eyelids already drooping.

As they closed the door behind them, Ryan turned to Phillips.

"Charming man."

"Oh, aye, a real fat heid," Phillips agreed, leaving Ryan to marvel at his singular turn of phrase.

It was almost three o'clock in the morning before Phillips let himself into the smart, three-bedroom semi he owned in an area of Newcastle known as Kingston Park. It rested on the western border of the city and had been chosen twenty years ago for its relative proximity to CID Headquarters. A lot had changed in the intervening years, he thought, as he toed off his comfortable brown loafers and slid them onto the shoe rack in the hallway next to MacKenzie's boots. For a start, he'd lost his first wife to cancer nearly eight years ago and never thought he'd find another woman he loved enough to ask to share his life a second time.

Well, he'd surprised himself there.

Then, there was the fact he took orders from Ryan, a man young enough to be his son. It made him smile to think of how uncomfortable they'd been in the early days, compared with their easy camaraderie now. He was going to be best man at Ryan's wedding and that made them more than just friends or work colleagues.

It made them family.

CID Headquarters had moved to new premises in another part of town and Phillips felt a pang of regret for the loss of the ugly, sixties-style building they'd called home for too many years to count. Its boxy design was no oil painting and he wouldn't miss the perpetual stench of sweat and detergent, but those greasy walls held memories. He supposed he should be grateful he'd been spared the process of uprooting his desk and dealing with the logistical nightmare of transferring operations, thanks to a three-month suspension from work.

Phillips scrubbed a tired hand over his face.

If he were a younger man, he might have been angry. As it was, he felt relieved that the outcome of the disciplinary hearing had been relatively lenient. He'd attacked a doorman in his quest to find Denise, who was being held by a known serial killer at the time. By following his instincts, he'd brought the force into disrepute through conduct unbecoming a detective sergeant. He'd undermined public confidence, according to the stony-faced panel who had considered his case. However, since CCTV proved he hadn't thrown the first punch and none of the other players was alive to make any further complaint, not to mention that his instincts had turned out to be *correct*, the Powers That Be had decided to hand down a three-month suspension without pay rather than resorting to dismissal.

Oh, and he was off the promotion list for the foreseeable future.

Thirty years of loyal service but it only took one misdemeanour to cancel it all out.

Phillips waited to feel some sense of disappointment but it never came. The fact was, he'd do the same all over again to protect the woman he loved and who had, against all the odds, survived. The Hacker had always planned to kill Denise and theirs had been a race against time. What was a setback in the workplace, compared with her life? Three months' suspension had enabled him to devote himself entirely to her recovery but, now he was back at work, he was finding it hard to keep his mind on the job. He worried about how she was coping on her own, particularly since she showed no inclination to come back to work herself.

That was a problem for another day.

When he stepped into their bedroom a few moments later, MacKenzie was not sleeping peacefully. She was sitting bolt upright in the double bed they shared, her fingers clutching the handle of a kitchen knife.

"Frank?"

Banking down the impotent anger he always felt when he saw that look in her eyes, the fear another man had put there, he moved quickly across to the bed and curled his hands around hers.

"Aye, lass. It's me."

He watched the fight drain out of her body, leaving her limp and tired. The knife shook and he tugged it gently from her fingers.

When she tried to reach for it again, he took her in his arms.

"Shh, now." He began to rock her, rubbing wide circles against her back. "He's gone, he's dead and gone."

MacKenzie buried her face in his shoulder and breathed in the comforting smell of him.

"He's dead," she repeated, thinking of the Hacker's remains lying on a cold, impersonal slab at the mortuary. "He's dead."

"You saw him." Phillips knew the drill. They'd been through it numerous times but it seemed to help her to remember that the man who haunted her nightmares was reduced to ash, his body incinerated and incapable of hurting another living soul.

MacKenzie nodded and let her eyelids droop, snuggling into the hollow of Phillips' neck until her breathing became even and he knew that she slept. With infinite care, he laid her down against the pillows, drew the covers over her slender body and held her hand for a while longer, wishing he had been taken instead.

The wait was agonising. It had been two hours since they'd given their statements to the police and more time had been wasted listening to a long-winded rehash of the life of Victor Swann, whose dubious character had taken on the quality of a martyred saint in the eyes of his co-workers. The place had been awash with tearful anecdotes and sob stories about the many times Victor had saved the day, forcing disingenuous smiles and polite murmurs from anybody required to listen.

The man was dead and he'd been an average man at best.

End of story.

But no, the caterwauling had continued as people piled into the minibus that had been laid on to ferry them all back to their respective homes, mostly within the grounds of the estate or in the nearby town of Rothbury. There'd been precious few minutes to change clothes and gulp down a glass of water before slipping out again.

The police lingered into the early hours of the morning. Their voices carried across the quiet gardens down into the shadows of the forest, their clumsy feet crunching across the gravel driveway while Ryan presided over it all like a Mother Goose, clucking around as if he were master of all he surveyed.

Arrogant bastard.

But so long as they didn't stray too far, there was time to make one final, very important house call.

CHAPTER 4

Sunday 14th August

Ryan opened his eyes one at a time and made a swift assessment of the damage. His head was pounding but the ache was low grade, nothing a couple of painkillers wouldn't cure. His throat felt scratchy and dry, which was no more than he deserved after an evening quaffing red wine as if it were going out of fashion. He could have done with another eight hours' solid sleep but that was wishful thinking. After all the drama of the previous evening, he and Phillips had eventually classified Victor Swann's untimely demise as 'not suspicious' but that didn't mean there wasn't paperwork to clear up and calls to make, even at the weekend.

They needed to find Swann's next of kin, for starters. Nobody seemed to know much about Victor's private life beyond the fact he was a familiar face at Cragside. But by the time the body had been collected for transportation to the mortuary and Faulkner had completed his work, it had been after two o'clock in the morning and they were all exhausted. Ryan had taken the decision to go through the dead man's personal effects with the benefit of a few hours' sleep and some natural light.

Technically, Ryan knew Victor's death should be passed on to another team to free up resources for the more serious cases that were the domain of CID. There was no evidence to suggest foul play; an extensive search of the crime scene had shown no indication of it. Yet, it continued to trouble him and so, until the results of the post-mortem came back in a few days' time, he planned to keep hold of the case for as long as he could.

Caseloads and budgeting ran through Ryan's mind as he weighed up all the active investigations into murder, manslaughter, rape and GBH alongside the officers attached to each. He considered who he could enlist to deal with the mind-numbing bureaucracy of a non-suspicious death and thought immediately of PC Melanie Yates. It was character building for an ambitious young officer and he happened to know that Yates hoped to get her stripes working in CID. She had a solid backbone, which was a crucial component in all the staff on his division, and she held up well at a crime scene. Maybe it was time to authorise a permanent transfer to see what she was made of.

Ryan glanced at his watch and was dismayed to find it wasn't even eight o'clock. Weren't Sunday mornings supposed to be slumberous days of rest, spent in bed with the object of one's desire?

"Ryan! Get your arse out of bed, y' lazy lump!"

Speak of the devil.

He huffed out a laugh, then swung down into a few quick press-ups on the floor to get his blood flowing. His nose detected the scent of smoked bacon as it wafted upstairs and his mood perked up considerably.

A few minutes later, Ryan was towelling himself after a quick shower and looking forward to breakfast when his mobile phone began to shrill.

He made a dive for it.

"Ryan?"

He was caught off-guard and unconsciously squared his shoulders when he recognised that the caller was Chief Constable Sandra Morrison.

"Good morning, ma'am. Has there been an incident?"

"No, nothing like that. I'm sorry to disturb you at home but there was a matter I wanted to discuss with you privately."

"Oh?"

There was a short pause while Morrison fiddled with the biro she twirled in her hand and searched for the right words.

"Phillips has been back at work for three weeks now."

"Yes."

Morrison was already aware of Ryan's feelings on the subject, which he'd told her in no uncertain terms. As far as he was concerned, Frank Phillips should never have been put through the humiliation of a disciplinary inquiry, especially when his actions had been instrumental in leading them to find the Hacker. Furthermore, his sergeant should never have been subjected to a three-month suspension.

At the other end of the line, Morrison sighed.

"Let's try to put it behind us." She refused to justify what she considered to be appropriate actions, taken with the best interests of the constabulary in mind. Much as it might have pained her to do it, much as she might have suffered a few sleepless nights, it was not enough to know that Phillips had acted with the best of intentions. They had to be *seen* to be trustworthy in the eyes of the ever-watchful public.

It was that detachment and ability to consider the politics of a situation that had allowed Sandra Morrison to rise quickly through the ranks of the police hierarchy.

It was also the reason why Ryan preferred to remain exactly where he was.

"The fact is, I'm concerned." She came straight to the point. "I'm glad to see Phillips return to the office but he seems very distracted."

Ryan's jaw set.

"That's hardly surprising, is it? He's been dragged through the wringer these last four months and he's been caring for MacKenzie at home."

"I realise that but the HR team tell me she's refusing to see the occupational therapist and they haven't heard a peep from MacKenzie about when, or whether, she's planning to come back to work."

"She's entitled to take up to twelve months' leave. For God's sake, she was kidnapped, psychologically tortured, physically battered. Do you expect her to shrug it off?"

His words came out like bullets, every one of them hitting their mark.

"I expect her to *recover*," Morrison threw back. "You forget, I've known Denise a lot longer than you have and she's always been strong. Hiding away at home for months will only reinforce her fear."

It was on the tip of Ryan's tongue to make some snide remark about Morrison being a psychologist in her spare time but he recognised more than a grain of truth in what she was saying. He'd seen his own share of trauma over the years and it had always helped to get back on the proverbial horse rather than staying at home, brooding about the what-ifs.

"Ryan—"

"Look, I'll talk to Phillips about it."

Morrison breathed a quiet sigh of relief and set the biro back down on her little writing desk at home.

"I appreciate that."

She groped around for a change of subject when Ryan offered none.

"I, ah, heard you caught a new one last night?"

"Nothing major. One of the staff here at Cragside fell down a flight of stairs. I discussed it with Phillips and it looks like an accidental death but I'm keeping it on the radar."

His tone was clipped and formal, his voice bearing the mark of years spent at a southern boarding school. Among his friends, Ryan could be warm and generous but not a whisper of that was evident now.

Sitting at home in faded running gear, her sandy blonde hair pulled back into a merciless ponytail, Sandra Morrison recognised the civil tone and swallowed an unexpected lump in her throat; she was no longer privy to the warmth Ryan reserved only for those he considered a friend.

In his eyes, it was the price she paid for betrayal.

"I see," she murmured. And she *did* see. "Ryan, you know we discussed the prospect of your promotion to superintendent a few months ago?"

He shifted the handset to his other ear and walked to the bedroom window to look out across the gardens towards the edge of the forest. Cragside was hidden somewhere among those trees, he thought, like a sleeping giant.

The position of detective chief superintendent had been vacant for almost a year since DCS Gregson, his former boss, had fallen from grace in spectacular fashion and was now living at Her Majesty's pleasure. Although it wasn't part of the Chief Constable's job description, Morrison had been forced to oversee much of their operations in CID until Gregson's successor could be appointed, but they all knew it was a temporary arrangement. In many ways, Ryan had been a shoo-in for the job. He had solved a series of high-profile cases and, much to his own surprise, was a popular figure in the press. The role of superintendent was unappealing not only because he'd be chained to a desk. Thanks to Gregson and the rot that had spread throughout CID, the position was tainted by association and Ryan wasn't sure he was ready to accept such a poisoned chalice.

Ryan leaned his long body against the window frame and watched a bird swoop down from the trees to perch on the birdhouse Anna filled with fresh seed every morning.

"My position is unchanged," he said eventually.

"I realise that and, since you have no interest in proceeding, I wanted to let you know we have another strong candidate in mind."

He raised a single dark eyebrow.

"Anyone I know?"

"Perhaps. Her name is Jennifer Lucas and she would be coming to us from the Met. She's acting DCS while the present incumbent is on a leave of absence, but they're due to return in the next couple of months so she's interested in accepting a permanent post and making a fresh start elsewhere."

Morrison paused but no comment was forthcoming.

"She's coming in next week for an informal discussion and there are a couple of other candidates we'll be speaking to but Lucas has the strongest credentials on paper. I'd appreciate your input, Ryan, because whoever we appoint will be the person you'll be reporting to directly from now on."

Ryan pinched the bridge of his nose between thumb and forefinger to stifle the tension that was developing behind his eyes.

"I...yes, I know Jen Lucas. She was my DI, back when I started at the Met."

"Oh! I must have missed that connection. That's great, you two can pick up right where you left off."

Hardly, Ryan thought.

"She was a good inspector," he said. "But—"

"Yes?"

Integrity prevented him from fabricating a list of professional blunders because the plain truth was that Jennifer Lucas had always been an outstanding detective. Any relationship that had existed between them had ended years ago and should have no bearing on her appointment as DCS.

Ancient history, he decided.

"Nothing. Who are the other candidates?"

When Morrison rang off a couple of minutes later, Ryan slipped the phone into the back pocket of his dark jeans and continued to stare out over the flower beds blooming in the garden below. He watched Anna step onto the patio with a cup of coffee and a newspaper, making herself comfortable at the bistro table. She tipped her face up to the sun that turned her dark hair to burnished mahogany and warmed her long legs as she stretched out in shorts and sandals. When she caught sight of him at the window she raised a hand to wave, crooking a finger for him to join her.

He rested his forehead against the glass pane and thought of how their lives had altered in the space of one short phone call.

CHAPTER 5

Police Constable Melanie Yates grasped the opportunity to work on Ryan's team with both hands and bundled herself quickly into the blue VW Golf parked on her parents' driveway. She was saving up a deposit for her own little place closer to the centre of town, where she could be on hand for any urgent cases at the new CID Headquarters. Until then, she was relying on her parents' goodwill.

As she pulled onto the A1 and headed north from the city towards Cragside, her thoughts strayed back to her first week out of cadet training and the first time she had seen Ryan striding down the corridor. Melanie had been grappling with the vending machine and, with a distracted air, he'd paused to thump the side of the ancient metal frame, giving her a friendly smile when the machine had promptly coughed up a chocolate bar.

"Don't be afraid to give it a good kick," he'd said, with a smile.

On that occasion, she had stared at him like a rabbit caught in the headlights and he'd moved off again, already having forgotten she existed. Melanie imagined she wasn't the only person ever to be affected by him and the fact he was engaged to be married seemed to have no dimming effect on the people who mooned over him in the staff canteen or down at the pub after work.

As she drove towards the Northumberland National Park, the rolling countryside eventually gave way to a dense forest that grew all the way up to the tarmac, its tall emergent trees blotting out the morning sun except for a few beams of white light cutting through the branches. She enjoyed the way the sunshine played through the trees and sent dappled streams of light across the windscreen until, a few minutes later, she slowed for the turn that would lead her along a winding driveway towards Cragside. The driveway curved past a large lake on her left, then over an old stone bridge leading through the trees until the house appeared, its towers and chimneys peeping through the uppermost branches.

Melanie schooled her features into a professional mask. It would be disastrous if Ryan were ever to read her innermost thoughts, the childish desires she harboured only in private. Work was her passion and she had been given an opportunity to shine.

She planned to make the most of it.

Ryan stood outside the main entrance to Cragside fielding irate questions from Martin Henderson. The estate manager's balding head reflected the glare of the summer sun and, as she parked her car in the circular driveway, Yates could see pearls of sweat glistening against his skin. By contrast, Ryan looked very much at ease with his hands tucked into the back pockets of his jeans, in a stance that could have signified boredom, or contempt. Catching sight of her, he looked across the driveway and raised a hand in greeting before turning his attention back to Henderson. Yates locked the car and made her way towards them, smoothing a nervous hand over the curly brown hair she'd bundled into a ponytail.

"I've told you repeatedly," Ryan was saying. "We will do all we can not to disrupt the normal running of the estate. The area surrounding where Victor fell has been cordoned off, as has the drawing room and exterior staircase but otherwise people should be able to move freely."

Henderson shifted his feet.

"I don't know whether you're aware, but I have a responsibility—"

"As do I," Ryan interjected, very quietly. "My first responsibility is to Victor Swann, not to a stack of bricks and mortar, pretty though it is, or to your employers. If the Gilberts have any grievances to raise, I'm sure they know where to find me."

With that, he gestured for Yates to follow him inside the house, leaving Henderson blustering on the steps outside.

"Thanks for getting up here so quickly," he said, barely glancing in her direction.

"Not at all, sir, I'm happy to help. Thank you for bringing me on board."

Ryan jerked his head back over his shoulder.

"That was Martin Henderson, otherwise known as The Big Cheese. He's the estate manager and seems to spend most of his time being high-handed with the other staff. Giving them all a pain in the arse, no doubt."

"I understand."

Ryan's lips twitched.

"Good. Are you up to speed?"

"Yes, I read your summary. It doesn't seem to be a priority case," she said.

Ryan stopped briefly inside the dim, wood-panelled hallway.

"First rule of CID, Yates. They're *all* priority."

She filed that little nugget away and followed him into what appeared to be a staff common room, through a door to the right of the reception area. Formerly the butler's pantry, it was a mixture of old and new, with corniced ceilings and antique side tables offset by jarring, overstuffed foam easy chairs and plastic coffee tables. A bank of metal lockers, the kind you might see in the changing rooms of a leisure centre, lined one of the walls. It was nearly empty except for a man and a woman who were huddled over one of the tables in hushed conversation.

The man looked across at their arrival and stood up.

"Morning, Ryan." He stepped towards them and held out a hand.

"Dave."

"Hell of a business," the other remarked, with the long-faced expression of one who didn't know what to say. "We're all still in shock."

Ryan angled his body and made the introductions.

"This is PC Melanie Yates," he said. "She'll be handling some of the loose ends relating to Victor's death."

She held out a hand, which was shaken enthusiastically.

"Dave Quibble, conservation manager." He gave her an appreciative smile. "I'm responsible for overseeing the general conservation of the site here, thanks to the Gilberts' generosity. There's a team of specialists who take care of all the different elements, from the gardens to the artefacts and the electrics. Anything we can do to help you, just say the word."

"Thank you." She nodded towards the lockers. "Did Victor have one of those?"

"Yes, indeed. Alice? Do you know which one was Victor's? Alice is one of our specialist staff members working on painting restoration," Dave explained.

A pretty, dark-haired young woman in her late twenties looked up from a copy of *Cosmopolitan*.

"Ah, I think it was the one at the end."

"Let me see if I can find an access key," Dave began but Ryan shook his head and they watched as Yates drew on a pair of nitrile gloves and used her index finger to open the locker. It let out a metallic whine as it fell back on its hinges.

"It's empty," she said. "And the lock appears to have been forced, sir."

Ryan flicked his eyes back to Dave's face, which was a comical mask of surprise. He turned to Alice, who gave a startled shrug of incomprehension.

"Yates? I want to know where Victor lived. If somebody's cleaned out his locker, it's possible they also paid a visit to his home." Ryan turned to the other two people in the room. "Unless either of you happen to know his address?"

"It was somewhere in Rothbury," Dave piped up. "But if you ask the Gilberts, or Maggie, she might know exactly. I think she's working down at the tea room today, helping out because one of the staff is off sick."

"Maggie?" Yates queried.

"The housekeeper," Ryan provided. "She and Victor were close, I think."

Alice nodded her agreement.

"It was nice to think of two people finding love later in life," she said wistfully. "Sort of makes you think it's never too late. But I suppose accidents happen all the time."

Her sentiments echoed Ryan's own thoughts when he'd found Victor the previous evening. But if Victor's death was an accident, why had somebody broken into the dead man's locker?

He came to an instant decision.

"Yates, I'm bumping this back up to 'suspicious'. See what else you can dig up around here and have a word with the Gilberts to make them aware. Make sure nobody touches that locker in the meantime, or any of them, for that matter. I'll be back shortly."

With that, he made a beeline for the tea room.

CHAPTER 6

Ryan walked along a narrow access road from the main house towards a grand cluster of buildings which had formerly been the stables but was now an education centre and a tea room. He entered the latter and found Maggie arranging scones on a frosted glass display plate on the stainless-steel countertop running along one wall. She was dressed in the ubiquitous black and white uniform of a waitress and her hands moved deftly as she fiddled with sachets of butter, turning them so their little cow-faces could be seen. The tea room was full of visitors enjoying a mid-morning snack as they wandered the vast grounds of the estate and there was a pleasant aroma of baked goods and minced meat which foretold of shepherd's pie on the lunch menu.

Sensing his presence, Maggie looked up from her task and gave Ryan a watery smile.

"Hello, pet. Why don't you take a seat? I'll be with you in a minute."

Ryan selected a chair beside the window and waited while Maggie hung up her apron, exchanged a quick word with one of the other waitresses and joined him at the table. She seemed to be full of energy and her feet were quick but he noticed a pronounced hobble to her gait. Reading his thoughts, she tapped a hand against her right hip.

"Rheumatoid arthritis," she explained, settling herself opposite him. "I need another hip replacement but to be honest I can't face it."

"I'm sorry."

"It's just a fact of life. Not that I should be complaining, after what happened to poor Victor." Fresh tears welled in her eyes and Ryan noticed they were a very pale blue. He found himself wondering if they had been a bolder shade in her youth, and whether their pigment had faded with the passage of time.

Ryan gave her a moment to compose herself.

"I know you gave a statement last night but I was hoping to ask you a few more questions, if I may."

Maggie blew her nose into a cloth handkerchief and Ryan was reminded of his grandmother, who had always kept one tucked inside her sleeve.

"I'll do my best," she said, her voice muffled by the material.

"Tell me a bit about your relationship with Victor."

She tucked her handkerchief away again and gave him a no-nonsense look.

"We were friends," she said emphatically. "Oh, I know everyone else around here thinks there was more to it but, really, it's ridiculous. At our time of life—"

"Don't tell me you're a day over forty," he put in, with the flash of a smile.

"Oh, go on!" She made a dismissive gesture but the fine lines at the corners of her eyes crinkled and she flushed with pleasure. "You could charm the birds from the trees."

Ryan had heard 'grumpy' and 'bastard' used frequently in the same sentence when describing his character but seldom 'charming'.

He came back to the point.

"Can you tell me anything about Victor's family? We're having difficulty locating his next of kin."

Maggie shook her head sadly.

"I asked him if he'd ever been married or whether he had any children but he told me he'd always been happy living alone. I think life as Lionel's valet suited him and he loved to travel, which was a big perk of the job."

"Any brothers or sisters?"

"He never mentioned any." Her hands flapped as she tried to remember. "I'm sorry, love, but Victor was one of those people who could talk about everything and nothing. He knew all about the history of the house and grounds and he could write a book about art and culture. But when it came to the everyday stuff, he just clammed up."

Ryan considered the little he had seen of Victor Swann and thought it was an accurate description.

"He never spoke of anything troubling him? Nobody who had given him cause for concern?"

Maggie's eyes widened a bit.

"No, nothing like that. Why? I thought…I thought it was an accident?"

Ryan reached across to clasp her hand, which had started flapping again as the enormity of his question struck her.

"These are all routine questions I have to ask. There's just one more thing, for now. Do you know where Victor lived?"

Maggie put a shaking finger to her temple and squeezed her eyes shut.

"Yes!" Her eyes flew open again. "It was in one of those new-builds on Windy Drive in Rothbury." She referred to the nearest town, a couple of miles away. "I seem to remember him saying he'd painted the front door bright red. He has a room in the big house but he decided to buy a place of his own in one of those sheltered housing estates. He was long past retirement age and I think he knew there would come a day when he'd have to stop."

"He didn't live in, like you?"

She shook her head.

"The Gilberts only ever spend four or five months of the year at Cragside," she explained. "The rest of the time, I keep the home fires burning for them and it makes sense for me to live in. But Victor travelled everywhere with them and used a spare room whenever he needed one. Since they've started spending longer periods at home, he decided it was time to buy his own place nearby. I suppose I'll have to think about that, one day," she said. Time had a worrying habit of marching on.

Ryan gave her hand a final squeeze.

"Thanks, Maggie. Save one of those scones for me."

While Ryan drove the short distance to Victor Swann's former residence, Frank Phillips struggled to concentrate on the computer screen at his desk at the new CID Headquarters. Everything was horribly *new*, from the ultra-modern glass frontage to the carpet tiles and white-washed paint. It still smelled new, too, but that would change soon enough. Offices like these were not built to last, not like the fine Victorian buildings in the city centre that had withstood over a century of wind and rain. The creamy-white rendered walls would quickly fade to murky-grey and damp spots would develop on the ceiling tiles. Peculiar stains and scuff marks would appear overnight and, instead of paint, the corridors would begin to smell of tuna casserole and drains. As far as Phillips was concerned, all would be right with the world again.

"You should try one of these smoothies from the juice bar."

Detective Constable Jack Lowerson strolled across the open-plan office to join him, draining the last of a bright pink concoction from an eco-friendly, recyclable plastic container in the shape of a miniature milk bottle.

Phillips spun around in his ergonomic desk chair and surveyed the young man with incredulity.

"Juice bar? Lad, you might as well ask me to scale Everest. Give me a cup of milky tea and a few digestives any day of the week."

Lowerson grinned, displaying a row of freshly-whitened teeth.

"Did you know, the bloke who used to run the pie van outside the old offices has moved over here with us? He's tripled his business because all the other office buildings want a piece of the action."

Phillips scowled.

"Probably because all they've been getting is vegetable juice and quinoa until now. The pie van was one of our best-kept secrets," he grumbled. "I'll have to queue up to get a corned beef pasty, now."

Lowerson shrugged inside his trendy Air Force blue suit.

"Heard anything from Ryan?"

"He's reclassified the body he found at Cragside. Apparently, the victim's locker was broken into sometime during the night."

Lowerson didn't miss the fact that Swann was now being referred to as a 'victim'.

"Why would anybody want to hurt a harmless old man?"

Phillips linked his fingers across his paunch.

"You should know by now, there's no such thing as 'harmless.'"

Lowerson nodded, then licked his lips.

"Ah, I wanted to ask how MacKenzie's getting on? I don't want to be a nuisance, if she'd rather be left alone."

Phillips looked away and cleared his throat.

"Aye, she'll be grand."

Jack might have been a bit green around the edges but he still recognised a dodge when he heard one. Denise MacKenzie had, after all, been the one to teach him how to see beneath the surface to the bones of a case and to read a person's body language rather than just the words they said. For Phillips to brush him off like that, things must be bad.

He laid a hand on the older man's shoulder.

"It's only been a few weeks," he said quietly. "She just needs more time."

In the silence that followed, they wondered whether time would ever bring back the woman they loved, in their different ways.

Anna decided to take a break from Northumbrian history and drive into the city. The morning's sunshine had given way to an overcast afternoon and rainclouds now gathered over Newcastle, threatening a downpour later in the day. The house MacKenzie shared with Phillips was in a cul-de-sac on an estate in Kingston Park. The area was well-kept, with fresh paint on the doors and neatly trimmed front gardens. Children played out in the street under the watchful eye of their parents and she could hear an ice-cream van booming out a tinny rendition of *Greensleeves* somewhere nearby. Anna scanned the houses and pulled up at the kerb outside one with a green door. She rested her hands on the steering wheel for a moment before reaching across to retrieve a bouquet of flowers sitting on the passenger seat, then slammed out of the car.

When MacKenzie heard the doorbell ringing, she nearly dropped the kettle of boiling water she held in her hand.

She stood, frozen for a moment, until the sound came again.

Buzz, buzz, buzz.

The kettle clattered onto the countertop and she reached for one of the carving knives from a wooden block, remembering another time when she'd answered the front door without thinking and without protecting herself. It had nearly cost her life.

She edged into the hallway and waited.

Buzzzzzz.

"Hello! Denise, are you in there? It's me, Anna!"

MacKenzie swiped away tears of relief and hid the knife inside the pocket of her coat, which hung from the peg in the hallway. She looked down at the old pyjamas she wore and thought seriously about not answering the door.

"Come on, Denise! I'm desperate for the loo!"

Outside, Anna didn't flinch at the white lie and was pleased when she heard the tread of footsteps, followed by the sound of several locks unbolting.

She had a big smile in place when the door finally opened. It didn't falter an inch, even when she saw how thin her friend had become, or how dark the shadows were beneath her eyes.

Anna enveloped Denise in a warm hug.

"It's wonderful to see you," she said, feeling the sharp edges of her ribs through the thick cotton pyjamas.

MacKenzie let herself be held and enjoyed the scent of fresh flowers Anna had brought with her.

"Come in," she murmured. "I'm sorry, I wasn't expecting company."

Once inside, Anna dutifully went to the bathroom, allowing MacKenzie a few precious minutes to run a brush through her hair and clear up the breakfast paraphernalia she still hadn't managed to tidy away.

She was staring at the washing-up liquid when Anna stepped back into the kitchen and summed up the situation at once.

"You need to get out of the house," she said, gently.

MacKenzie turned to her with wild green eyes that were suddenly spitting with anger.

"How would you know what I need?" she snarled, letting the washing-up bottle slip from her fingers into the sink. "You have no *idea* how I feel, cooped up in here all day…or how I feel when I'm out *there*. You waltz in here, with your perfect life—"

"That's enough."

Anna's voice cracked like a whip and MacKenzie was taken aback by the hard tone, so seldom used.

"I know all about loss, about suffering," Anna bit out. "I lost my entire family, or did you forget?"

She moved further into the kitchen until she stood in front of her friend, eye-to-eye.

"I remember the fear I felt when Steven Walker drugged me, tied me up and sat above me with a dagger in his hands. I'll never forget the look in his eyes, the madness."

Anna thought back to that night two years ago and felt a shudder rack her entire body. Yes, she knew about fear, the kind that dug deep into the bones of a person and took root there.

"Denise, you're surrounded by people who understand what you're going through—Phillips, Ryan, even Jack. But me? I don't just understand, I *empathise*, because I've been there myself. That night, when I lay there… I thought my life was over. I thought I wasn't coming back."

MacKenzie's throat was so tight she couldn't have said a word.

"I'm not standing here pretending I know what it feels like to have gone through what you went through in that farmhouse. Only you know that. But I can tell you that I remember what it felt like to make my peace with God, like you must have done."

That brought a measure of surprise, which momentarily replaced the sadness in MacKenzie's eyes.

Anna nodded, self-deprecatingly.

"Oh yes, even though I say all the time I don't believe in a god, I don't mind telling you I made my peace with him, or her, or whatever the hell it is, just in case. I said my 'goodbyes' and wondered if God would consider I'd been a decent person when the time of reckoning came."

Anna's voice quietened, almost to a whisper.

"I still don't know the answer to that. I only know I've never felt such relief, and such guilt, for being alive when others weren't so lucky."

"Yes," MacKenzie choked out, thinking of the Hacker's many victims who hadn't managed to escape. Their faces filled her mind, images of them alive and dead, until she could barely sleep at night.

Anna reached out for MacKenzie's limp hands, clasping them tightly.

"It's time to come back, Denise. You aren't responsible for their deaths. Do you hear me? You aren't responsible. Only one person is answerable for that and he's paid the ultimate price now. Don't let the Hacker win, not after you fought so hard to beat him."

There was a short silence as the words began to penetrate.

"You're right," MacKenzie whispered and moved into Anna's open arms, holding on tightly. "I'm sorry."

"No need to be sorry," came the reply. "But it's time to bury the past. Somebody said once that living well is the best revenge."

"They were right."

There was a contented silence while the women held onto each other by the sink in Phillips' kitchen, punctuated only by the sound of the refrigerator humming. When they pulled apart, MacKenzie's eyes were clear again.

"I never said 'thank you' for the part you played in finishing it."

Shock frittered over Anna's face and she took half a step back, unconsciously defensive.

"I don't know what you—"

"I think you do." MacKenzie reached out for Anna's hand again. "That man was a monster. If you hadn't acted, Ryan might have been the one lying dead at the foot of a waterfall, not the other way around."

Anna didn't deny it. Four months ago, Ryan had fought a killer who was more animal than human, who would have stopped at nothing.

"The official inquest found no evidence of a bullet wound in his body," she said carefully, referring to the post-mortem that had been conducted shortly after the Hacker's death. "His injuries were so extensive after being battered about on the rocks, *if* a bullet was fired, it must have passed through him as a flesh wound."

As a light rain began to fall outside, MacKenzie smiled beautifully for the first time in four months.

"A flesh wound was enough to distract him and the water did the rest. I had a rifle aimed but I was too slow to use it. Phillips says he had his firearm with him but the angle was so bad he couldn't get a clear shot. The tactical teams were three or four minutes behind us. There was only one other person who was in position and who had the ability to take a shot. I believe that person was you."

Anna said nothing at first, turning her face to look out the kitchen window into the small back garden with its big terracotta plant pots.

"I took Ryan's gun from his lock-box at home," she said quietly. "It could cause trouble for him, if he knew."

Anna hugged her arms around her body, feeling a chill at the thought of it.

"He's adamant he heard a shot being fired and he thinks the CSIs must have missed something, or else the pathologist. He can't understand why nobody will admit to discharging a weapon and I don't want to keep lying to him."

"Is it such a bad thing for him to know you helped him?"

"No, but he might feel compelled to report it, officially, which could affect his professional standing. Even if the outcome was the best for everyone, that's not necessarily how the Independent Police Complaints Commission will see it. I'm a civilian and I had access to his authorised firearm. They'd make out it was negligence on his part."

MacKenzie acknowledged that was a possibility.

"I think the past should stay buried."

Anna looked back at that, with a smile that held no mirth.

"Oh, but it never does."

CHAPTER 7

Unlike the stately architecture that constituted most of the small town of Rothbury, Victor Swann's home was unremarkable at first glance. The bungalow formed part of a sheltered housing estate with an on-site caretaker, gardener and automatic membership of the Neighbourhood Watch. There were six identical bungalows arranged in a semi-circle around a central flower bed that was in full, glorious bloom and, of the six, only one had a bright red front door.

Ryan headed directly for it.

The curtains were closed and a quick inspection of the front door told him it was still securely locked. A wooden gate gave access to a paved pathway leading to the rear of the house and, as soon as he rounded the corner, Ryan spotted the tell-tale fragments of broken glass indicating there had been a break-in. The back door was standard white UPVC and it had been an easy job for someone to smash the panelling and let themselves in. A garden shovel was propped against the wall beside it and he'd bet the heavy metal handle had been used to drive through the glass.

Ryan took a moment to slip on some plastic shoe coverings and a pair of nitrile gloves before stepping inside.

The back door led directly into a small kitchen with top-of-the-range appliances. There was a fancy-looking breakfast table with a polished glass top and seating for four, in the centre of which was a ceramic fruit bowl containing a few bananas on the turn. A couple of the cupboard doors stood open with their contents spilling like entrails onto the tiled floor. The fridge hadn't been closed properly and a nasty smell of raw meat permeated the air, which did nothing to alleviate the overall impression that the house had been disembowelled.

Ryan made his way through to the sitting room, where he found a hoard of treasures. Fine quality paintings hung in brass frames on the walls and objets d'art had been meticulously arranged across every available surface and inside a glass-fronted corner unit. An expensive wall-mounted television took up one wall and a soft brown leather sofa was set out with matching armchairs around an antique chest, on top of which a pile of heavy books on Renaissance art and contemporary photography had been arranged in a fan shape.

Everything else was in total disarray.

The contents of every drawer and cupboard had been strewn onto the thick-pile carpet, even the DVDs, which seemed to consist mostly of the complete collection of *Dad's Army* and *Monty Python*.

At least he'd had a sense of humour.

The single cupboard in the hallway had been ransacked, with shoes and coats left in a heap on the floor. Turning to the master bedroom, Ryan found three wardrobes full of menswear for all occasions. Shirts had fallen from their hangers as the intruder had thrust them aside during their frantic search. The room was decorated lavishly, with pearl-grey silk wallpaper and a top-quality bedspread that had been swept onto the floor. The mattress had been dislodged from the base unit and one of the side tables lay upturned on the floor.

Apart from the bathroom, the only remaining room in the single-level house was a box bedroom which Victor appeared to have used as a reading room. There were more paintings on the walls and another pricey-looking armchair but there was also a substantial bookcase filled with tomes on art, music and local history. A slimline antique bureau in elm wood had been systematically broken apart and its elegant curved legs were scattered on the floor alongside a drawer full of receipts and paperwork.

Ryan stood for a moment looking at the destruction and thought that the unknown intruder could not have been clearer in his message.

Victor had something specific that you wanted, didn't he?

Just then, he heard shuffling footsteps near the back door and Ryan moved quickly through the house to intercept them.

"Stop right there!"

A young man of around twenty stood outside the back door wielding a garden rake and Ryan assumed he must be the resident caretaker.

"I've—I've called the police! There's no use making a run for it!"

Ryan couldn't help but smile. It wasn't the first time he'd been mistaken for a criminal and he wondered if he looked like a reprobate.

He reached for his warrant card and held it out for inspection.

"Here—satisfied?"

"That could be a forgery!"

Ryan had to give the man points for enthusiasm but he didn't have time for any more games.

"You've been watching too many episodes of *Law & Order*. Now, put that bloody rake down, before you take somebody's eye out with it."

Phillips told himself to concentrate on the road ahead and not on the fact he hadn't heard from Denise in over four hours. He'd tried calling her several times without success and he was starting to worry. What if she'd hurt herself or had another panic attack? *He could make a quick detour, just to check...*

"Frank?"

From his position in the passenger seat of Phillips' Volvo, Lowerson realised the man hadn't heard a word he'd said.

"Sorry, I was miles away."

"I was just saying, I don't have a date lined up for Ryan's wedding. Does Anna have any single friends?"

Phillips looked across to where Lowerson was patting his quiff back into place and shook his head. The lad was constantly thinking with his glands.

"What happened with that lass from the estate agents?"

"She met a gym instructor," came the surly reply. "His biceps are bigger than my entire body."

Phillips smiled.

"Take it from me, lad—it's not all about brawn. Women like a man who can make them laugh, who appreciates them. Doesn't hurt if you can dance, either."

Lowerson turned to him with disbelief writ large on his cleanly-shaven face.

"You must be kidding—I've seen the way they fall over themselves with Ryan. I'd hate him, if he wasn't such a decent bloke."

Phillips snorted out a laugh.

"Aye, well, I never said they were struck blind, did I? But you need more than looks to win the day. Take me," he jerked a thumb towards his own chest. "Did you ever think, in a million years, that Denise would look twice in my direction?"

Lowerson considered the question. Phillips was an intelligent man with a unique capacity to put even the frostiest witness at their ease. He was universally liked around CID and, despite being a bit rough around the edges, he was known for being a gentleman. He might not have the body of an Adonis, but what he lacked in physique he made up for in charm and humour.

"Maybe you're right," Lowerson conceded and let his hand fall away from his hair.

Phillips smiled to himself and made the turn for Cragside.

"You know, I hear Melanie Yates has come on board to help out with the legwork," he added, casual as you like.

Lowerson's ears pricked.

"Oh?"

"Mm-hmm. Nice lass, that one."

When Phillips glanced back across, Lowerson was checking his hair again in the vanity mirror. He let out a muffled laugh which petered out as he thought of MacKenzie, alone and frightened inside the four walls of his house in Kingston Park.

———

MacKenzie swore softly when she realised she'd forgotten to bring her mobile phone. Forgetfulness was becoming a problem these days. The 'self-help' books Phillips had subtly left around the house told her that memory loss was a common side-effect following severe trauma. Over time, she hoped her skills would improve and return to normal, as would her sleep patterns, so long as she continued with the cognitive behavioural therapy she'd been trying to do a little of every day. All the same, it was frustrating.

"Are you feeling alright?"

Anna walked beside her as they made their way along a woodland path towards the main house at Cragside. It was a fair question to ask, considering the last time MacKenzie had been inside a forest she'd been running for her life.

She looked deeply into the shadows of the trees, imagining who or what might be lurking in the undergrowth. Then, she looked firmly away, concentrating on the path ahead.

"I'm fine," she said shortly.

A light sweat trickled down her back but she told herself that was to be expected on a warm afternoon in August. The air was close and heavy with rain that would surely fall later in the day but, for now, sun flooded through the trees and cast long hazy beams to guide their way. Insects buzzed somewhere in the brush and butterflies seemed to float on the air, moving from one patch to the next.

Whenever she heard MacKenzie utter a sharp intake of breath or sensed that panic wanted to take a stranglehold, Anna paused, ostensibly to point out a flower or bird. She chattered about the wedding that was fast approaching or about current affairs, anything to distract her friend from the horrors of the past.

Her kindness was almost MacKenzie's undoing.

"Strange there aren't more visitors," Anna remarked, suddenly realising they hadn't come across a single visitor or estate worker on their travels.

They stopped and peered through the trees, looking for the usual groups of families going on a bear hunt or collecting pine cones.

A twig snapped somewhere behind them and both women spun around in reflex, but there was nobody there.

The main house was equally deserted and the reason soon became apparent. Following the escalation of Victor Swann's death to 'suspicious', visitor access had been suspended for a period of twenty-four hours to give the police a chance to conduct more detailed enquiries. Faulkner's team of CSIs had been recalled, this time to give the staff room and Victor's locker a thorough going-over, in addition to the man's home in Rothbury. Only a skeleton staff remained to keep Cragside house and grounds operational, the others having been given the rest of the day off. The entrance was manned by a shiny-faced young constable who told them to enter their names into a log book. He scrutinised MacKenzie's warrant card before handing it back to her.

"Sorry, ma'am, I almost didn't recognise you."

MacKenzie chose not to be offended but it stung nonetheless.

Had she changed so much?

They paused to cover their shoes in elasticated plastic, then made their way inside the house. To their right, they could see the CSIs already hard at work sweeping the staff room and they headed upstairs to the drawing room, where they found Ryan setting out the sequence of last night's events for Yates' benefit.

"There are two entrances to this room, one at the north end and one at the south end, which leads you through the billiards room and back around in a loop to the main corridor off the gallery," he was saying. "Including Cassandra Gilbert, there were twenty-two people gathered in this room last night. Some seated around the dining table, others grouped together chatting, accounting for eight who had already gone home by the time Swann died."

"Thirty guests in total, twenty-two remaining by the time Swann died," Yates repeated, making a swift note in her book. "Does that include Lionel Gilbert?"

"No, that would make thirty-one."

"Ah-ha." Yates amended the note. "And, it was too dark to tell who might, or might not, have been absent while Swann made his way down to the fuse box?"

Ryan gave a brisk nod.

"We'll re-interview everyone over the next couple of days while it's fresh in their minds but I can tell you it was like a cave. You could barely see more than a few metres in front of your own hand, let alone be able to tell who might have slipped out of a room this size. I can start by listing who was in my immediate vicinity and we can ask the other guests what they can remember but that's the best we've got."

"I suppose it's too much to hope for any CCTV?"

"You suppose correctly," Ryan confirmed. "The Gilberts prefer to keep everything authentic, as close as possible to how things would have been during the Victorian era."

Yates opened her mouth to ask another question but Ryan's attention was immediately drawn elsewhere as he spotted Anna and MacKenzie entering the room.

He flashed a smile and strode across to greet them.

"This is a very pleasant surprise," he said, leaning in to bestow a kiss on Anna's upturned face.

Turning to MacKenzie, he couldn't fail to notice the weight loss and general air of exhaustion but he had the Chief Constable's words ringing in his ears from earlier that morning and felt optimistic that her arrival was a big step in the right direction.

"Are you sure you're ready to come back to work?"

MacKenzie lifted her chin.

"I'm going to start with part-time duties and see how it goes."

Ryan searched her face and whatever he read there seemed to satisfy him.

"That sounds sensible but don't be shy to tell me if you change your mind." He gave her a warm smile. "Welcome back, Mac."

"Thanks," she said and felt a weight lift from her shoulders.

Behind them, the floorboards creaked beneath the weight of two pairs of feet and Phillips entered the drawing room with Lowerson at his heels.

Their footsteps slowed when they caught sight of MacKenzie.

"*Denise*?" Phillips' jaw fell open.

Uninhibited by the crowd of onlookers, he hurried across the room.

"Are you alright? I tried to call you—"

MacKenzie stifled a sigh.

"I'm sorry, Frank, I left my mobile phone at home. Anna came to see me and we drove out here together."

Phillips sent Anna a frustrated glare.

"Out here? To the *woods*? Surely—"

"I asked her to," MacKenzie put in firmly. "It's time I started living again. I can't hide away forever."

He had questions, a lot of questions, but he decided to save them for when they had less of an audience.

"That's good." He rubbed his hands up and down her arms and then stepped back again, giving her the space she needed. When they were at work, Denise remained his superior officer and Phillips was always careful to respect that distinction.

"Hasn't been the same without you," Lowerson put in, with a wide smile.

"There's no telling what mischief you'd get up to, left to your own devices," she teased.

At the other end of the room, Yates watched them with a stab of envy. They were bonded together, a close-knit team of colleagues who behaved more like family, whereas she was on the periphery. She wondered if she would ever be welcomed with open arms, without the cool, professional formality Ryan employed as a default.

As if sensing her observation, he turned and gestured for her to join them.

"Yates?"

She hurried forward.

"I think you've all met PC Melanie Yates but I don't know if you've met my fiancée, Anna?"

Yates pasted a friendly smile on her face and held out a hand to the tall, slim woman with the face of an angel.

"Doctor Taylor," she said, politely.

Anna laughed but it wasn't an unkind sound.

"Please, call me Anna. Only my students call me 'Doctor Taylor'. Or Ryan, when he's being facetious."

Yates watched a smile pass between them and something lurched in her stomach. She nodded as the others drew her into conversation but her eyes strayed back to where their two dark heads leaned together, fingers touching now and then in the kind of natural gesture that spoke of two people who were supremely comfortable with one other.

When Anna excused herself to return to her own work, Yates raised a friendly hand to wave her off.

Ryan guided his team on a walkthrough of Victor Swann's movements the previous evening. As they moved from room to room, daylight filtered through the windows and lent the house a different character but it was still easy to imagine the forbidding atmosphere once night fell. "That's another thing," Ryan said, and turned to them as they stepped outside into the courtyard where Victor's body had been found. "I want to know why the lights failed and whether it was by accident or design."

"You think somebody might have deliberately fused the lights and used the darkness as a cover to push him down the stairs?"

MacKenzie had always been a quick study.

"There are three possibilities, as far as I can tell." Ryan tapped the index finger of his left hand. "First, Swann's death was entirely accidental, as was the electrical failure. But, if that's the case, why was his locker and house ransacked?"

"Opportunism?" Lowerson and Yates spoke in unison, then turned to one another in awkward surprise.

"It's possible," Ryan agreed. "In which case, we need to dig a bit deeper to understand why. None of his valuable possessions has been taken, so what did Victor have that was so important?"

He tapped his middle finger.

"Second, somebody fused the lights deliberately to provide cover for themselves. But how did they know Victor would offer to check the fuse box? It could easily have been me, or Dave Quibble…any number of people."

"Might have been a case of mistaken identity," Phillips put in. "Easy enough to mistake one person for another, especially in the dark."

Ryan nodded.

"That's another possibility, if an assailant mistook Swann for somebody else. But who?"

He shook his head and tapped the third finger of his left hand.

"Finally, the lights fusing was sheer coincidence and somebody took the opportunity to slip out and kill Victor Swann. Once again, we have to ask ourselves why."

There was a short silence while they digested each possibility and Ryan swept his gaze over each of their faces.

"Let's start digging."

CHAPTER 8

By late afternoon, the rainclouds had migrated from the city to settle heavily over Cragside. They brought with them a strong summer wind that buffeted against the white forensic tents and threw up dust from the long gravel driveway. It howled through the uppermost layers of the trees until their branches swayed wildly against the darkening sky and rattled the windows of the old house which, like its master, remained defiant against the gathering storm.

Conscious that the day was slipping away, Ryan dispatched Lowerson and Yates to oversee a thorough search of Victor Swann's house in Rothbury, always hopeful that it might turn up something useful. Phillips and MacKenzie stayed to supervise the work at Cragside, taking secondary statements from its remaining staff and the Gilberts, who looked on with mounting disapproval as their home was invaded. Crime analysts had been instructed to conduct a search of their intelligence databases, just in case Victor Swann had a sheet. The old valet might have seemed the quintessential country gentleman, too refined to have embroiled himself in anything untoward, but if Ryan had learned anything during his timé as a policeman, it was that appearances could often be deceptive.

While those investigations were underway, Ryan went in search of Dave Quibble and a tour of Cragside's electrical systems. He found the conservation manager hunched over a computer in his office, cataloguing what appeared to be a plank of wood.

Ryan rapped a knuckle against the door, which had been left open to visitors.

"Got a minute?"

Dave leaned back in his chair and removed his glasses, blinking a couple of times to clear the glare from his computer screen.

"Of course," he said as he gestured Ryan inside. "What can I do for you?"

Ryan looked around the tiny office space. It was full to brimming with what looked like pieces of junk to the untrained eye but were probably artefacts of great historical importance.

"Working on a Sunday?"

Quibble slid his glasses back onto his nose and indicated the boxes stacked beside his desk. "Always something to keep me busy," he said. "Alice is working on one of the family portraits upstairs and I had another couple of students cataloguing the old nursery upstairs but they've been sent home. What can I help you with?"

"I'd like to take you up on that offer of a guided tour of the electrics but, if this isn't a convenient time...?"

Dave nodded sagely.

"You want to know why the lights went out last night, eh?"

Ryan inclined his head.

"That's easy enough," Dave said, tapping a few keys to save his work. "How much do you know about electrical circuitry?"

"Perhaps the question should be, 'How much do I know about *nineteenth-century* electrical circuitry?' In which case, my answer would be, 'Not much.'"

Quibble laughed and drew himself up.

"Alright, let's start from the top."

Ryan could already feel the beginnings of a headache.

Twenty minutes later, Ryan found himself looking at what could only be described as a giant, fifty-foot corkscrew. A short stroll downhill from the house had taken them along a winding driveway flanked by Douglas firs, conifers and thick rhododendrons until Quibble stopped beside a stone bridge. He pointed towards an enormous turbine leading down to a narrow river which snaked through the trees.

"It's an inverse Archimedes screw." Dave raised his voice above the sound of the water bubbling furiously below.

"How does it work?" Ryan rested his forearms on the edge of the bridge and watched the machine in action.

A swathe of mist covered his face in a fine sheen of moisture.

"Well, normally, an Archimedes screw pumps low-lying water upwards but, in this case, we're taking water from higher ground and forcing it downwards." Dave bobbed his head towards an expanse of water on the other side of the bridge. "Water from Tumbleton Lake feeds through the screw at the top and the weight of it forces the blades to turn, which allows the water to fall to the bottom and the screw rotates."

Ryan nodded, watching the powerful blades undulating in rhythmic motion as the water made its journey through the turbine.

"Then what?"

"The energy produced by the rotational action is harnessed in an electrical generator that's connected to the main turbine shaft."

"How much energy are we talking about here?"

They turned away from the bridge and began to walk back towards the house, while Dave removed his glasses and rubbed the lenses against the edge of his jacket to clear them of condensation.

"If Cragside were your average house, the energy produced by that screw would be enough to power it for more than a year. That's because the average house only has around twenty light bulbs, whereas Cragside has over three hundred."

Ryan looked up at the mansion and stood still for a moment, considering.

"And each bulb has twenty or forty watts?"

"No," Dave stuck his hands in the pockets of his padded gilet. "The family wanted to use hydroelectricity, just like old Armstrong would have wanted it, and we use energy-saving LED bulbs to conserve power and maintain the historical ambience."

"What about the other electrics?"

"The screw only provides enough power to light the house," Quibble explained. "There isn't enough hydro-power to operate large items, like fridges or washing machines. The house is connected to the National Grid, of course, so we can always rely on mains electricity for that. Sometimes, we produce excess power and store it in a giant battery but it's not usually enough for a consistent output."

A light drizzle began to fall as their feet crunched over twigs and fallen leaves.

"So, you're saying you can choose whether to rely solely on hydro-power?"

"Sure," Quibble shrugged, as if it were obvious. "But the Gilberts prefer to avoid mainstream electricity wherever possible."

"When do they use it?" Ryan prodded.

"Only on set days—usually Mondays and Fridays, which is when the housekeeper does the laundry and whatnot." Quibble chuckled to himself. "That's when we have the radio playing in the staff room."

"How about yesterday? Surely, mains power would have been needed to prepare dinner for the party?"

Quibble scratched the side of his nose.

"Ordinary cooking for the family or small parties can be done in the house kitchens but large-scale catering comes from the tea room in the old stable block. We keep that area connected to the National Grid continuously, so there's never any disruption to visitors' amenities. The best person to ask about that would be Maggie but I think the catering staff transferred the food and drink from the tea room across to the main house last night using the servants' stairs."

The same staircase Victor had tumbled down, Ryan thought.

"But the main part of the house was entirely disconnected from the National Grid?"

"Yes, that's right."

"One final question, Dave. Who knows when the house will be connected to mains power and when it won't?"

Quibble gave him a searching look.

"Well, everybody, I suppose. It's part of the initial staff training, to prevent people turning on a dishwasher and inadvertently fusing the circuit. All the family and staff know which days are safe to use large electricals. The only possible exception would be when the Gilberts decide to use mains electric on a different day and forget to tell anybody about it but that rarely happens."

Ryan fell silent as the drizzle turned to fat raindrops and soaked through his thin cotton shirt. He looked up at the whimsical house that appeared like a mirage, hazy and fantastical with its turrets and towers, and wondered what festered beneath its picturesque exterior.

"Found anything interesting?"

Melanie Yates looked up from her inspection of the chest of drawers in Victor Swann's bedroom as Lowerson sauntered into the room. "Not yet," she replied, turning back to her search. "Just clothes and trinkets. You?"

Lowerson cleared his throat in what he hoped was a manly fashion.

"It's more a question of what I *haven't* found," he said. "There's hardly any photographs around the house and no letters or cards from family. Bit weird, don't you think?"

"Maybe."

"Victor certainly liked the finer things in life, didn't he?" Lowerson went on, taking in the upscale furnishings and extravagant clothes hanging in the wardrobe. "I didn't realise valets were paid so well."

"I wouldn't have a clue," Yates admitted, then made a small sound of surprise when her fingers brushed against something hard. She pushed aside a mound of folded boxer shorts and grasped a brown, A4-sized envelope.

"What's that?"

Lowerson came to stand beside her, leaning in a little too close for comfort. Yates took a subtle half-step away, so she would not be suffocated by the overpowering scent of whatever aftershave he'd doused himself in that morning.

"Looks like photographs," she said, then pulled out a wad of colour prints with a gloved hand.

The first few images were innocent enough, just snapshots of a garden and of the house at Cragside. The prints seemed to be a few years old judging by the yellowing edges and general hue, but they had been carefully stored away from the light so their quality was preserved.

As she turned to the next print, the content changed dramatically.

The images that followed were all of Cassandra Gilbert in various poses, out on the lawn or beside the trees, mostly in the nude or half-dressed. At a glance, they might have been taken at least ten years earlier.

"Well—"

"Ah—"

Lowerson and Yates looked at each other in a combination of startled embarrassment and genuine surprise.

"Who said the younger generation have all the fun? Judging by these photos, it's the older ones who like to let loose." Lowerson tried for levity but his attempt fell on deaf ears.

"Do you think Victor took these photos?"

Lowerson shrugged.

"Impossible to say for sure."

Yates returned the photos to their envelope and looked across at him.

"Why else would Victor have these pictures? It puts a different slant on Cassandra Gilbert's relationship with her husband's valet, doesn't it?"

"Let's not go jumping to conclusions, pet." His tone was ever-so-slightly condescending and he immediately wished he could snatch the words back. Perhaps he should do himself a favour and stop talking altogether.

"I am not your pet."

Too late, Lowerson thought weakly.

Yates raised a single, unimpressed eyebrow and then stalked out of the room with her spine ramrod straight.

After she'd left, Lowerson slapped a palm against his own face and blew out a long, frustrated breath.

"And I wonder why I'm still single," he muttered, before trailing after her to issue an apology.

CHAPTER 9

The rain continued for the rest of the afternoon, casting a daytime shadow over the landscape so that it seemed much later than five o'clock when the CSI team packed away their equipment and Cragside closed its doors to the outside world.

Ryan waved off Faulkner's team as they trundled along the winding driveway back towards the city and remained standing for a while longer watching the rain from the relative shelter of a covered stone archway.

Phillips and MacKenzie found him there, lost in thought.

"Penny for them, lad?"

"I'm not sure they're worth that much," Ryan replied, turning away from the rain. "I was wondering whether we're barking up the wrong tree. Faulkner says they haven't found any meaningful trace evidence, although they'll be running tests over the next few days. No fingerprints other than Swann's on his locker or at his house, so I'm asking myself why it still feels off."

MacKenzie zipped up her jacket as the wind whipped through the archway.

"Your instincts are usually good. If there's anything to find, we'll find it."

Ryan gave a slight shake of his head.

"I can't afford to rely on instinct, not when there's a pile of other cases waiting for me back at CID. They deserve at least as much attention as an old man who might have lost his footing."

Phillips heard the irritation in his voice and wondered what else was causing it. It wasn't like Ryan to doubt himself.

"Everything's taken care of," Phillips said. "There's a capable team manning the fort and if something crops up, you can easily step in."

Ryan nodded, his eyes straying upwards to where Lionel Gilbert watched them from a window on the first floor. He didn't shy away from the scrutiny or raise a hand to wave.

It was unnerving.

"If Swann's home hadn't been ransacked, I would have signed it off as accidental death pending the post-mortem," Ryan lowered his voice so that they could not be overheard above the sound of the pattering rain. "But Yates tells me they found a stack of compromising photographs in Swann's bottom drawer, all of Cassandra Gilbert."

"In the buff?" Phillips exclaimed, with his usual finesse.

"For God's sake, keep your voice down. There are eyes and ears everywhere in this place," Ryan muttered.

"Maybe that's what the intruder was looking for? Cassandra might have been embarrassed to think somebody would find them, so she tried to recover them before we found them, or asked somebody else to do it," MacKenzie suggested.

"It's possible," Ryan said but he was dubious. "The thing is, both Yates and Lowerson agree the photographs weren't hard to find, especially considering our unknown perp pulled out almost every drawer in the house. He must have seen those photographs and discarded them."

They watched the rain for a moment while they considered other possibilities.

"All the same, it's a bit saucy, isn't it?" Phillips pronounced.

"More *importantly*"—MacKenzie gave him a withering look—"it calls her credibility into question because when we took another statement from her less than an hour ago, Cassandra was adamant she barely knew Victor Swann beyond social niceties and the usual employer-employee relationship."

"Either she's telling porky-pies or Swann got hold of those photographs some other way," Phillips said.

"He could have stolen them," Ryan agreed. "Which calls *his* integrity into question and forces me to wonder what else Victor Swann might have done to upset person or persons unknown."

His eyes strayed up to the first-floor window again but this time it was empty.

"I don't know that the circumstances of his death justify me bandying around accusations about what could have been a private dalliance that has no bearing on Swann's death. If I raise it with Cassandra Gilbert, we could cause a lot of embarrassment and potential trouble with her husband."

"It's not for us to judge people's private affairs," MacKenzie agreed but Phillips shook his head.

"I dunno, love. Living in the nineteenth century with no telly, gaddin' about the countryside in their birthday suits… they seem mad as hatters, if you ask me."

"Eccentric." Ryan gave him a quick slap on the back. "Not mad, old boy. Rich people are always *eccentric*."

Their laughter echoed around the stone walls as they bade each other farewell but when Ryan turned away to make the short journey back to his rental cottage he felt the same creeping sensation return, trailing its way up his back.

Alice Chapman didn't notice the rain, or that she'd worked long past her contractual hours. Within the cosy confines of Cragside's uppermost turret room, she had become engrossed in the intricate business of returning an old painting to its former glory. Her hair hung in a shining curtain down her back, tucked behind her ears with two clips at either side, and her face was covered by a jeweller's headset complete with visor and built-in magnifying lens. Her jeans were crusted with drying paint and the scent of turpentine was ripe on the air. Shifting slightly on the wooden stool she'd positioned at an angle to the window, Alice considered the painting on the easel in front of her. When Dave Quibble had first commissioned her to restore the portrait, it had been coated in a brownish-yellow tint which she knew had been caused by natural degeneration of the original varnish. Since then, it had taken several days inside a borrowed laboratory to meticulously clean away the discoloured varnish and dirt with cotton swabs, peeling away the delicate layers to reveal the true image beneath. It had taken almost as long to blend the right oils to match the original colour palette, systematically checking individual colours against UV light, or their chemical reaction with varying degrees of solvent to find just the right blend.

Thankfully, she was a patient woman.

Four years studying Art History at Cambridge and a further three as apprentice to one of the best restorers in London had taught her perseverance. Slow and steady hands were required to do justice to great masterpieces and hers would have made any surgeon proud.

Today, she had finally begun the process of repainting the damaged areas of the portrait and, because it was the part she enjoyed the most, time had slipped by without her noticing. It was only when she heard the *crack* of thunder outside that she realised it was well after six o'clock and the light was no longer good enough to use. Reluctantly, she set her paintbrush down and stepped away from the easel, regarding it with a critical eye.

"Two more minutes," she promised herself, reaching for the brush again.

Fifteen minutes later, she found her throat was bone dry. Looking across to the window ledge, she spotted a cup of cold coffee she'd left untouched hours earlier. A milky skin now floated on top, next to the half-eaten sandwich she'd also neglected to finish.

"Time to go," she murmured, stretching her arms above her head to ease her cramped muscles.

It took another twenty minutes to pack away the equipment and clean her paintbrushes, by which time her stomach was rumbling and she had the beginnings of a dehydration headache. Alice grabbed her summer coat and started to shrug into it as she left the room, pausing to collect the dirty dishes and lock the door securely behind her. She made her way down a narrow flight of stairs and emerged onto the galleried landing to find it silent and empty but for the sound of the rain hammering against the windows. She wondered where everybody was.

"Hello?"

They've probably gone home already, she realised.

The Gilberts were nowhere to be seen, either, and she wondered whether she should look into the main rooms to let them know she was still there.

Deciding against it, she made her way down to the ground floor and dipped her head inside the staff common room, which bore the remnants of a forensic search earlier in the day.

That, too, was empty.

Feeling suddenly cold, Alice turned towards the kitchen. Another wave of dehydration washed over her and dark spots swam in front of her eyes.

Foolish, she told herself. It was stupid to become so engrossed in work that she neglected to eat or drink.

She entered the kitchen and flicked on the lights, which did little to relieve the melancholic atmosphere. She stacked her dishes beside the sink and decided to grab a quick glass of water, which ought to tide her over until she got home. The drive to Rothbury wasn't long and she had a fully stocked fridge back at the little one-bedroom flat she'd rented for the duration of her assignment. After a bowl of pasta or maybe a nice homemade paella, she'd get an early night and rest her tired eyes.

Another *crack* of thunder rumbled outside, bouncing off the walls.

Alice gulped down a few mouthfuls of water and hurried out of the room. There was still no sign of anybody in the reception foyer and the hallways were eerily quiet; there was no distant sound of conversation nor the murmur of a television, not even Lionel's booming voice carried on the air.

But she was not alone.

The house seemed to breathe around her, whispering secrets through its wooden walls, watching her. Waiting.

Warning.

Alice had reached the front door when she heard a clattering sound somewhere over her shoulder. She tugged open the door and looked out at the rainy driveway, feeling the warm summer wind brush against her skin. Freedom awaited her and held the promise of a lifetime of rewarding work, perhaps a husband and children one day.

But it was not to be, and the noise came again.

She looked over her shoulder at the empty, shadowed corridor. It beckoned her to turn back and she began to wonder if one of the Gilberts needed her help. Lionel might have fallen, or Cassandra, for that matter. They were getting on, after all. Or it could be Dave, struggling with a box of artefacts in his office further down the hall. Her hand fell away from the doorknob and the door clicked softly shut again.

Like Pandora, she was unable to resist her own fatal curiosity.

CHAPTER 10

The lights were blazing through the windows of their rental cottage when Ryan returned home. He'd taken the walk through the trees more quickly than usual, dodging puddles as he went. He didn't mind getting wet, especially when the rain was warm against his face and smelled of freshly-cut grass, but he minded the overwhelming sense of disquiet he'd been feeling all day and sought the comfort of home to remind him of everything that was right and good in the world.

"Hello?"

Ryan kicked off his sodden boots and began to shrug out of his wet shirt. Summertime in the north of England was universally acknowledged to be a temperamental season and he should have known better than to leave the house without a jacket. Clearly, the brief bout of warm weather had addled his brain and the sooner winter came, the better.

He dipped into the downstairs bathroom to retrieve a hand towel and was in the process of scrubbing at his hair when Anna came to greet him.

"Hi," she said, lifting the edge of the towel to bestow a kiss. "How was the rest of your day?"

"Tedious," he replied. "Long, unproductive and full of unanswered questions."

"Welcome to my world," she laughed, thinking of the hours she had spent poring over texts about the first Viking raids in Northumberland.

Hearing her laughter was just the tonic he needed. Ryan moved forward and looped the towel around her waist like a lasso. She chuckled as he drew her towards him with a definite glint in his eye.

"You sound as if you need a distraction," he said, when they stood toe to toe.

Anna pretended to consider the question.

"I do enjoy a game of Scrabble."

"Mm," he agreed, dipping his head to nuzzle at the sensitive skin of her neck. His breath was warm against her skin and she sighed.

"Or chess," she managed. "I like chess."

He lifted his head and kissed her deeply, letting the towel fall to the floor so he could spear his fingers through her hair to cradle her head.

"I'll show you my best gambits," he promised.

A good while later, Ryan followed Anna through to the spacious kitchen where she had been working for several hours using the large oak breakfast table in lieu of a desk.

He scented the air like a hungry lion and almost growled when he caught a whiff of meat roasting in the oven. "You didn't need to go to all this trouble," he said.

Ryan didn't expect anybody else to cook or clean for him; he could rustle up a pretty good meal and he enjoyed singing along to a spot of classic rock while he did the vacuuming, which thankfully drowned out any flat notes.

"I had a yen for some comfort food and it was a welcome relief from reading Bede's ecclesiastical history," Anna told him. "You can do the washing up, if you like."

"It's a deal."

While Anna tidied away lever arch files and closed her laptop computer, Ryan went in search of a bottle of red wine and a couple of glasses. It was the weekend, after all, and it would complement the meat nicely. If it managed to soothe his taut nerves, that wouldn't be such a bad thing either.

"So"—Anna re-entered the kitchen having deposited her paperwork elsewhere and accepted a generous glass of Malbec—"before I was carried off, you were telling me about your day."

They clinked glasses and took a sip of wine.

"I've had worse," Ryan conceded, thinking of recent history with a flashing smile. "There were no crazed psychopaths running amok, for one thing. If anything, the estate has been strangely quiet. I don't know what it says about my psyche but I almost wish something *would* happen."

Anna frowned.

"What do you mean?"

"I don't know." He set his wine down again, his thirst having disappeared. "I've had a sense of foreboding all day. I can't explain it."

"You think something bad is going to happen?"

He walked across to the kitchen window and braced his hands on the countertop, eyes scanning the dusky garden outside.

"I'm trying to figure it out," he said quietly. "I know there's something I've seen or that I'm missing and it feels important. I wish I knew what it was."

Anna rested a hand on his back in silent support.

"You can't stop somebody committing a crime, if they've set their mind to it."

He laughed shortly.

"If I could, I'd be out of a job."

The smile died on his lips when he remembered the discussion he'd had with his Chief Constable. The intended candidate for Detective Chief Superintendent had been troubling him all day. He didn't want the position himself and had never intended to apply but it might be better than allowing ghosts from the past to haunt his present and the future he hoped for with Anna. He made up his mind, there and then, to tell Morrison that he wanted the job after all. He'd tell her first thing tomorrow morning.

Anna gave him a searching look.

"Is something else on your mind?"

Ryan had never lied to Anna and had no intention of starting, particularly on the cusp of their wedding.

On the other hand, he saw no reason to worry her if a simple solution presented itself. That being the case, he tugged her against him so that the top of her head tucked snugly beneath his chin and wrapped his arms around her protectively.

"Nothing to worry about," he murmured, rubbing his cheek against her soft hair.

He hoped it was true.

Phillips muted the evening news when MacKenzie walked back into the living room. He wrapped a sturdy arm around her shoulders as she sank onto the sofa beside him and snuggled into his chest. He noticed she'd washed and dried her hair into shining red waves and he could smell the aroma of coconut body cream on her skin. Until recently, it was all he could do to help her get out of bed in the mornings and his heart soared with optimism. "Nice bath, love?"

"Mmm." She listened to the strong *thud* of his heartbeat and felt relaxed for the first time in months.

"How did it feel to be back on the job today?"

MacKenzie heard his heartbeat quicken and guessed he'd been worried about her.

"I had a few uncomfortable moments," she admitted, thinking back to the panic she'd felt walking through the trees earlier in the day. "I needed to do it, otherwise these walls would start to become a prison. It felt good to be part of the team again."

Phillips kissed the top of her head.

"You never stopped being part of the team."

She nodded, watching silent newscasters mouthing their report on the television. The screen cut to images of drunken revelry in the city centre and a straitlaced reporter reciting statistics about binge drinking.

MacKenzie reached across to stab the remote control and the screen went blank. What she was about to say required no distractions.

"Frank, you've been a rock these last four months."

"Oh, I hardly—" he began but she cut him off firmly.

"No, let me get this out. I want you to know how much it's meant to me, knowing you were beside me every step of the way. Hearing you breathing next to me when I woke up scared during the night or knowing you were only a phone call away helped me to push through. I don't know what I would have done without you."

"You'd have been just fine," he said quietly.

"I've always been one to manage alone," she agreed. "The women in my family were so constrained, so tied to their roles, when I grew up I never wanted to rely on anyone or become too dependent."

"The day you become the Little Woman will be the day hell freezes over."

She smiled against the side of his cotton shirt.

"I know I've been difficult at times."

Phillips sat back so he could look directly into her sad green eyes.

"You are one of the strongest people I've ever known. What you went through…" His jaw clenched as he thought of it. "Some people would have buckled but not you. Not my Denise."

Her eyes glittered with emotional tears.

"I've got two questions I want to ask you, Frank."

"Aye, lass?"

"The first is whether you'll teach me to box. I've done a bit of kickboxing in my time, but I'm talking about the real thing. I never want to feel weak or defenceless ever again."

Phillips simply stared, momentarily lost for words.

He'd grown up sparring with his friends on the street and had spent many of his formative years training at Buddle's Boxing Gym, which was a local institution in Newcastle. He knew a thing or two about the sport and he considered himself an enlightened man in all things, but he'd never been asked to teach a woman, especially one he happened to love.

"I don't want to hurt you," he said, gruffly.

"What makes you think you would? It's only sport, Frank." There was a light of challenge in her eyes, one he knew very well. "Perhaps you're worried I'll run rings around you, boyo?"

He grinned.

"Alright, you're on. We can start whenever you like."

Pleased, she leaned over to plant a smacking kiss on his ruddy cheek.

"What was the second question?"

"Well…"

Phillips detected a serious tone to her voice and wondered whether he'd forgotten to empty the dishwasher or left the toilet seat up.

MacKenzie watched panic flit across his face and almost laughed. Instead, she folded her arms across her chest and looked him dead in the eye.

"I want to know what your intentions are."

His eyebrows flew into his receding hairline.

"I—my intentions?"

"I might be a modern woman, Frank Phillips, but I want to know how much longer you expect me to carry on living in sin with you like this."

She tightened the belt of her towelling robe, for added effect.

"Let's not forget I'm a good Catholic," she continued, although she couldn't remember the last time she'd stepped inside a church other than to investigate a crime.

Phillips recovered himself quickly.

"Well, if that's the way you feel about it, I'd better tell you that I expect you to marry me as soon as possible and I won't take 'no' for an answer. As it happens, I asked your Da a couple of weeks ago and he tells me that I'll do right enough."

MacKenzie felt a lump rise in her throat.

"You did? Frank, you know, I was only joking, you don't have to—"

He silenced her with a brush of his lips against hers, then heaved himself off the sofa.

"Wait there."

He was gone for a minute, leaving MacKenzie to wonder whether she was ready, whether he was ready and whether he still loved his first wife who had passed away a few years earlier. Thoughts and doubts circled her mind until he returned with a small black box clutched in his hand.

He hovered there, not quite knowing where to begin.

"Denise, you know I was married before."

"Yes, Frank, and it's alright. I understand if you don't feel the same—"

"Will you let me get a word in edgewise?"

He laughed and shook his head.

"Laura was a wonderful woman," he said honestly. "It hurt, more than I can say, when cancer took her from me. You probably remember how it was," he added, for they had been work colleagues at the time.

She nodded soberly.

"I remember."

"I grieved for her and, for a while, I didn't think I'd be able to love like that again." He looked over to where she fiddled nervously with the ends of her dressing gown. "But I never bargained on you, Denise. It hit me like an arrow between the eyes, the way I feel for you. Even in the old days when I fought against it, you'd find a way to get under my skin and make me feel like a daft teenager. I don't like to think of how empty my life would be without you in it."

Her lips trembled and he came to perch on the sofa beside her.

"Four months ago, I thought I had lost you. I said to myself, if we both came through it, I wasn't going to be frightened of loving again. If you didn't want to get married, that was okay. That was just fine, so long as you loved me as I love you."

"Oh, now you've gone and done it," she sniffled.

"But since you're so worried about what the neighbours might think"—he grinned and held open the box— "I thought I'd better have this ready just in case your Da came after me with a shotgun."

She giggled. Nearly forty-four years on planet Earth and she giggled like a girl.

It felt wonderful.

CHAPTER 11

"Is anybody there?"

Alice's voice was lost inside the deserted hallway. Lamps fizzed and dipped ominously as the storm gathered momentum outside, flickering their weak light at regular intervals as she crept along the corridor, listening intently for sounds of life.

"Hello?"

She pushed open the doors as she made her way down the hallway but found each room empty. Eventually, she stopped and turned around a complete circle. There *had* been a clattering noise, she was sure of it.

Perhaps she was hearing things.

She was about to turn away when the noise came again.

Alice took a couple of steps further down the corridor and almost jumped out of her skin when a figure stepped through one of the panelled doorways.

"Oh! You gave me such a fright!"

She let out a bright, nervous laugh.

115

"I *thought* I heard someone," she prattled on, failing to notice the look of profound shock on the other person's face.

"I thought everyone had gone home," they whispered, glancing in both directions down the hallway.

"I haven't seen anyone else," Alice said, helpfully.

She adjusted the strap on her bag, which was overfull and weighed heavily against her shoulder. She happened to glance down and noticed they were clutching a bag tightly, angled away from her direct line of sight. It was a white and blue plastic affair bearing the name of a large supermarket chain and appeared to be full of odds and ends.

"You're as bad as me," she observed, cheerfully. "I seem to hoard junk. Be careful, it looks like the handle is about to—"

And she was right.

The plastic buckled, spilling its contents onto the carpeted floor at their feet.

"*Damn!*"

The sharp expletive surprised Alice and she bent down to help tidy the clutter back inside its miserable plastic carrier.

"Don't worry, I'll help you clear it up."

"No. Don't."

"Would you like another one?" Alice continued, failing to hear the stark warning. "I'm sure I have a spare bag in here, somewhere," she began to search for one inside her own voluminous leather bag.

"I think you should go home."

"Honestly, it's no trouble," she parried.

With an exclamation of triumph, she tugged out a foldaway carrier bag and held it out.

"Here," she smiled.

They looked at each other for a long moment.

"Go ahead, it won't bite!"

The smile froze on Alice's face as she looked more closely at the contents of the spillage, seeing them properly for the first time. She recognised an expensive silver cartridge pen bearing the monogram 'VS' and frowned, not immediately understanding its significance.

Then, she noticed their hands.

Why wear gloves inside the house?

Realisation came crashing down like a tonne of bricks. Alice's eyes flew to the person who watched her closely with a tinge of regret. Slowly, she retracted her hand, staring into the eyes of someone she thought she had known.

"I—I should be getting home."

"Alice."

Her legs seemed to have turned to jelly. She needed to *move*, to get up and *run*, but she could only manage to edge away like a startled deer. She drew herself up and clung to the strap of her bag for support, praying all the while that somebody—anybody—would interrupt them.

But they were completely alone.

"It's getting late…" Her voice wobbled and she began to step backwards. Her mouth opened and then shut again, unable to voice the scream that welled inside her belly.

"Is there something you want to ask me, Alice?"

She shook her head wildly.

"No. I'm not thinking anything. I just want to go home. I *am* going home," she gabbled. "It's been a long day and I—I need to go home now."

The figure shoved the contents of Victor's locker back into the broken carrier bag, grasped the ends in a firm grip and then stood up.

"Why don't you stay awhile and tell me how the portrait is coming along?"

She heard the words but the eyes held a different message as they watched her like a predator. Alice read the intent as clearly as if it had been spoken and her stomach did a slow flip.

They stood facing one another for one humming second before she whirled around and ran for the door.

Thirty miles away, Jack Lowerson let himself into the two-bedroom flat he had recently bought in Newcastle and was in the slow process of renovating. He couldn't quite stretch to one of the swanky new apartments on the Quayside or a Georgian terrace in Jesmond but he was working up to it. For now, he'd taken the little garden flat in Heaton and was polishing it until it gleamed. He enjoyed the sense of achievement it gave him each time he looked at the kitchen he'd helped to install, or at the floorboards he'd sanded, stained and varnished himself. But, God, it was lonely to come home to a microwave dinner and Marbles, his cat.

The feline in question skipped into the hallway as he entered and wound her way through his legs, purring loudly when he bent down to give her a scratch between the ears.

"There's my girl," he crooned. "Did you miss me, hmm?"

Uncaring of the mess it would make of his suit, he scooped her up and headed into the open-plan kitchen diner. The purring grew louder as she identified the direction he was headed and she leapt down to stand beside the cupboard where he kept the cat treats.

Lowerson laughed and shook his head.

"Always on the make," he grumbled but dutifully fed her a packet of meaty biscuits.

He leaned back against the counter and folded his arms across his chest, looked around the immaculate empty kitchen and wondered what Ryan or Phillips would be doing around now. Probably relaxing with their partners in life, chatting over the events of the day or breaking open a bottle of wine.

They certainly wouldn't be talking to mute animals.

He sighed and flung open the fridge to reach for a microwaveable lasagne.

Alice flew down the hallway towards the front door. The wind shook the walls of the house until they seemed to cry out, whining against the force of the summer storm and drowning out the sound of thundering footsteps following her down the corridor.

She reached the front door and yanked it open, the air catching in her throat as she turned and caught sight of the person who followed. For a moment in time, their eyes locked and she saw only grim determination.

No remorse, no madness.

Just purpose.

She stumbled outside onto the gravel driveway and into the rain that fell like a deluge. It plastered her long hair down her back and poured into her eyes so that she could hardly see which way to turn. Her car was parked in the staff car park along an access road to the left but she found herself veering right, skidding down a wet gravel pathway leading into the trees.

She heard panting breaths not far behind and she ran faster, feeling the soles of her shoes slipping against the pathway. She sobbed as she scrambled down the slight incline, tripping against the potholes but pushing herself to reach the iron bridge which spanned a small river running between the crag where the house stood and the trees on the other side. Once she crossed the bridge, it was only a few minutes' run through the trees until she reached her destination.

If she could only make it to Ryan's cottage, she'd be safe.

The footsteps were getting closer.

Melanie Yates let herself into the front door of her parents' house and immediately heard the refrain of a well-known soap opera playing on the television in the living room. "Mel? Is that you?"

"Yes, Mum. I'll be through in a minute!"

She took her time hanging up her coat and slotting her shoes neatly into the rack her father had built from scraps of MDF wood, back in the days when home improvement shows had dominated Saturday night prime time telly. Twenty years had passed since the country's obsession with *Changing Rooms* but still the little shoe rack remained to remind her of the passage of time.

Melanie thought of all the years she'd been coming home and slotting her shoes onto the flimsy rack and experienced a wave of cabin fever. She loved her parents but it was time to strike out, to be independent.

Her mother came into the hallway to seek her out and clucked her tongue.

"You're late for dinner, love."

"I'm sorry, Mum. Remember, I told you I'd be working odd hours over the next while. I've been seconded to CID," she said proudly.

Her mother's face didn't alter.

"That's nice, dear. I've kept some shepherd's pie warm for you in the oven."

Melanie forced a smile.

She had never, in all her life, liked shepherd's pie. But it was her father's favourite and, in their household, that was all that mattered.

"Thank you," she said, and leaned in to peck her mother's cheek.

She smelled the gin immediately, although there had been a liberal dose of mouthwash to try to hide it. Some days, you couldn't smell the booze, which usually meant the tipple of choice had been vodka. Either way you looked at it, her mother was a functioning alcoholic and had been for over ten years.

Ever since Gemma died.

Her twin had been the shiny half of the coin, the glossy version of herself that she could never hope to emulate. Much as Melanie tried to carve out her own existence, the knowledge that she was a pale comparison to the child they'd lost was a constant wound and every day she continued to spend beneath her parents' roof was a reminder of her own inadequacy.

Melanie watched her mother stumble back through to the living room and decided to bypass dinner. She headed upstairs to the room she'd had all her life and closed the door quietly behind her.

———

Thunder crashed in the skies far above where Alice Chapman dashed along the rocky pathway. It led down from Cragside house towards a vast wrought-iron bridge spanning two sides of the steep gorge which separated the house from the forest and gardens on the other side. It was also the route towards Ryan and Anna's rental cottage, and safety.

Adrenaline compelled her to run faster, to push her aching muscles to the limit of endurance, but shock and fear worked together with the driving rain to make progress impossible. Her feet tripped and stumbled against the stone steps that were slick with water and her heavy bag knocked her off-balance.

Alice cast it away and the bag thudded into the shrubbery as she scampered past.

Behind her, the person who raced after her made a mental note of its position, in case they would need to recover it. Their lungs screamed for release as their feet pounded after her and, remarkably, tears began to fall.

It was not supposed to be this way.

If only she hadn't seen the bag.

No time to think about that now.

Fear was a powerful motivating force and their stride lengthened, closing the gap between them and their quarry.

CHAPTER 12

Less than a ten-minute walk away, Anna watched Ryan pace the living room floor for the hundredth time and wondered what she could do to ease his mind. He'd changed into a fresh shirt of wash-worn cotton and had rolled up the sleeves in deference to the humidity but he had no appetite for dinner.

"Why don't you come and sit down beside me?" Anna patted the cushion next to her on the squishy, oatmeal-coloured sofa.

Ryan ran an agitated hand through his black hair and let it fall again.

"I'm going to ring the pathologist," he said. "Pinter should have done the autopsy on Swann's body by now."

"It's been less than twenty-four hours," Anna reminded him. "You told me yourself, he has more urgent cases to deal with. Besides, it's"—she paused to consult her watch—"almost seven-thirty. Would he be at work at this hour on a Sunday?"

Ryan swallowed his frustration because she was perfectly correct. There was no sense in hurrying the pathologist, who he knew to be highly competent and dedicated to his work. Harassing the man at home would only hinder the process.

He would just have to wait.

"Without any physical evidence, all I've got is a very bad gut feeling."

He rapped a fist against his abdomen.

"I can't justify any more man hours spent diving into Swann's personal history unless I have something to substantiate it."

Anna nodded her understanding.

"You're doing all you can."

She studied him as he roamed about the room like a caged tiger. The compassion he felt for the dead and their loved ones swam so close to the surface it was almost tangible. Ryan's vocation was to seek justice for the dead, to avenge them and re-balance the scales, but that came with a weight of responsibility. She wondered how he coped with the ones he couldn't avenge; the families to whom he couldn't bring justice, whatever that meant.

"Come and sit down," she urged. "You're making me seasick."

Ryan drummed his fingers against the side of his jeans and made a conscious effort to shrug off the tension. He joined her on the sofa and they sat quietly with their hands clasped together while Billie Holiday sang dulcetly about summertime on the stereo system.

Moments later, there came a tremendous crash of thunder and they both jerked around in shock. Outside, lightning blazed through the sky and the wind circled, wailing like a banshee.

"Did you hear that?" Ryan said urgently, rearing off the sofa to draw back the curtains and look out the window.

"It was only the storm," Anna soothed.

But Ryan shook his head and strode out into the hallway to shove his feet back into his damp boots.

Anna sprang up after him.

"Where are you going? It's blowing a gale out there!"

He said nothing and continued to lace up the boots with short, sharp movements.

"I'll be back shortly."

"Stuff that," she said roundly. "I'm coming with you."

Alice didn't have to look over her shoulder to know they were gaining on her. She could *feel* their proximity in every cell and nerve ending of her body, which was vibrating with fear. She was shaking with fatigue and her feet were starting to drag against the wet ground, scuffing against the turf leading up to the foot of the bridge. *Just a bit further.*

Her knees buckled as she reached the entrance to the long, gracefully arched bridge and she groped for the handrail to prevent a fall, but it was inevitable.

She hit the ground hard, grazing the palms of her hands and twisting her ankle with a painful *crunch.*

Alice cried out and tried to drag herself back up, but the delay cost her precious seconds she couldn't afford.

A pair of strong hands hauled her upwards and she opened her mouth to scream. The sound echoed around the trees, penetrating the stormy sky until a hard hand clamped over her mouth to silence her.

"Shut up," they ground out, wrestling with her as she fought to break free. "I don't want to hurt you."

The plastic bag swayed with the movement of their bodies as they grappled on the narrow bridge and Alice kicked out her legs, clawing at the hand blocking her nose and mouth. She tried to bite at the skin but the pressure was so tight she could hardly move her jaw.

She couldn't breathe and her nostrils flared as she sucked thin streams of air through her nose.

"I don't want to hurt you," they repeated, but a knee drove into Alice's back so that her spine arched forward and she was pushed towards the edge of the railing. She could hear their harsh breathing in her ear, could feel their spittle against her skin, and her mind began to shut down. In a final surge, she reared up and twisted against the hands which held her like iron rods but her body was exhausted and succumbing to shock.

"I'm sorry. I don't have any other choice."

Alice's heart leapt into her throat and then she found she was floating, falling, suspended in mid-air for endless seconds before the ground rose up to meet her in the valley far below.

Through the darkness, the lone figure on the bridge heard the distant sound of heavy impact and shuddered.

Pity.

Looking up at the outline of the house they saw lights glimmering in its uppermost windows and hoped fortune had been on their side. The rain would wash away their footprints. What else was there for the police to find?

Only then did they realise Alice had taken the plastic bag with her and it lay scattered in the depths of the valley beside the broken shell of what had once been a person.

Ryan ran out into the night and was immediately bathed in a shower of rain.

"Which way?" Anna joined him, blinking through the heavy fall of water.

"Let's take the path," he called to her above the rainfall and pointed towards their usual walkway through the trees.

They jogged across the saturated ground, their boots sinking into thick mud as they made their way through the gathering darkness. The trees provided some shelter, allowing them to take stock of their surroundings until they reached the iron bridge connecting the two sides of the valley. The outline of the house could be seen on the other side, glorious in all weather and impervious to the petty follies of mortal man.

"I can't see anyone," Anna said, shivering slightly as the rain turned colder and night descended. "Are you sure you heard something?"

Ryan's hair was matted to his head and gleamed black, even in the half-light of the solar-powered lamps lining the bridge at their feet. To either side, there was a sheer drop into the gorge beneath which was, by now, cloaked in darkness.

He lifted his hands in mute appeal but there was nothing to find and nobody to save.

"Maybe I was wrong," he said. "Perhaps it was the thunder, after all."

"Let's check up at the house," she suggested. Another person might have complained about the conditions and gone home at the earliest opportunity, but not Anna.

They climbed the stone steps that Alice had run down only minutes before, until they connected with the driveway and the main entrance to the house. They didn't see the plain black leather bag hidden among the shrubs, nor the tail lights of the car as it rounded the furthermost edge of the driveway and sped out into the night.

CHAPTER 13

Monday 15ᵗʰ August

Sleep eluded Ryan for most of the night.

Dark dreams filled with faces from the past had chased sleep away until, finally, he gave up altogether and left Anna to slumber peacefully. The storm had died sometime during the early hours, leaving a blank canvas for the new day. There wasn't a cloud in the sky when Ryan stepped out onto the patio with a mug of steaming coffee and waited for the sun to rise.

If he had been the sort of person to find celestial meaning in the ordinary world, Ryan might have said it was a spiritual experience to stand quietly and watch Nature in all her illustrious glory. The grass was coated with a layer of fresh dew and the trees were a patchwork of green and brown. The scent of lavender and magnolias filled the morning air and he breathed deeply, finding peace in the solitude.

Slowly, the sky began to change before his eyes, melting from darkest midnight to cardinal blue, then into a sweeping lilac as the sun's rays spread over the horizon.

The birds awakened and their song became a cacophony, their cries shrieking through his quiet repose and reminding him of the voice he had heard the night before, raised in terror. He'd asked himself time and again whether he'd misheard or whether it could have been the storm that had let out that piercing, animalistic cry, but he had a nagging feeling it had been human.

In fact, he was sure of it.

The weather conditions had prevented a search last night and it had taken several irate attempts to ring the old-fashioned brass bell before the doors to the main house had opened. They'd been informed by Cragside's short-tempered mistress that everyone had returned home for the evening and they might think of doing the same themselves. It seemed Cassandra Gilbert had now caught whatever virus her husband had recently suffered and wasn't best pleased to have been woken up by her cottage tenants, especially when there appeared to be no emergency to warrant it.

But Ryan felt that *itch* again, the irrepressible feeling that something was very badly wrong.

He took a long gulp of coffee and looked up at the sky one last time before resigning himself to whatever the day might bring.

Half an hour later, Charlotte Shapiro drove the short distance from her house in Rothbury towards Cragside. She sang along to *Smooth Hits* at the top of her voice, safe in the knowledge that she could not be overheard from the confines of her snazzy little Fiat. As head gardener, she had access to several more practical vehicles for use around the estate but she much preferred her nippy little Italian car. The north of England might not share the same climate as those balmy Mediterranean clifftops but there was precious little she found more satisfying than pootling around the countryside with the sunroof open and the wind rushing through her short, choppy blonde hair. As Sting began to sing about fields of gold, Charlotte whizzed through one of the service gates to the estate and followed the road until she reached the staff car park, where she selected her usual parking space and stepped out into the early morning sunshine. It was barely six-thirty but she enjoyed this part of the day, puttering around the estate attending to business before the rest of the staff and the family awakened. She could almost pretend she had the place to herself.

She zipped up a lightweight, forest-green gilet emblazoned with 'CHARLIE' in gold embroidery on the breast pocket and slid a pair of sunglasses onto her nose. Her eyes fell on the battered little silver Clio parked a few spaces further along and she frowned, remembering she was not alone after all.

Anna opened her eyes to find Ryan buttoning a crisp white shirt. He was wearing smart navy suit trousers and the matching blazer hung on the back of a chair. "What time is it?"

"Seven o'clock," he replied, leaning across to plant a kiss on her cheek. "You should try to sleep a bit longer."

Anna sat up and watched him knot his tie with efficiency. Ryan never usually bothered to wear a suit to the office, preferring casual dress wherever possible.

"Where are you going? You look as if you're heading to a job interview," she joked and his fingers paused in their action.

He met her eyes through the bedroom mirror.

"I am—in a manner of speaking."

"What do you mean? This is the first I've heard of it."

Ryan reached across for his cufflinks and began looping them through the little holes at his sleeves.

"It's the superintendent job," he explained. "I've been thinking, perhaps it might not be such a bad idea, after all."

Anna almost laughed.

"*What*? You told me categorically that you would rather spend your life watching paint dry."

"I've changed my mind."

Anna's brows drew together at the sharp tone of his voice.

"What's brought this about?"

"Is there anything wrong with taking the next step on the career ladder?"

He snatched up his suit blazer and tugged it on with more haste than finesse.

"Well, of course, if you really want the job, then you should go for it," Anna said, not wishing to hold him back.

Ryan opened his mouth, wanting so desperately to tell her about Jennifer Lucas. He wanted to tell her all the reasons why he didn't want that woman's poison to infect their lives and how he would do anything—even take the job as DCS—to prevent her coming close.

"I love you," was all he said.

Forty minutes later, Ryan entered the clinical-looking foyer of the new and improved CID Headquarters in an area of North Tyneside known as Wallsend. Lying three miles east of Newcastle city centre, its name held a literal meaning, being situated at the eastern end of Hadrian's Wall not far from the North Sea. The area was famous for its long history of shipbuilding, its yards having raised the RMS Mauretania to the water among many others and it had an even longer history of coal mining before that. Nowadays, it was better known for its sprawling retail park.

Ryan raised a hand to greet the desk sergeant and then headed towards the secure double doors that would lead him to the main office suite. The rows of visitors' chairs were already filled with people of varying ages, gender and race which served to remind him that crime did not discriminate and nor did it stick to a nine to five schedule, more's the pity.

Ryan ignored the lift and took the stairs to the third floor which housed the command suite. He knew that the Chief Constable was often one of the first to arrive and he was counting on today being one of those occasions.

He made his way down a long corridor covered in ugly grey carpet tiles, which was a small improvement on the mud brown they had enjoyed in their previous building. Posters advertising everything from victim support groups to pub quiz nights had been tacked up on the wall and he wondered how long it would take for them to be defaced.

Ryan spotted something from the corner of his eye and ground to a halt before turning back to get a better look. He peered at an A4-sized colour photograph and shook his head in amused dismay.

It was a glossy poster of *him*, dressed head-to-toe in Victorian fancy dress, taken covertly outside the house at Cragside. Someone with a knack for graphic design had added the text: "HAVE YOU SEEN THIS MAN?"

"Phillips," he muttered, with a quirk of his lips.

Ryan was about to take it down, then thought better of it. Life was too short not to have a sense of humour and, in their line of work, they could do with all the laughs they could get.

Charlotte made her way from the staff car park towards Debdon Burn, the narrow river meandering its way through the fold of the valley. She stopped now and then to test the bark of a tree or to feel the soil between her fingers, assessing its texture and colour. She made a mental note of fallen trees and dangerous fungus or weeds that might damage existing ecosystems until she found herself near the bottom of the valley. Towering above her, the house stood atop its mighty crag. Sunlight bounced off its windows so that it seemed to wink at her like a fellow conspirator, watching her every move. The burn trickled between the rocks and made its journey through the valley as it had done for over a hundred years and, looking at the Arcadian scene, it was hard to believe the picture was almost entirely man-made or that the forest had not existed before one visionary person had decided to revolutionise the drab landscape.

It took a person of vision to maintain it, too.

Charlotte reached the burn and hopped across a couple of stepping stones before dropping onto her haunches beside the shallows. She ran her fingers through the tinkling water and raised her face to the sun, dabbing some of the cool water on the back of her neck. She cupped more in her hands to drink.

She wiped her wet hands on the back of her khaki trousers and, as she stood up, her eye caught something glinting in the water further downstream. Even with sunglasses, it was difficult to see past the glare of the sun that turned the little burn into a river of molten silver.

Charlotte shielded her eyes with the back of her hand, then hopped onto the next rocky stepping stone and rolled up her sleeve. She reached down into the water and fished out a silver cartridge pen. She felt its weight and rolled it between her fingers for a moment, wondering what to do with it.

She slipped it into her pocket and stood up again, squinting down at the water to see if there was more to find.

There was.

Charlotte was so focused on the water that she smelled the body long before she saw it. The stench of rotting flesh wasn't new to her; working as head gardener on an estate of that size entailed a degree of familiarity with the natural cycle of life and death, including regular discoveries of woodland animals or sheep from a neighbouring farm.

But nothing could have prepared her for what she found.

The mangled body of what had once been a young woman lay half-in, half-out of the burn, its head submerged beneath the rushing water and surrounded by long dark hair, tangled and matted with leaves. The limbs and torso lay like a ragdoll, torn apart by scavengers throughout the night.

Ryan stopped outside a freshly-painted door bearing a brass plaque that informed him he had reached the domain of the Chief Constable. He rapped a knuckle against it and didn't wait for a response before walking straight in. The speech he'd rehearsed died immediately in his throat.

"Ryan?"

Sandra Morrison looked up in surprise, pausing in the act of pouring fresh coffee into the pretty china cups she'd bought to make her new office feel homely.

"Ma'am. I'm sorry, I didn't think to make an appointment."

"On the contrary, this is very fortuitous," Morrison beamed at him and waved him inside. "I'm sure I don't need to introduce you to our new superintendent?"

Ryan's stomach plummeted as he flicked his eyes to the woman seated in one of the tub chairs arranged in front of Morrison's desk.

"DCI Lucas."

His voice was entirely devoid of emotion, his eyes completely shuttered.

Jennifer Lucas was in her late forties with dark, carefully highlighted hair styled into a sleek bob around a striking face dominated by a pair of big, baby-blue eyes. It had been nearly ten years since he'd last seen her but he was forced to admit she hadn't changed much.

It was not intended as a compliment.

"Hello, Ryan." She stood up and extended a manicured hand. "I'm so pleased to see you again."

He made no move to take it until he became aware of Morrison watching him with disapproval. Only then did he offer the briefest of handshakes before turning back to his Chief Constable.

"Ma'am, excuse me, but I understood that no final decision had been made regarding the superintendent position?"

Morrison gave him a look that told him the question was both unwarranted and rude.

"The committee discussed it informally over the weekend and DCI Lucas kindly agreed to meet me first thing this morning. After a detailed discussion, I'm very satisfied that she will make an admirable superintendent for the criminal investigation department. But I'm sure I don't need to remind you of her credentials."

"Ryan knows me well enough," Lucas put in, with a small smile.

Her voice remained entirely professional but Ryan was aware of the double entendre and refused to be party to it.

"Ma'am, I feel I should make you aware that DCI Lucas and I once had a personal relationship—"

But Morrison waved it away with a hint of irritation.

"DCI Lucas has already discussed the circumstances with me and I understand that your relationship ended nearly ten years ago. Is that correct?"

"Yes," he admitted. That much was true.

"Then, I'm surprised you feel it necessary to raise it in a professional context," she snapped. "Your private life is no concern of mine and I'm sure DCI Lucas finds this all very embarrassing."

"Please, don't worry on my account," she murmured, keeping her back to Morrison. "I'm sure Ryan will agree that nothing should be allowed to influence our relationship and the important work we have ahead of us."

Morrison nodded her agreement and found herself disappointed by Ryan's behaviour. As far as she could gather, the two had enjoyed a brief fling that had ended amicably enough, following which Ryan had transferred north. She saw no reason for there to be bad blood between them and, frankly, it was inconvenient. CID had been crying out for a new superintendent ever since the Gregson debacle and she couldn't continue to oversee CID as well as fulfil her wider duties as Chief Constable. It was past time they had a new leader and Lucas seemed capable and firm, both of which were qualities required of anyone hoping to manage Ryan and his staff.

"DCI Lucas will be taking up her new position here from the end of next month," Morrison made a point of saying. "Just after you return from your honeymoon."

Something flickered in Lucas's eyes.

"You're getting married?"

Ryan inclined his head.

"Congratulations," she murmured.

Five minutes later, Ryan stormed out of Morrison's office and headed blindly down the corridor, nearly colliding with Phillips as he rounded a corner balancing a white polystyrene cup and a paper bag containing a freshly-baked corned beef pasty. "Oi! Where's the fire?"

Ryan took a couple of deep breaths and eyeballed the coffee.

"I've just come from Morrison's office. She's appointed a new DCS."

"Oh, aye? That was quick," Phillips replied. "I s'pose it's a good thing, since you didn't fancy the job yourself."

Ryan stuck his hands in the pockets of his trousers.

"I'm not so sure."

"What's wrong with the new bloke? You don't march down here with a face like thunder unless there's something bothering you, lad. Might as well spit it out."

"It's a woman called Jennifer Lucas," Ryan said. "I knew her from my days at the Met."

Phillips gave him a bland stare.

"You knew her? Or you *knew* her?"

Ryan turned to him with serious grey eyes.

"We had a very brief thing nine years ago."

Phillips handed over the coffee cup, having decided the man's need was greater than his own. Ryan took a grateful swig and glanced down the corridor, waiting for a group of staff to pass before speaking again.

"Lucas is the reason I left London."

Phillips wanted to make a joke of it, to laugh about ex-girlfriends or manfully reminisce about past conquests but one look at Ryan's face silenced him.

"If it's that bad, can't you speak to Morrison about it?"

"I've tried." Ryan took another sip of coffee and waited for the caffeine to hit his veins. "She thinks I'm behaving unprofessionally by even raising it. Morrison has no idea who she's dealing with."

Phillips tugged his lip between thumb and forefinger.

"What kind of thing are we talking about here? Is Lucas bent? On the take?"

Ryan shook his head.

"As far as her record is concerned, she's whiter than white." He passed a weary hand over his eyes. "I have absolutely no evidence to corroborate what happened between us. Not a damn thing."

He looked over Phillips' shoulder and thought of his life in London, a lifetime ago.

"All I have are memories."

Phillips declared a state of temporary emergency and directed Ryan to the staff canteen, where he ordered two sausage stotties with brown sauce and found a quiet corner where they would not be disturbed. "Eat," he ordered Ryan, who obeyed without question.

After the second bite, he started to feel better.

"I'm telling you, it's an old Geordie remedy," Phillips proclaimed but didn't touch his own sandwich.

He folded his hands on the shiny-clean table top and waited until Ryan had eaten his fill before raising another important matter.

"I've got something to ask you."

Ryan frowned.

"Shoot."

"Will you be best man, at my wedding?"

It took a second or two, then Ryan forgot his own troubles and broke into a wide grin and stood up to give him a hard hug.

"It would be an honour," he said. "That's assuming MacKenzie doesn't come to her senses before then. Congratulations, Frank."

Phillips shook his head, hardly believing his own luck.

"I hope it isn't the anxiety talking," he thought aloud. "What if she changes her mind, once she's back to her old self?"

"Don't be daft."

"I'm older than she is," Phillips continued. "I don't want to be a burden to her in years to come."

"I'm sure MacKenzie's realised that you're a few years her senior, using the magical power of simple arithmetic," he said. "Besides, you're already a burden, so it makes no difference."

That earned him a hard punch on the arm.

"Look, stop questioning it, just be grateful you've found someone who'll put up with you for the rest of your life."

"With sentiments like that, you could have been a poet," Phillips said.

"If my career in law enforcement goes down the pan, I'll give it a try. You realise, this gives me some excellent leverage."

Phillips gave him a beady-eyed look.

"My stag do is fast approaching," Ryan explained. "You've been threatening a night I'll never forget for months. Now, you know you can't do anything too outlandish because, whatever you do, I'll quadruple it when your turn comes around."

Phillips gave him a pitying look.

"Lad, I've been on more stag dos than you've had hot dinners. The question you need to ask yourself is: do you have sufficient life insurance cover?"

Ryan looked up at that.

"Welcome to big school, son," Phillips said, and took a hearty bite of his sandwich.

CHAPTER 14

News of the discovery of a body at Cragside suspended any further discussion and they made their way back to the estate with all speed, leaving instructions for Lowerson and Yates to meet them there. Thanks to a loose interpretation of the Highway Code, Ryan managed to cut the journey time by almost half. However, as he steered his car through the pillared gates and Phillips sent up a prayer of thanks for their safe arrival, it quickly became obvious that the media had still beaten them to it.

Ryan slowed the car to a crawl and scanned the faces of the crowd that had gathered outside the entrance to the house and were spilling onto the driveway. For all he knew, they could be trampling across an active crime scene and he had a good mind to book them for obstruction. His mood did not improve when he spotted four news vans parked haphazardly along the grassy verge leading up to the main entrance.

"For God's sake. Who tipped them off?"

Ryan pulled up behind one of the vans and cut the engine.

"My money's on the family," Phillips said. "I reckon old Lionel fancies himself on the telly."

But Ryan shook his head.

"There's only one person who could be stupid enough, and egotistical enough, to enjoy this kind of spectacle."

With that, he slammed out of the car and went in search of Martin Henderson.

———

The estate manager was not hard to find. He stood on the stone steps outside the main doors of the house dressed in what Phillips would have called his Sunday Best, holding court over a group of baying journalists who were eager to capture a soundbite in time for the lunchtime news.

"It's a terrible, terrible tragedy," he was saying, injecting just the right note of sympathy into his nasal voice. "As spokesperson for the Gilbert family, I would like to offer our sincere condolences to Alice Chapman's family and to assure them that we will be doing all we can to make sure an accident like this never happens again."

"What if it wasn't an accident? Two deaths in two days looks suspicious, doesn't it, Mr Henderson?"

He shook his head sadly.

"I don't think we can draw any particular conclusions from these unprecedented events," he said, as if he knew what he was talking about.

"Turn those cameras *off*!"

The crowd parted like the Red Sea and several stunned faces spun around as Ryan's voice carried across the driveway. His long legs covered the ground at speed and he was coldly, furiously angry.

"You!"—he jabbed a finger towards Henderson—"Get your arse back inside the house or I'll book you for wilful obstruction!"

The estate manager hesitated and was obviously tempted to argue against the edict but Ryan took a step closer and looked him dead in the eye.

"Go on," he purred. "Try me."

Henderson might have had a monstrous ego but he didn't have a death wish. He scurried back inside the house and Ryan's lip curled.

"As for you vultures"—he turned scathing eyes on the men and women who remained, making no move to switch off their cameras or microphones—"you should know better than to release the name of a victim of a fatality before their identity has been confirmed or the family informed. Have some integrity, for pity's sake. Now, bugger off, before I report you to Ofcom!"

They scattered like rats and Ryan watched them with a fulminating glare.

"That'll not be the end of it," Phillips warned, as he came to stand beside Ryan. "They love a bit of nonsense to feed the masses. Fake news and all that."

Ryan sighed and thought of what Morrison would have to say about it all.

"I don't have time to worry about PR. I want some order injected into this chaos," he said as he swept a disgusted hand over the driveway, which was still teeming with people who had come to watch the drama unfold. "Where are the first responders?"

Two young police constables loitered on the far side of the driveway with their hands in their pockets and Ryan saw red.

"Go easy, lad," Phillips advised him but settled back to enjoy a good dressing down.

"Oi, Tweedle-Dum and Tweedle-Dee!"

The constables promptly shat themselves at the sight of a senior officer heading in their direction with a bloodthirsty look in his eye.

"Report!"

"Y—yes, sir," one of them babbled. "Control Room received an emergency call at around seven-fifteen this morning. We were dispatched to attend the scene and secure it. The head gardener discovered the body of a young woman down by the burn she believes to be that of Alice Chapman."

"Who called it in?"

"Ms Shapiro says she rang 999 straight away, from her mobile."

"Has anybody tried to contact Alice Chapman?"

"Not yet, sir, but Ms Shapiro says her car is parked in the staff car park, which Mr Henderson and several other staff members have since corroborated. It's a silver Renault Clio, '09 plate."

Ryan looked between the pair of them, noting their names for future reference.

"Tell me, at what point did you feel it was acceptable to allow the press—or anybody, for that matter—to invade a crime scene?"

"Sir, honestly, we tried to keep them out—"

"Are you aware of the appropriate procedure as first responders to a crime scene?"

"Yes, but—"

"Did you, or did you not, fail to follow that procedure?"

"Well, yes, but—"

"Then you're lucky I'm not writing you up for a disciplinary. Get your fingers out of your arses and start doing the job you're paid to do," he ground out. "One of you start moving these people along and the other one get down to the entrance and guard the scene. Anybody could have slipped along the path to take pictures of the victim, thanks to your negligence," he spat. "Now, *move!*"

Nodding like seals, they scarpered.

Lowerson and Yates arrived shortly afterwards and set to work restoring proper procedure, taking statements from those present and closing all access routes to the house within a half-mile radius leading down to the burn, which effectively made the entire house and gardens a crime scene. Constables were stationed at each access point and were armed with log books to record all those seeking to enter or leave. When they were satisfied that things were returning to some semblance of order, Ryan and Phillips joined Tom Faulkner and headed down to the bottom of the valley. Ryan gave one of the local constables—he couldn't remember whether it was Tweedle-Dee or Tweedle-Dum—a level look as they passed by where he stood guarding the access route to the river, clutching a log book which they dutifully signed.

"What's the story, then?"

Sweltering inside his plastic suit, Faulkner led the way down a narrow pathway towards the burn, brushing past pampas grass and sprouting perennials as he went.

"A call came into the Control Room at around seven-fifteen," Ryan told him. "It seems the head gardener, Charlotte Shapiro, was doing her early rounds of the estate and stumbled on the body. She put a call through to 999 and the local boys arrived around fifteen minutes later."

"Henderson seems to think it's been identified already," Phillips said, bringing up the rear.

"Henderson's a prat," Ryan said succinctly. "But, as it happens, Alice's car is parked in the staff car park and there's been no sign of her since yesterday. It's hard not to draw conclusions from that."

Each man fell silent, preparing themselves for what was to come.

Sure enough, a distinctive bouquet assailed them as they reached the lower part of the valley and the burn came into view. Death possessed its own unique scent, the kind of sickly-sweet odour that clung to your clothes and stayed in your memory for a long while after. On a warm day in summer, it was especially potent.

They pushed through the undergrowth near the banks of the burn and came to a gradual, horrified standstill.

The body lay ten or twelve feet ahead of them, half-submerged beneath the water. Maggots were already swarming to feast on the remains and the high-pitched whine of newly hatched flies was almost deafening above the rippling water.

"Dear God," Phillips whispered. "That poor girl."

Ryan's face betrayed very little of the emotions swirling through his body and his eyes remained impassive as he continued his silent observation of the scene. But rage flooded through his veins as he thought of the wasted life; the love, the laughter, the people she left behind. Nobody had the right to take that from her.

Nobody.

"Is it her?" Phillips asked.

Ryan looked at the clothing and the hair and nodded. Alice Chapman had been wearing a pale green summer dress with printed daisies and white plimsolls on her feet. The dress was now sodden and stained, twisted around the remnants of her body and only one shoe remained on her feet. The other lay upturned beside the water.

"Yes, it looks like Alice."

"The, ah, position of the body would be consistent with a fall from the bridge," Faulkner said quietly, his throat working again.

Ryan looked up at the iron bridge rising above them with its fine arches and engineered metal, then back at the body.

"The torso has been moved," Faulkner continued, in a low voice that shook with feeling. "I can see that at a glance."

Phillips nodded sombrely but didn't bother to ask who or what had been responsible for displacing the body; it was obvious from the open wounds on the girl's torso that animals had played their part.

Faulkner cleared his throat and stepped forward, snapping his mask into place.

"Better make a start," he mumbled.

Ryan and Phillips held back, allowing him to conduct his assessment without cross-contamination. They watched him move carefully around the body, swiping a hand through the air every now and then to clear the flies, taking pictures as he went.

"Could've been a suicide," Phillips pointed out, and wished he could light up a cigarette to mask the unfortunate smell.

"It's possible," Ryan agreed but his gut told him otherwise.

"If someone was going to do her in, there are easier ways," Phillips said. "Throwing someone over the side of a bridge takes a bit of strength and speed."

"Not all killers plan ahead."

Phillips watched Faulkner shuffle around the body, not envying him the task. After a few minutes, he made his way back to them.

"This is going to take a while," he said grimly. "Better send the troops in, and tell them to bring plastic sheeting."

Ryan nodded and began to turn away, then paused and looked back up at the bridge.

"Do you think she jumped?"

Faulkner lifted his hands in a helpless gesture.

"Given the state of the body, it's hard to say," Faulkner replied. "I'll take some swabs and we'll see what we see."

Ryan nodded, recalling times when an apparently suspicious death had been ruled a suicide or the coroner had left the verdict open. There were borderline cases where the wider circumstances leaned towards accidental death, too.

But after two deaths in as many days, he didn't like the odds.

"Could be a coincidence, two deaths happening in the same place," Phillips said, reading his mind. "I can't see what Victor and Alice have in common, apart from both working up at the big house."

"That's what we need to find out, Frank."

CHAPTER 15

The staff were fully assembled in the library when Ryan and Phillips returned.

It was one of the larger reception rooms on the ground floor and happened to have been the first room in the world to be lit by an electric lightbulb, according to Dave Quibble's guided tour the previous day. No artificial lighting was necessary now, as late morning light streamed through a large bay window overlooking the valley and warmed the apricot-coloured walls which provided a contrast to the heavier décor throughout the rest of the house.

"Oh, Ryan, I'm so glad to see you." Cassandra Gilbert bustled across the room, looking as if she had spent most of the morning in tears. Her husband had roused himself from his sick bed and was installed in an armchair beside the fireplace.

"About bloody time you coppers came to see us!" he boomed. "No use palming us off on the junior staff. I want to know what you're doing about all this!"

Cassandra winced.

"I'm sorry." She kept her voice low, so that only they could catch what she said. "He's a bit hard of hearing."

She bore the martyred look of one who was well versed in making excuses for her errant husband and Phillips found himself feeling sorry for her.

"Why don't you take a seat, Mrs Gilbert?" He led her back to one of the sofas arranged in a u-shape in the centre of the room.

"I don't know what to do." She sniffled, partly from grief and partly thanks to the virus she was coming down with. "What *can* I do, to make it up to that poor girl's parents?"

"It wasn't your fault," Phillips said as he patted her arm.

"But she was here, under my roof, doing such marvellous work on our paintings. I feel responsible. Why would she do a thing like that?" Tears spilled over again. "She had her whole life ahead of her, everything to live for."

Phillips decided to hold his tongue rather than raise the prospect of murder and left Cassandra to be comforted by Charlotte Shapiro, who was seated beside her.

"Thank you for your cooperation this morning." Ryan raised his voice so that he could be heard in all four corners of the room. "As some of you may already be aware, we have identified the body found underneath the iron bridge as being that of Alice Chapman."

There were murmurs around the room, more tears and a degree of fear that hadn't been there before. He passed his gaze across each of their faces and thought: one of you *knows*.

His jaw hardened.

"I understand that each of you has provided a statement to my colleagues but, for the time being, I would appreciate it if you would make yourselves available for further questioning should the need arise."

"Is that really necessary, chief inspector? Of course, we're all devastated about what happened to Victor, and now Alice, but I don't see what any of us has to do with it." This came from Henderson, who stood near the door with a sullen look on his pinched face.

Ryan gave him a hard stare.

"For the avoidance of doubt, the deaths of Victor Swann and Alice Chapman are being treated as suspicious and as potentially linked."

Realisation dawned on each of their faces and he made a careful note of their varied expressions. He saw Maggie clutch a hand to her throat and was sorry for it, but the facts could not be helped.

"On any analysis, two serious incidents within a twenty-four-hour period cannot be ignored and, therefore, will be jointly investigated until new information comes to light."

Cassandra blew her nose loudly and then said what they were all thinking.

"Chief inspector, if Victor and Alice were…if their deaths weren't accidental, do you think one of *us* might have been involved?"

Ryan could have given her a safe, roundabout answer, but he wasn't in the habit of dishing out empty platitudes.

"Yes," he said. "I do. For the time being, I would urge you to be vigilant and to report any suspicious activities to myself or one of my colleagues. Direct contact numbers will be made available but, failing that, you can always call the emergency number."

His words fell like a death knell.

"There must be a mistake, chief inspector." Dave Quibble was the one to break the residual silence. "Nobody in the room is capable of hurting anyone. We're like a family, here at Cragside."

There were nods of agreement around the room, more tears, but Ryan remained resolute.

"Anybody is capable, given the right motivation."

As Ryan faced the room, one person looked on and almost laughed. He was so serious, so wholesome and dedicated to the scales of justice. How easy it must be, to live in a world of black and white and never any shades of grey. Perhaps he hadn't lived enough of life to learn that, sometimes, action must be taken for the greater good. It was not enough to forgive and forget, or to go on with your life as if none of it mattered.

It was remarkable, really, how one individual action could trigger a sequence of events with such far-ranging consequences, some of which wouldn't become obvious until much later. A person was forced to go on living with those consequences, putting up with the pain and the hardship, until the day arrived when there was an opportunity to balance the scales.

The girl's death was unfortunate but, really, in the grand scheme of things, Alice had been a casualty in the war against a greater evil.

One that must be stamped out for good.

It took several hours for the CSIs to complete their work for the day, during which time Alice Chapman's body was transferred to the mortuary for post-mortem and Ryan had the unenviable job of breaking the news of her death to the girl's parents. They were based in Cambridgeshire, so Ryan delegated the task of paying a house call to a local family liaison officer. It gave him no pleasure to hand over a duty he felt he owed to her family and he intended to follow up with another phone call the following day, as much in solidarity as anything else.

A search of the immediate vicinity had provided the police team with their first breakthrough in the form of a solid link between two deaths which had, at first glance, appeared unconnected. Articles of menswear and other small items had been recovered from the shallow waters of the burn and had been found scattered in the rocky undergrowth in a twenty-foot radius around Alice's body. They were undergoing forensic examination, but Lionel Gilbert had already confirmed that he recognised at least one article of clothing as belonging to his valet, Victor Swann.

A separate search of the gardens near the house had unearthed Alice's large black shoulder bag among the rhododendron bushes, which begged the question of why a woman intending to take her own life would choose to leave it in such an odd place unless it had fallen from her body in some other way.

Lowerson and Yates had taken detailed statements from every member of the household who was present, amounting to twelve in total. That number narrowed to eight when they considered who had remained on site at Cragside the previous day, after the rest of the staff were sent home. A cross-check confirmed that all eight had been at the party on Saturday night too.

There was always a margin of error, thanks to numerous available access points to the estate which might feasibly allow an intruder to enter and leave without being noticed, but the police could not legislate for that. It was at moments like these that Ryan wished for modern conveniences like closed circuit television.

Ryan scheduled the first briefing of 'OPERATION LIGHTBULB' for five o'clock and approved his rental cottage as an authorised police site, enabling them to use it as a base rather than travelling forty minutes each way to CID Headquarters back in Newcastle. Proximity was a definite advantage in close-knit communities like Cragside.

There was no better way to smoke out a killer than being right on his doorstep.

Back in the city, Denise MacKenzie braved the late afternoon shopping crowd to meet her friend for an al fresco lunch in the city centre. It felt good to be alive, she thought, as she strolled down Grey Street towards their chosen restaurant. She had walked these pavements so many times before and yet it was only after her visit to Cragside that she found herself looking at the architecture afresh. It was incredible to think that one man—admittedly, one man with a vast fortune—had built the city landscape as they knew it. Few people could lay claim to such a legacy and MacKenzie found herself considering the kind of legacy she wanted to leave behind when she was gone. What difference had she made to the world, really?

There was her family back in Ireland, her parents who continued to be as robust as ever. She loved them and enjoyed visiting but could she imagine living in the little village in County Kerry where she had grown up?

No, not any more.

Her life was here. Frank was here.

Then, there was her work. She had spent twenty years carving out a career in law enforcement and, with no false modesty, considered herself to be a damn good murder detective. She knew she had helped to prevent dangerous criminals from committing further crimes and without the long arm of the law, their deeds would have gone unchecked.

She smiled as a group of teenage girls wandered across the road, laughing raucously at some private joke known only to their generation. Without rules, without order, they would not be able to live so freely. Her smile dimmed and she was forced to admit that, even with all those rules and officers on the beat, there were still people out there for whom social laws meant nothing. For them, inflicting harm on others was a kind of blood sport.

Immediately, his face swam into her mind.

"Oh, no," she whispered, and panic gripped her unexpectedly by the throat.

MacKenzie collapsed to her knees, right there in the middle of the city's finest street, and shoppers slowed down to get a better look.

"Drunk," one of them muttered.

"Drugs," another said, with a superior smirk.

She saw them through the fog that covered her eyes and mumbled something unintelligible before the world slipped away.

"Denise?" MacKenzie came around a few seconds later to see a pair of sandal-clad feet hurrying across the pavement, then a set of neat, red-painted toenails came into view. Her body felt weak and shaky and there was a cut on her knee, burned through the material of her best jeans.

"Oh, my God. Denise, are you alright?"

Anna dropped down beside her friend and gave the crowd a scornful look, wondering what the world had come to.

"Have you hurt yourself?"

Now that the faintness had passed, MacKenzie felt a greater sense of embarrassment and pushed herself upwards.

"No, no. I'm fine. I'm alright."

But she swayed a bit and Anna wrapped an arm around her waist.

"Let's find somewhere to sit down," she suggested, looking around for a convenient spot but finding none.

"No, really, let's just get out of here," MacKenzie muttered, eyeing the gaping faces of the herd.

Anna started to move in the direction of the restaurant.

"Haven't you got homes to go to?" she couldn't resist calling out, and made MacKenzie laugh.

"Human nature," she commented.

"Yeah, it's a bitch."

Just before five o'clock, Ryan returned to the cottage to set up a makeshift incident room. He knew Anna was spending the afternoon with MacKenzie and was heartened to see the two women growing even closer than before. Whether they admitted it openly or not, they needed each other. Entering the kitchen, he slid his navy blazer onto the back of a chair, removed his cufflinks and rolled up the sleeves of his shirt to the elbows. He was eager to shed his suit altogether and exchange it for something more comfortable but there wasn't time.

The kitchen boasted a supersized oak table with enough seating for ten or twelve people. He laid out a jug of water and some glasses, then disappeared into one of the bedrooms where they kept a printer to run off some copies of the reports generated so far.

The doorbell went as he was coming back downstairs, bang on five o'clock.

It was Melanie Yates.

"Come in," Ryan said as he glanced over her shoulder. "Where's Lowerson?"

"He said to tell you he'd be five minutes late," she replied, slipping off her shoes. She looked for an MDF shoe rack but found instead a smart antique priest's chair with purpose-built slots for shoes. "He's, ah, sorting out the voluntary consent forms so we can take DNA swabs from everybody."

Ryan led the way through to the kitchen and moved across to the kettle.

"Is anyone kicking up a fuss?"

"I think there were a couple of murmurs but, thankfully, everyone has complied without needing to get the lawyers involved."

"Amen to that." Ryan jiggled the kettle. "Want some coffee?"

"Yes, please."

Yates lingered in the doorway for a moment and then stepped inside the room, casting curious eyes around the airy space.

"It's a pretty cottage," she remarked, taking in the Aga range and old beams, so unlike her parents' modern, nineties house. She wondered what it would be like to settle down with a good book beside the fire in the sitting room, or to cook a meal in here.

Ryan spooned instant coffee into two mugs and added water.

"It's only temporary," he said, "but it's been great for us to get out of the city for a while. Milk and sugar?"

"Milk, no sugar, please." She licked her lips and wondered whether to ask a personal question. "Have you, ah, found somewhere more permanent?"

To her surprise, Ryan looked over his shoulder and tapped the side of his nose.

"That's classified information," he smiled. "But let's just say, I have something up my sleeve."

He turned and held out a cup with a picture of a Christmas elf on the side, then nodded towards the table.

"Take a seat, the others won't be long." He settled himself on one of the chairs and crossed one long, suit-clad leg over the other.

He waited for her to select a chair.

"How did you find it today?"

Yates cradled the coffee in her hands and wondered whether she should give him the short answer or the honest one.

"I prefer honesty," he added, reading her mind with ease.

"It was—well, it was hard to see the body like that. I've seen one before, sir, when I responded to a call out on the Hacker case but this one seemed more disturbing, somehow."

Ryan understood what she meant. The victim she had found previously had been a local gangster whose badly mutilated body had been the Hacker's handiwork. In CID, it was a point of principle that every victim was afforded the same standard of care and the same level of professionalism as any other, but they were only human. It was far easier to feel sympathy for a young woman who had died badly than a man who had made his living from the misery of others.

"We do our best for all of them," he said. "But sometimes you feel it more than others."

He looked up from his coffee.

"Lowerson tells me you held up well at the scene," he remarked. "If you've got a good stomach for the darker side of life in CID, that's half the battle. You need to be able to look at a set of facts objectively but be unafraid to follow your gut when it feels justified. Do you think that's for you?"

Yates drank her coffee and let the warm liquid settle the butterflies in her stomach.

"Yes, sir, I think I can do it."

Ryan nodded and gave her a direct, unwavering stare.

"Tell me, Yates, why do you want to work in my department?"

She had expected the question to come at one stage or another but her palms still turned clammy.

"When I was sixteen, my twin sister was murdered. It devastated my whole family, particularly because they never found her killer. They could be out there, right now, killing other people." She swallowed the acid rolling in her stomach and met his eyes. "When I was younger, I thought

I wanted revenge. I don't feel that way anymore, but I do feel compelled to try to stop the same thing happening to other people, or at least try to give the families closure so they can move on with their lives."

Unlike my family, she added silently, thinking of the stale environment of her parents' home and the tears her mother still shed every night.

Ryan listened and heard the pain buried beneath the softly-spoken exterior. Nobody was better placed to understand the pain of losing a sibling but it also meant he was uniquely placed to warn her of the potential pitfalls of policing for the wrong reasons.

"Is this a personal crusade, Yates? Vengeance has a time and place"—he could hardly argue otherwise, given his chequered past—"but you need to be able to see past your own life experience. Not every victim is your sister."

She set her cup down on the table and lifted her chin.

"I can do it," she repeated firmly.

Ryan nodded and stood up again to answer the doorbell.

"Good. In that case, consider yourself part of CID from now on; I'll square it with Morrison and we'll see about getting you on the training pathway to become a detective. Six months' probationary period."

Her eyes lit up, animating her face.

"Thank you, sir."

As he left the room to open the front door, Melanie smiled broadly and thought that everything was beginning to slot nicely into place.

CHAPTER 16

The sun was low in the sky by the time Ryan's team had all gathered around the kitchen table. For now, he had decided to keep things simple and brief his core staff, leaving the various support staff based out of CID Headquarters—administrators, intelligence analysts, telephone operatives, IT specialists, to name a few— to provide their assistance remotely. The only exception to this rule was the presence of Tom Faulkner who, although not employed by the Northumbria Police Constabulary as a permanent member of staff, fulfilled that role in all but name.

Forensic services were outsourced, as were the services of their police pathologist, who could usually be found in the basement mortuary of the Royal Victoria Infirmary in Newcastle. Ryan planned to pay a visit to the pathologist as soon as he'd had an opportunity to assess Alice Chapman's body and Victor Swann's post-mortem had also been bumped up the list.

For now, Ryan waited while his team availed themselves of coffee and let off a bit of steam before they got down to business. Phillips had taken a seat next to Lowerson and was pulling his leg about being vegetarian, gluten-free and lactose-intolerant, which were three cardinal sins in Phillips' carnivorous world. Yates watched them from her position on the other side of the table while giving a very good impression of listening to Faulkner droning on about various flora and fauna he'd spotted in the gardens at Cragside.

Ryan judged it was time to step in.

"Alright, let's get started."

The group fell quiet and looked at him expectantly.

"First, I want to thank you all for your hard work today. It's not a barrel of laughs, dealing with a DB on one of the hottest days of the year but I'm sure Alice's family appreciate everything you've done for her today."

There were nods around the table.

"Second, I want to formally welcome Melanie Yates to the team. She'll be joining us in CID and I know you'll make her feel welcome. Lowerson? I'm hoping you'll show her the ropes."

Lowerson barely held off a grin.

"Happy to," he said, keeping his face as nonchalant as possible.

If Yates was disappointed that she would not be taken under Ryan's wing, she didn't let it show.

"I'm looking forward to working with you all," she said, and meant it.

"Just give us a shout if you need anything, lass." Phillips smiled at her warmly. "We don't stand on ceremony round here."

"He's right. I'm constantly faced with insubordination in the ranks," Ryan said, before tapping his fingers against the pages of the summaries he'd printed earlier. "Now we've got the preliminaries out of the way, let's talk about Victor Swann."

They looked down at a recent photograph of the former valet provided by Maggie, then compared it with pictures Faulkner had snapped of him as he'd lain at the foot of the stone staircase.

"To recap, on Saturday evening, Anna and I attended the staff murder mystery party at Cragside house. It's an annual party that Lionel and Cassandra Gilbert have thrown every year since they first bought the place in '98. It was supposed to be an evening of harmless fun but, at around eleven o'clock, the lights failed. I can bear witness that Victor Swann volunteered himself to go downstairs, from the drawing room where we were all assembled, to check the fuse box. The house was completely dark but Swann did have a small torch he kept on his person and there was some solar-powered lighting on the exterior stairs."

Ryan paused and leaned back in his chair, casting his mind back to the events that night.

"At the start of the evening, it's been confirmed there were forty people at the party, including Cassandra Gilbert. Her husband, Lionel, was present in the house but states that he remained in his room the entire evening. By the time the lights went out, there were twenty-two people present in the drawing room—twenty-three people still in the house including Gilbert."

"How can you be sure of the number?" Yates asked.

"We have to rely on witness statements. Having gone through all of them, I've eliminated people who left the house at least an hour before the power failure." Ryan said. "There's always the chance that somebody pretended to go home and doubled back. That's a secondary line of enquiry but we have no way of knowing for sure given the fact there's no CCTV around the house and nobody other than Victor himself to tell us otherwise."

"We found no trace evidence around Swann's body," Faulkner chimed in. "The lab is testing his clothing and we'll compare the swabs we took from his body against the DNA samples provided to us by the people at Cragside, as soon as we have them."

Ryan nodded. That was an urgent job for tomorrow morning.

"Thanks Tom." He turned to the rest of them and spread his hands. "As you can see, it looks a lot like accidental death up to this point. I'm waiting to receive Jeff Pinter's pathology report and that will likely shed some light on cause of death and tell us the extent to which foul play was involved."

"Why else would somebody raid his locker and house?" Lowerson asked.

"That's where Alice Chapman comes in." Ryan flicked a page and looked down into the open, smiling face of a young woman who had been destroyed, along with her incredible artistry.

"Her body was discovered at around seven-fifteen this morning by the head gardener, Charlotte Shapiro. A fingertip search was made throughout today, in expanding circles from where her body was found."

Ryan turned to a list of items recovered by the search team.

"Various small items and clothing have already been identified by Lionel and Cassandra Gilbert as belonging to Victor Swann. One or two items were recovered still within a blue and white plastic carrier bag which had become entangled in the undergrowth. I think this points to a strong possibility that Alice, or her attacker, was in possession of the missing items taken from Victor's locker sometime in the early hours of Sunday morning."

"D' you reckon she might have done away with Swann and then killed herself?"

Phillips dunked another custard cream into his lukewarm coffee.

"Until Pinter gives us his report, we don't have any evidence to suggest Alice was attacked and thrown from the bridge, so suicide can't be ruled out yet," Ryan was obliged to say. "But, in my opinion, it doesn't fit the wider circumstances or the girl's behaviour."

He nodded towards Yates, who sat up a bit straighter in her seat.

"We spoke with Alice in the staff room, yesterday. What were your impressions?"

"She seemed a very steady sort of person, sir. Quiet, studious, very dedicated to her work. Although she was saddened by Swann's death, she didn't exhibit any unusual behaviour that would give cause for concern."

"I came to the same conclusion. And there's something else to consider. Alice Chapman was one of the party-goers who left *early* on Saturday night, over half an hour before the power failure and Swann's death, so it's even less likely she was responsible."

The table fell silent for a long moment until Phillips spoke up again.

"The thing is, guv, I can't see what was so bloody important that somebody would kill an old man and then snuff out somebody else just to keep it quiet."

"We may not have found the answer to that yet, but there was obviously something and it was obviously highly motivating. Until we hear from Pinter and the lab, we need to focus on the paper trail and a process of elimination."

"Alice's body was exposed to the elements last night and, apart from the rain damage, there was a lot of animal contamination. We'll do our best," Faulkner assured them, "but I need to manage expectations."

Ryan steepled his fingers and looked at each of them in turn, the light of battle shining in his eyes.

"Looks like we'll have to use our little grey cells."

By the time they were settled at a table in the late afternoon sunshine, MacKenzie was feeling much better. When a friendly waiter approached their table with a cocktail menu, she felt even better still. "I could get used to this," she sighed, rubbing absently at her knee. It was throbbing after the fall and she wondered if she ought to look out some antiseptic cream.

The waiter asked to take their order and, after feigning indecision for the sake of appearances, she ordered a caipirinha.

"It's happy hour," they were told, "two-for-one, until seven p.m."

"I'm driving," Anna said, with considerable regret, and ordered its non-alcoholic equivalent. When the waiter departed, she rested an elbow on the table and cupped her chin in her hand.

"How's your knee?"

MacKenzie made a sound of frustration.

"It'll be fine. I didn't fall flat on my face—I managed to do it in stages." She smiled weakly. "It's mostly the embarrassment that gets to me."

Anna pursed her lips.

"Are you speaking to anyone about the panic attacks?"

MacKenzie shrugged a shoulder.

"I went to the GP and got some beta-blockers but I've been doing a cognitive behavioural therapy course online, while Frank's at work. It works better when I'm alone," she explained.

"That's good," Anna said, encouragingly. "Do you think it's helping?"

MacKenzie thought about how to answer.

"Hard to say. Yes, I think it helped me through a hard patch because it trains me to focus my mind on the good things in life, rather than harkening back to…to what happened."

She paused briefly as her cocktail arrived and she took a generous sip.

"I haven't needed to take any medication for two days now," she added, tapping a fingernail against the edge of the glass. "Actually, ever since you swept into my house like a force of nature and told me to get a grip on myself."

Anna opened her mouth to object and MacKenzie laughed.

"Four months of CBT and all I really needed was a one-woman whirlwind to come and lay down some home truths," she continued. "It's done me the world of good."

She raised her glass to toast her friend and, in doing so, the sunlight caught the square-cut emerald glinting on the ring finger of her left hand.

Anna did a double take.

"What is *that*?"

MacKenzie looked down at her hand and realised she'd become so comfortable wearing the ring, she'd forgotten it was there.

"Oh, this old thing?"

She wriggled her fingers and gave a sly smile.

"You dark horse!" Anna squealed—it was the only word for it—and leapt from her chair to wrap her arms around MacKenzie, who couldn't help but laugh.

"We got engaged last night."

"Where? How? Tell me everything," Anna demanded, taking a long slurp of her drink.

"Well, I was dressed in my ancient dressing gown and the evening news was on," MacKenzie said, dead-pan. "It wasn't moonlight and roses but, you know what? I didn't need them. I realised something last night, something I don't think I'd really known until then."

Her hand came to rest on her heart.

"I've been in love with Frank Phillips for years and I was so clueless, I didn't even know it. Maybe even when his wife was still alive because I saw how he looked after her, how he nursed her. It's hard not to appreciate that kind of devotion. He's a good, kind man and I love him."

"He'll want corned beef pasties and Newcastle Brown Ale at the wedding," Anna warned, her eyes shining. "And he's bound to sing a rendition of *Fog on the Tyne*."

MacKenzie laughed delightedly.

"He'll have to do it in front of my Irish family, then, since we're planning to have the ceremony on the Emerald Isle," she said, and then waved her hands in the air as if to clear the thought. "I don't want to start planning anything until after your big day. I'm excited enough about seeing you and Ryan finally tie the knot."

Anna's smile slipped, just a fraction, but MacKenzie caught it.

"What's the matter?" She was instantly serious. "You're not getting cold feet?"

"No," Anna replied, "but I'm a bit worried that he might be. These last few days, Ryan hasn't been himself. It feels like he's keeping something from me."

"He's been tied up with the Cragside investigation," MacKenzie offered but Anna shook her head.

"It's not just that. It's probably paranoia but I'm worried he's having second thoughts."

MacKenzie was having none of it.

"That man adores you," she said firmly. "There might be something on his mind but I'll eat my hat if it has anything to do with you."

"You're probably right," Anna said brightly, polishing off her drink.

MacKenzie saw the hurt and confusion in the younger woman's eyes and wished she could tell her that there would always be a fairy tale ending to every story.

Unfortunately, life didn't work that way.

CHAPTER 17

"As far as I can see, there are eight potential suspects."

With a blithe disregard for his tenancy agreement, Ryan began tacking photographs in an even row along one of the kitchen walls. Phillips scratched his chin and wondered if it had been painted recently.

"Ah, not to piss on your bonfire, lad, but how can there be suspects without a confirmed crime?"

"Because if Alice Chapman threw herself over that bridge, then my name is Rita Hayworth," Ryan snapped, without bothering to turn around.

"Fair point, well made," Phillips said cheerfully, settling back to listen.

Ryan tacked up the last photograph and moved to the side, so they could see the full line-up.

"Dave Quibble was Alice Chapman's line manager during the painting restoration work at Cragside. In his statement, he says that he last saw her at approximately four-thirty, when she came down to the kitchen for a cup of tea. This is corroborated by Cassandra Gilbert, who was in the hallway next to the kitchen with Quibble looking at the fuse box and discussing how the power might have failed on Saturday night. We'll come to that," Ryan added. "The important thing is, those two were the last to see Alice alive yesterday."

Other than the person who killed her.

He pointed to the eight faces he'd tacked up on the wall.

"These are the people who were on site until at least five o'clock, when most of the staff were due to go home. Given the lack of CCTV surveillance, we have no way of knowing who actually *did* go home but these are the people who were due to come to Cragside and were seen to be on site yesterday."

Ryan watched his team look from one face to the next.

"First and most obviously, we have Cassandra and Lionel Gilbert, both of whom were in the house all day." He tapped a finger against the faces of the old couple. "Lionel spent most of yesterday in his rooms, whereas Cassandra was more active helping the police teams in their investigation following Swann's death. After the teams packed up, she states that she went upstairs because she felt unwell, having come down with the same flu virus as her husband."

"Can anybody confirm that?" Lowerson asked.

"The housekeeper, Maggie." Ryan moved to a picture of an approachable woman of around seventy. "She lives in a small apartment inside the main house, so was on site the whole evening. She says that she made the Gilberts a light supper which she took up on a tray at five-thirty. Lionel Gilbert was awake and listening to the radio, whereas Cassandra Gilbert was fast asleep and seemed under the weather. She asked if they needed anything further, then headed to her own room for the night. Her movements have been confirmed by Lionel Gilbert and Dave Quibble."

"None of them saw Alice after then?" Yates asked.

Ryan shook his head.

"Anna and I went up to the house during the storm last night, after seven o'clock. The conditions were bad," he recalled, thinking of the near darkness wrought by the storm clouds. "I was sure I heard a scream and we went out to look. It was a fruitless journey but we asked up at the house to see if anything had happened. They hadn't seen or heard anything and only the Gilberts were present."

"How do you know?" Yates asked, and Ryan had to admire her eye for detail.

"Because I walked through every room in the main part of the house while Anna stayed with the Gilberts," he replied silkily.

"Anybody ever tell you, you're the suspicious sort?" Phillips let out a rumble of laughter.

"I was merely concerned for their safety," Ryan grinned, then looked back at the photos of the Gilberts. "Generally, they operate an 'open-door' policy because they employ so many staff who are constantly coming and going during working hours. Only a small number have keys to the house but they tend to leave the main door unlocked anyway, except after ten o'clock when they lock up for the night. The crime rate is extremely low around here."

"Can't see your average burglar getting away with a smash 'n' grab in that fortress of a place," Lowerson agreed. "They'd need a battering ram and a fork-lift truck."

That got a few laughs around the table and even brought a smile to Yates's face.

"Moving on to David Quibble, the conservation manager." Ryan indicated the next picture on his line-up, taken of a smiling man in his mid-fifties with endearingly crooked teeth, glasses and wiry grey hair.

In short, he was a living stereotype of the average historian.

"In his statement, he tells us that he went home to his house in Morpeth at around five-thirty. He didn't see anybody else in the staff room and, although he remembers seeing Alice's car still parked in the staff car park, he didn't think much of it because he didn't tend to micromanage or disturb her while she was engrossed in her work."

"Convenient," Phillips snorted. "Which other cars did he see in the staff car park, out of interest?"

"The housekeeper's car was still there, obviously, as was Charlotte Shapiro's. Martin Henderson's BMW too, since he has the estate manager's cottage within the grounds and it's more convenient to keep it there, or so he tells me."

Ryan blew out a long breath.

"All of that assumes Quibble is telling the truth, but it seems to be borne out by what the others say."

Just then, they heard the front door opening and Phillips' superior nose detected the scent of calorific goods even before Anna stepped into the kitchen, carrying two enormous paper bags full of Chinese takeaway.

"Anybody hungry?"

They fell upon the food like a pack of starving hyenas.

"Lad, I've said it before but I'll say it again. She's too good for the likes of you." Phillips dabbed soy sauce from the side of his mouth and gave Ryan a sideways glance.

"She's one in a million," the other agreed, looking across to where she chatted with Melanie Yates, already helping to put the other woman at her ease.

"If it were left to you, we'd all waste away to nothing."

It was Ryan's turn to give his sergeant a sideways glance.

"No immediate fear of that," he drawled.

"Didn't anyone ever teach you to respect your elders?"

Ryan grinned, then checked his watch. It was almost six-thirty and he needed to move things along.

Anna caught the action and began to stand up.

"Well, I'll leave you all to it," she said, blowing them a kiss.

Yates watched Ryan's face soften as he waved Anna off and wondered what it would feel like to have somebody look at her with even a tenth of that affection.

"We've covered the first four suspects on my list, so let's move on to mug shot number five." Ryan gestured towards the photographs with a prawn cracker.

"Martin Henderson is the new estate manager. He gets a cottage as part of the job and free rein to swagger around the estate," Ryan couldn't resist adding. "He says he didn't see Alice Chapman all day, except in passing sometime during the morning as they were all assembled to speak to the police and consent to a search of their lockers."

Ryan paused and took a bite of the cracker.

"He further states that he was attending to his agricultural duties throughout the afternoon on the Home Farm." He referred to the farm owned by the estate, some five miles yonder. "He went directly home, without stopping into the main house, at five o'clock or thereabouts."

"Nobody can substantiate his whereabouts because he lives on his own and didn't run into any timely passers-by," Lowerson put in. "Although the farm staff agree he was there until four-thirty."

Ryan crunched the last of his cracker and nodded at the picture of a smarmy-looking man in his early sixties, leering at the camera as if he were a matinee idol.

"At this point, Yates, let me reiterate my words to you about objectivity," Ryan said. "For example, I am presently thinking that Martin Henderson is one of the greasiest little buggers I've met in a good long while, but it would be wrong of me to rely on personal dislike because that leads to bias."

He leaned back against the wall and crossed his ankles.

"What I'm going to do instead is ask you and Lowerson to delve into his history with a fine-toothed comb. I want to know every little misdemeanour, every time he cheated the tax man, every wife, girlfriend, husband, boyfriend or sheep he's ever had."

Phillips laughed, then promptly choked on a piece of stir-fry chicken.

"I'd like to know how Henderson can afford a brand new electric BMW, handmade shoes and a fat Omega watch, on his salary. While you're at it, I want you to look at Victor Swann's finances, because I'm damned if I know how he could afford to live like Midas on a valet's salary."

"I smell a rat," Phillips agreed.

"We'll get onto it first thing," Lowerson said, thinking of the old man's penchant for fine things. "Do you think they were on the fiddle?"

"We'll find out," Ryan muttered, then nodded at the sixth photograph.

"Charlotte Shapiro is the head gardener." They looked at the attractive face of a fifty-something blonde. "She doesn't spend much time up at the main house because the gardening staff have their own digs and an extensive nursery. She tends to park her car in the staff car park then go for a wander through the grounds towards wherever she's working that day. She has a team of six staff who tend to the formal gardens around the house and access to contractors whenever she needs them."

"She looks like the outdoorsy type," Phillips remarked, with a wink for Faulkner. The other man blushed hotly and shuffled in his seat.

"She's a very nice woman."

All conversation stopped as the team turned to Faulkner, who looked to Phillips for divine intervention.

"Too late now, son," Phillips held his hands up.

"Well, um, I happened to get chatting with her yesterday morning. She was telling me a bit about the types of coniferous trees they have in the forest."

"Much as I hate to remind you, Tom, your woodland nymph could be a killer," Ryan pointed out.

"Aww, now, don't go breaking the man's heart before he's had a chance to show her the stars," Phillips grumbled. "She might *not* be a killer, after all."

"Gee, thanks," Faulkner chuckled and Ryan resumed their conversation.

"Charlotte Shapiro knows the grounds like the back of her hand. She says she didn't see Alice Chapman at all yesterday, only when she found her body at seven-fifteen this morning."

"What was she doing, hanging around the burn, anyway?" Lowerson demanded.

"She says there are plans afoot to cut back all the overgrown foliage beside the riverbank, which is becoming unmanageable and choking the life out of some of the other plants," Ryan said. "She was assessing what needs to be done and stumbled on the body. You wouldn't have been able to see her from the top of the bank or from the house because of the placement of the rocks and plants," Ryan added.

"Shapiro could have been heading back to the scene of a crime," Lowerson persisted, and Phillips gave him a clap on the back.

"Alreet, *Columbo*," he laughed.

"Well, I'm just saying, it's possible."

"I'm with Lowerson on this," Ryan said. "Victor Swann's things were scattered all around the area where she was found, so it's possible somebody would return to the scene in daylight to recover a particular item of importance."

"But what?" Yates asked.

"That's what we need to find out."

The remaining suspects on Ryan's list were two under-gardeners who had been working in the grounds the previous day; their alibis had not yet been confirmed for the period between four and seven o'clock, when it seemed most likely Alice Chapman went missing. The team spent another twenty minutes or so discussing possible lines of enquiry and, having agreed that it was useless to theorise further without evidence to hand, they said goodnight. Once the house was quiet again, Ryan returned to the kitchen and spent another minute or two studying the faces of the people he had tacked up on the wall. The clock told him it was just shy of seven o'clock and he decided it was time to go in search of his fiancée.

Anna was sitting at the little antique dressing table in the master bedroom, which she'd commandeered as a desk. A lamp burned brightly against one side of her face, so that the other side remained in shadow and illuminated her profile like one of those Victorian miniatures he'd seen scattered around the main house.

Ryan watched her fiddle with the pencil she held in one hand while she turned the pages of a hefty-looking textbook with the other and felt love wash over him.

"Hi," he murmured, leaning against the doorframe. "Do you want me to leave you to work a bit longer?"

Anna was so engrossed in first-century history that she hadn't heard him enter the room.

"Hi, yourself!" She leaned back and stretched her arms behind her back to ease out the kinks and was happy when he strolled across to plant a kiss on her upturned face.

"Thank you for dinner, earlier," he said. "It's getting to be a habit but everyone appreciated it. Especially Frank."

Anna chuckled.

"I'm used to the way you all work, by now," she said. "You have 'down' periods, where there's a sort of plateau of ordinary casework then, every so often, there'll be a case that taxes you a bit harder. Something out of the ordinary and more urgent than the rest. During those times, you barely remember to eat a slice of toast in the morning so I don't mind doing what I can to keep the cogs turning."

"You make me sound like a battered old machine."

"Well, you're not getting any younger," she teased him. "In fact, perhaps I should start buying some cod liver oil capsules to keep those cogs moving."

Ryan laughed, drawing her up for another kiss.

"Do you know what I love about you, Doctor Taylor?"

Anna smiled.

"My intelligence?"

"Apart from that."

"My rapier wit?"

"I do appreciate it, but, apart from that."

"What then?"

He wrapped his arms around her and drew her into the warmth of his body.

"You keep my feet planted firmly on the ground."

Anna smiled and was reminded of MacKenzie's words earlier in the day. Obviously, she was right and Ryan had been distracted by work, that was all.

"Happy to oblige," she said. "Oh, how did your interview go, this morning? I'm sorry, I forgot to ask."

He looked down into her expectant face and wondered where to begin.

"Morrison has already given the job to somebody else."

"Oh, that's a shame. Are you disappointed?"

"No, I never really wanted it."

"But, this morning…?" Anna was thoroughly confused.

Ryan sat down on the edge of the bed and prepared to delve into the past.

When it was done and Ryan had purged himself of that part of his life which he chose most often to forget, he looked down to where Anna's hand was clasped tightly in his own. "You should have told me before," she said softly. "Did you think I wouldn't understand?"

Ryan heaved a sigh.

"I don't know. I was ashamed; when I think back to that part of my life concerning Jennifer Lucas, I hardly recognise myself. I was afraid of her. I can say that now, although I didn't like to admit it at the time."

Anna could hardly imagine him being afraid of anything or anyone. She'd seen Ryan face down the most dangerous criminals and situations, and yet he was telling her he'd once felt so powerless that the only thing he could do was escape. It was that admission that gave her most cause for concern.

"Should I be worried?"

Ryan looked at her and saw the makings of fear already beginning to mar the happiness they'd worked so hard to find.

His hand tightened on hers, then he raised her hand to his lips to press a kiss against her palm.

"I'd never let anybody harm you, Anna."

But as she watched the bedroom light fall on the top of his bent head, Anna thought privately that it was not herself she was worried about.

Who was there to watch over *him*?

CHAPTER 18

Tuesday 16ᵗʰ August

The following morning, Ryan awoke to find an e-mail from the police pathologist to say he'd completed his preliminary report and, by nine-thirty, Ryan was pulling his car around to the service entrance of the Royal Victoria Infirmary, where he found Phillips already waiting for him.

"Morning!"

"How the hell do you manage to be so cheerful this early in the day?"

"I never kiss and tell..." Phillips winked.

Ryan snorted eloquently and joined his sergeant beneath a cheap perforated plastic canopy outside the service entrance. It was deserted apart from a junior doctor who stood a few metres away sucking rhythmically on a cigarette, staring out at the car park with a glazed expression that spoke of long-term sleep deprivation.

Phillips took a deep breath as they passed by.

"Two years and counting since I last had a cig."

"Just say 'no,'" Ryan advised him. "Think of cancer. Emphysema. Bad breath. Failing that, think of what MacKenzie would do if she caught you."

As a threat, it didn't get better than that.

"You've convinced me," Phillips said, turning his back resolutely. "Lead me away from temptation."

Together, they made their way down into the depths of the hospital until they found themselves on the basement level. A wide corridor led them to a set of secure metal doors at the end and the air was stifling, thanks to a set of powerful air vents which expelled hot air while keeping the mortuary cold.

"It's tropical down here," Phillips complained.

"You'll cool down soon enough," Ryan said, and entered the security code to buzz them through the doors.

Sure enough, there was an icy blast of cold air as they entered the main workspace of the mortuary. To their left, there was a line of lab coats hanging on pegs for visitor use and they selected a couple. They spent another minute signing into the log book and covering their heads in disposable hair caps.

"I feel like a dinner lady," Phillips muttered, fiddling with the elastic at his head.

But there was no appetizing scent of rice pudding in the clinical space surrounding them. Rather, the air carried a noxious combination of chemicals that didn't quite manage to disguise the insidious smell of death lingering beneath.

Phillips cleared his throat loudly and wished he'd had a cigarette after all. It might have masked the pong.

At that moment, the chief pathologist spotted them and made his way across the room. Doctor Jeffrey Pinter was a tall man in his early fifties whose gangly frame did nothing to improve the overall impression of a walking skeleton, which was an unfortunate comparator for someone in his line of work. His white lab coat covered just past his knees and they could see he wore a pair of conservative grey suit trousers beneath. There were deep shadows beneath his eyes, accentuating the overall pallor of his skin.

"You look like you need a holiday, mate," Phillips said, taking the man's outstretched hand.

"You're telling me," Pinter replied, transferring his hand to Ryan. "Good to see you both."

"Thanks for getting around to this so quickly," Ryan put in, eyeing the banks of metal drawers lining one wall of the chilly room.

"To tell you the truth, I'm intrigued. Two deaths in a matter of days could be a terrible coincidence but it looks fishy, doesn't it?"

Ryan gave him a small smile.

For all that Pinter could be pompous and socially awkward, he couldn't be faulted for his meticulous eye for detail and nose for the business.

"Precisely what we're thinking, Jeff."

"Well, I think I can shed some light on that," he said, with the air of someone who knew something they didn't.

Which, of course, he did.

Ryan and Phillips followed him past a row of central gurneys, one of which was presently occupied by the partially-shrouded figure of a recently deceased old man. A mortuary technician looked up as they passed and raised his scalpel in greeting.

With a sharp double take, they realised the cadaver was Victor Swann. His body was hardly recognisable as it went through the stages of putrefaction, causing his skin to turn a marbled greenish-black as the organs of his body self-digested.

Catching the direction of their gaze, Pinter paused.

"We're just getting around to him now," he explained. "Sorry, it's been a bit hectic in here the last few days."

"No problem," Ryan said, wincing at the sight of all that rubbery skin. "Let's focus on the girl, for now."

"That's what I thought." Pinter carried on past a large immersion tank towards another set of doors leading to the smaller examination rooms.

"She's in here," Pinter said, pausing beside a door marked 'EXAMINATION ROOM A'.

Pinter flicked on the overhead lighting to illuminate another shrouded figure resting atop the single metal slab in the centre of the room. A variety of Medieval-style implements rested beneath a pale blue covering on a trolley nearby.

Phillips had no time to steel his stomach before the shroud was peeled back to reveal the sad remains of Alice

Chapman and he felt his insides somersault. He trained his eyes towards the ceiling, counting to twenty until the sensation passed.

Ryan told himself to remain detached, to look upon the mass of assorted flesh and bone with an impersonal eye.

But, God, it was hard.

The mortuary staff had cleaned her up as best they could but, for the first time they could remember, Pinter had chosen not to reveal the girl's face so that only her long dark hair was visible beneath the paper covering.

Ryan raised sad grey eyes to the pathologist, who gave him an apologetic shrug.

"I…thought it best."

Phillips wrestled his system back under control and found himself more than happy to take Pinter at his word.

"What can you tell us?"

Pinter blew out a stream of air and produced a retractable pointer from one of the deep pockets of his lab coat.

"The overall picture isn't pretty, as you can plainly see," he began, as if he were delivering a lecture. "I'd say she'd been dead somewhere between twelve and fifteen hours, by the time she was discovered."

"Which puts her death roughly between the hours of four and seven p.m., yesterday," Ryan deduced.

"I'd say so. The remains are quite consistent with the type of injuries I would expect to see from a fall of that height onto jagged rocks and decomposition is well underway, probably helped along by some interference from local scavengers."

Ryan nodded gravely, forcing himself to look at the body. It would be easier to read the pathologist's report from the comfort of his armchair at home but that was no substitute in terms of impact. From now on, he would remember this image of Alice and think of it when he hunted for her killer.

For there had been a killer.

He was sure of it.

As it turned out, Pinter was of the same opinion. He flipped open his pointer and drew their attention to Alice's hands, which were encased in plastic bags that had inflated like small balloons as her body divested itself of natural gases.

"We've spent a lot of time looking at her hands and beneath her nails," he said. "It's unfortunate that some of the flesh is missing but, from what's still there, we were able to extract several useful samples."

Ryan's eyes swept upwards.

"And?"

"I can tell you we found traces of leather fibres beneath her nails and very small traces of human skin cells," Pinter said, puffing his chest out a bit. "The samples are with Faulkner's team now. They'll compare the DNA with the samples being taken from the people up at Cragside. I understand that's happening this morning?"

"Aye, MacKenzie's overseeing it now," Phillips put in. "They'll get the swabs down to the lab as soon as possible."

"I've authorised an expedited service," Ryan said. "If we have somebody operating up there, they're not afraid to move quickly. Even with a murder detective on site," he added.

"I remember when the crims used to have a healthy respect for the law," Phillips ruminated. "Those were the good old days."

Ryan and Pinter mumbled their agreement, then the pathologist moved onto the next point of interest.

"If you look down here at the left ankle, you'll see there's quite an obvious swelling." Pinter pointed at the decaying flesh.

Ryan could hardly see any difference between the swelling on the ankle in comparison with the rest of the body but he trusted that Pinter would explain the distinction.

"You can see that the flesh is starting to distend. Decay is most active around the open wound areas but the bruising around this area of swelling on the ankle could not have occurred post-mortem."

"Which means it was twisted before she died?"

"Yes, that's most likely," Pinter agreed. "It's sprained and the blood had to be circulating to pool in that area, which means it happened ante mortem."

Ryan searched the skin for signs of other bruising and, this time, he saw beyond the discolouration to the darker patches.

"And the bruising here?" Ryan's gloved finger hovered over the remaining skin of Alice's upper arms.

"Yes, that's quite telling." Pinter came to stand beside Ryan, while Phillips kept a safe distance. "You can see quite clearly there are deep imprints on the upper arms, in a circular formation that I would normally associate with aggressive handling."

Ryan folded his arms across his chest and thought of Alice Chapman's last moments, spent in fear.

"I'm still running blood tests and I'll put together my full report but I thought you'd want to see this straight away."

Ryan gave Pinter a grateful slap on the back.

"You were right. Let us know as soon as the DNA results come in."

He looked over his shoulder to where Phillips stood, a little green around the gills, and smiled fiercely.

"Looks like we've got a stupid killer on our hands, Frank."

"Oh, goody. They're my favourite kind."

CHAPTER 19

Lowerson told himself not to be put out by the fact Melanie Yates had just achieved something unprecedented. She had worked her magic on an uncooperative compliance officer at Victor Swann's bank, who had just sent through reams of personal account records without requiring a warrant of any kind. A mere thirty minutes earlier, Lowerson had ended a protracted phone call with the very same man without any success whatsoever.

Typical.

"Let's have a look-see," he declared, wriggling his fingers and then clicking open the files on his computer. He noticed Yates following suit at the desk cubicle beside him and they settled down to pore over Swann's accounts.

The numbers only covered the last three months but Yates had been promised more backdated accounts later in the day. Even looking at the most recent data, the neat little columns made for interesting reading.

For a start, they confirmed what the team already suspected of Victor Swann's character; namely, that he was a spendthrift, to the point of being completely profligate with money. Every week, there had been new luxury retail purchases—last week, he had spent over three thousand pounds on his costume for the party alone. That included a handmade suit, cut to the old Victorian style specifications, handmade Italian shoes, a Hermes silk tie and a bespoke hat from a well-known milliner in London. He'd also bought smaller trinkets, including expensive aftershave and toiletries she'd seen advertised in *Vogue* and recognised from the inventory taken at Victor's house. Then there was fancy fine dining, antiques and flashy membership of a local spa and golf resort.

That was just the tip of the iceberg.

Yates thought of the average pensioner in their seventies or eighties, of winter fuel allowance and supermarket coupons, and wondered how it was that the man had been able to spend so much. That led her to track the deposits into his account, which also made for interesting reading. While he had been paid a generous salary by the Gilberts, it was nowhere near enough to fund the kind of lifestyle Victor Swann had enjoyed.

However, when they added up all the regular cash deposits, that more than made up for the shortfall. Several times a month, deposits had been made into his account ranging between £500 and £2,000 a pop. The dates varied and, because they were made in cash, there was no account listed as the source.

She looked up and across to where Lowerson sat, his face trained on the computer screen. Yates opened her mouth to speak but found herself watching him for a moment longer, liking the way the sunshine fell on his dark hair, casting his face into a stronger profile than she'd noticed previously.

She promptly told herself to get a grip.

"Hey, Jack, did you see those cash payments last week?"

"Yeah," he replied, still preoccupied with the figures. "There are similar payments the week before and pretty much every week before that."

Yates got up and wandered over to his desk, sipping a bottle of sparkling water that had gone warm and flat sometime during the morning.

"Where was he getting all that cash?" she wondered aloud. "Do you think he had some kind of cottage business?"

"I definitely think he had something going on but I doubt it was above board. The question is, what was he selling?"

"If his finances *do* relate to how he died and one of the people working on the estate was involved, we really need to look at their accounts to match up withdrawals with the cash deposits here."

"Mm, yeah, we should contact the financial investigation unit first. We need to ask them to check their database to see if there are any suspicious activity reports listed against Swann."

"Or any of them," Yates added.

Lowerson nodded.

"Definitely. We can't use any of it without a warrant or a production order, but it would be a good start if they could point us in the right direction."

"I'll get onto the FIU right now," Yates offered.

"Check the National Database too," Lowerson told her, and surprised himself at how quickly he was taking to the whole mentoring malarkey. "You never know, there might be a marker on there for one of them."

"Will do, guv."

Lowerson almost burst with pride at being called 'guv' for the first time in his professional career but he managed to keep a lid on it.

"While you're doing that, I'm going to have a look at the old boy's mortgage papers, insurance and pensions documents, everything we found at his house. If he had that much cash flowing through his account, he might have tried to launder some of it elsewhere."

Yates blew out a long breath.

"We've stumbled onto something big here, haven't we?"

Lowerson recognised the tone of voice, which was a mix of awe and gratitude at being able to get stuck into some real detective work.

"Let's get cracking and see just how big."

MacKenzie arrived back at Cragside to supervise what was supposed to be a simple forensic process, along with

Tom Faulkner who came armed with a job lot of buccal swabs. He and his team of CSIs had returned for another day at Cragside to continue sweeping the area where Alice Chapman's body had been found the day before, as well as the uppermost tower room where she had spent most of her working day. It should have been an easy task to take half an hour away from his ordinary duties to swipe the inside of each person's cheek, having already obtained their voluntary consent on condition that the record would be destroyed afterward if it proved irrelevant to their investigation. Instead, they were met at the door by a smug-looking Martin Henderson, flanked by what could only be his solicitor. After so many years in the business, MacKenzie had learned to spot one at fifty paces.

"Good morning," she said mildly, reaching for her warrant card.

It was thoroughly inspected.

"I have an appointment at nine-thirty to take DNA swabs," she continued, in a no-nonsense tone. "Is everybody assembled?"

"I've told them all to get on with work as usual and you certainly can't disturb the Gilberts because they're resting," Henderson sneered. "I've discussed it with my solicitor and *she* tells me that the detective constable had no right to coerce our consent yesterday."

The solicitor bobbed her brassy blonde head and gave MacKenzie what could only be described as a very female look.

Her Irish hackles went up.

"There was no coercion involved whatsoever, and I resent the implication. Detective Constable Lowerson was fully within his rights to seek voluntary consent," MacKenzie shot back.

"Ah, but the consent isn't valid if we're bullied into it," Henderson told her. "Besides, you need to arrest me before you can take a sample. I know a bit about the law, you know. I did a night course."

"Well done," MacKenzie crooned, wondering if it was obtained from the University of Moronic Behaviour. "Would you like a medal?"

"Did you hear that?" he almost shouted at the woman standing silently beside him, racking up billable hours. "She *antagonised* me. I'm starting to feel harassed."

MacKenzie gave him a withering look.

"You know, I'm really starting to wonder why you're the only person raising obstacles to this enquiry," she said, ever so softly. "It makes me wonder what it is you're hiding, Mr Henderson."

"Don't be ridiculous," he spat.

MacKenzie held his skittish gaze for a moment, measuring the man, then smiled pleasantly.

"In any event, it's very convenient your lawyer is here. Since you are now repudiating your consent, that leaves me no choice but to enforce section sixty-three, sub-section four of the Police and Criminal Evidence Act 1984. Thanks to your extensive legal knowledge, I'm sure you're already aware, Mr Henderson, that it empowers me to take a non-intimate DNA sample prior to charging you with an offence where it will tend to disprove…or *prove* your involvement in a recordable offence."

His face lost colour and he turned to the woman standing beside him like a dummy.

"Melissa? Say something!"

"I'll be happy to stay on for an extra hour," she said, consulting an expensive watch on her bony wrist. "There'll be a surcharge, of course."

MacKenzie gave them another smile as she swept into the house.

"I'm so pleased we were able to clear up that little misunderstanding."

CHAPTER 20

Thanks to Henderson's interference, it took MacKenzie forty-five minutes to locate the eight people who had agreed to give a DNA sample. Having followed the advice of a seemingly legitimate solicitor and influenced by their officious estate manager, the staff had gone about their ordinary business. Unfortunately for the police, that took them to all corners of the vast estate and cost the investigation valuable time.

Which was surely the intention.

The Gilberts were the easiest to find. Cassandra and Lionel kept to their rooms upstairs while they recovered from the flu virus which, by now, was starting to spread to the rest of the household. Maggie, the housekeeper, was on hand to take care of them and had begun to develop a sniffle herself. Henderson had stormed off immediately after his cheek had been swabbed and hadn't been seen since. Charlotte Shapiro had been found in the nursery with all six under-gardeners, discussing plans for an undeveloped area in the north-west gardens. There were no other staff members on site while the estate remained cordoned off and the forensic work continued.

MacKenzie finally found Dave Quibble in the drawing room, where he was crouched beside a table near the door poring over a large porcelain lamp with a painted shepherdess on the side.

"Sorry to disturb you," MacKenzie said. "We're ready to take the swab from you now, Mr Quibble."

"Ah..." He stood up straight and turned to greet MacKenzie, whom he hadn't had the pleasure of meeting before.

He didn't know what he had expected from a female detective inspector, but it certainly wasn't an attractive redhead with direct green eyes and an Irish accent that could have melted butter.

"Very pleased to meet you," he said, a bit flustered.

MacKenzie dutifully shook his hand.

"This should only take a minute, Mr Quibble—"

"Dave."

"If you'd like to follow me to the staff room."

As they walked down the long gallery towards the main stairwell, MacKenzie tried to put him at his ease by asking some basic questions.

"I understand you're the conservation manager," she began. "That must be a lot of work."

"Oh, it never feels like work," he said. "I love my job, especially the electrics in this place. Absolutely fascinating."

MacKenzie had done a bit of research on the old house.

"I understand everything operates on hydro-power, as far as possible."

"Yes, that's right. You just caught me trying to figure out how on earth the fuse was blown the other night."

"And, have you figured it out yet?"

"Well, we've been looking around the house now that the CSIs have finished inside the main rooms to see where the problem lies, although I suspect I'll have to call in an electrician. I happened to notice that one of the old lamps had a frayed cord and there's a wine spillage on the carpet nearby. I wonder if somebody spilled a drink on it and managed to blow the fuse."

MacKenzie thought back to the statements she had taken on Sunday and of Charlotte Shapiro, but said nothing.

"I hope you get to the bottom of it," she murmured.

———

Following the completion of the DNA swabbing, Faulkner instructed one of his junior staff to transport the samples back to their lab and to press on with testing against the samples recovered from Alice Chapman's body. Afterwards, he took a short break and wandered around the side of the house and up into the rock gardens, which were impressive. Sandstone boulders covered the sloping hillsides to the west and south of the main house, interspersed with heathers, alpine plants and a couple of quaint waterfalls. He made his way to a boulder overlooking one of the smaller cascades and sat down to soak up the atmosphere before he returned to the less appealing task of sweeping a crime scene.

Charlotte Shapiro found him sitting there and was reminded for a moment of Bilbo Baggins in the Shire. Faulkner's scruffy-looking hair had been left to tangle in waves around his round, open face and he wore plain clothing that mirrored her own dark green canvas trousers and well-worn leather boots.

"Hello," she called out and watched him nearly topple off his perch.

"Oh, hello. Are they asking for me at the house?"

Charlotte shook her head and made her way along the footpath to join him. It wasn't yet noon but it was another sunny day and the temperature was already heating up.

"No, it seems we both had the same idea about where to come for a walk," she said. "Mind if I join you?"

Faulkner couldn't think of a thing to say, so watched mutely as she parked herself beside him. He looked across at the cascades and reminded himself that she was, at the very least, a material witness and it was important they should not discuss the case.

"So, how's the search going?" she asked brightly.

"Um, I'm sorry, but I can't discuss an active investigation with you," he replied stiffly, and she was delighted to note that the tips of his ears were burning a fiery red.

When his neck began to turn the same colour, she was suitably chastened.

"No, I'm sorry, I shouldn't have asked. I suppose I just want to know that you're doing all you can to find out what happened to Alice."

Her voice dipped low, thrumming with emotion, and Faulkner felt all the worse for not being able to reassure her of their progress.

"Ryan will get to the bottom of this, you can rely on it," he said, with conviction.

"Yes, he does inspire confidence," she said and her brows furrowed into a frown as she followed the lazy path of a bumble bee from one heather bush to the next.

"How did you come to be a CSI? Or am I not allowed to ask?"

She fixed him with a winning smile and his ears burned again.

"I, well, I sort of fell into it, I suppose. I did a chemistry degree when I was younger and there was a workshop on careers in forensics. I thought it sounded interesting." He paused, but when she didn't show any signs of becoming bored, continued tentatively. "I was always a big fan of Sherlock Holmes and of Conan-Doyle, of course. Back in those days, it was really the inception of my line of work. They were starting to look at blood spatter and trace evidence more systematically to deduce what had really happened at a crime scene."

"Aha, so you wanted to be a real-life Sherlock Holmes."

He looked to see if she was making fun of him but all he could see was genuine warmth.

"Yes, I suppose that's right," he grinned. "I'm a big kid at heart."

"Aren't we all?"

Faulkner forgot the time for a moment and asked her the same question in return.

"Why did you become a gardener?"

Charlotte looked away, out across the beautiful rock terraces where she could name every single plant, explain its origins and how long it was likely to survive.

"When I was growing up, we didn't have a big house," she began quietly, wondering how much to say. "It was just a little terraced place with a yard at the back but my mam and dad used to take me and my brother on the bus up here to Cragside or some other place in the country whenever they could."

She closed her eyes briefly, remembering.

"I'd never seen so much greenery," she recalled. "And when I found out this entire valley used to be flat and empty, I could hardly believe it was possible to create so much texture and beauty from a blank canvas."

"It sounds as if it's a kind of art to you," he said.

"I think it is," she smiled, happy that he understood. "I started growing little tomato plants on the window sill at home, or herbs. It was the start of a love affair that has lasted a lifetime."

Faulkner could appreciate the sentiment entirely and was content to sit for another minute watching the water until it was time to leave.

"It was…nice talking to you," he offered.

Charlotte smiled and watched him make his way back through the rocks to deal with death.

Beneath the shade of an old tree, one person looked out across the valley. How many people had walked the earth around those rocky hills? How many had carried on, unaware and ignorant of the people they left in their wake? They watched as a kestrel circled high and then dived downwards to capture an unsuspecting mouse.

Surely, it wouldn't be long before the police came. The investigation had been running for days now and Ryan had a reputation for closing cases quickly. DNA swabs had been taken earlier and there was usually something for the police to find. If that was the case, Ryan would be back to make an arrest.

On the other hand, perhaps the police wouldn't find anything. It was always a possibility, however remote.

Time to end this, they vowed.

CHAPTER 21

After a pit stop for lunch, Ryan and Phillips headed back to CID Headquarters. They had almost made it to their office when they were intercepted by the Chief Constable's overbearing personal assistant.

"Morrison wants a word with you," she barked out, without any niceties.

Ryan pasted a megawatt smile on his face.

"Good afternoon, Donna. How nice to see you again—I hope you're having a pleasant week?"

She didn't bat an eyelid.

"Morrison wants to see you in her office *now*," she repeated, before turning her back on him and stalking down the corridor.

"That woman should have a sinister theme tune," Ryan muttered. "Every time I run into her, she looks as if she's about to hack me to pieces with the blunt end of a machete."

From his position on the side lines, Phillips burst out laughing.

"It's a pity Jack wasn't here to see that," he said. "Might have made him feel better about the fact you're not universally admired by the opposite sex. Unlike me," Phillips tagged on.

Ryan rolled his eyes.

"Yeah, all those hordes of women throwing themselves at your feet. It's starting to become a health and safety issue."

"Aye, it's a problem but we each have our cross to bear."

Chief Constable Morrison was waiting for him when Ryan knocked on the door of her office, and she gestured towards one of the semi-comfortable tub chairs arranged in front of her desk. He noticed she'd put a few potted cacti on the window ledges and watercolour pictures of local seascapes hung on three of the walls to soften the stark white. Ryan came to stand in front of her desk.

"I understand you wanted to see me, ma'am?"

"Yes. Take a seat, Ryan, you're giving me a neck-ache."

She watched him settle himself, admiring the way he always managed to look unruffled, no matter what bubbled beneath the surface of those clear grey eyes.

"How are things up at Cragside?"

Ryan shifted in his seat, recognising the warm-up question for what it was. They both knew what Morrison really planned to talk about but he was happy to go along with the subterfuge if it bought him a few precious minutes.

"Progressing," he replied. "I had a word with Jeff Pinter earlier this morning and it's likely there was a struggle before Alice Chapman died. On that basis, we're treating her death as murder in the absence of any other plausible alternative. DNA testing is ongoing."

"What about the first victim?" Morrison racked her brains for a name. "Victor Swann? I understand you're treating his death as a linked investigation."

"Yes, ma'am. Although we're awaiting the pathologist's report, it would appear there is an evidential link between the two deaths. I suspect there is a strong financial motivation too. Swann lived like a king but his earnings capacity didn't match his spending. DC Lowerson and PC Yates have been following the money, digging around into any outstanding SARs to see if there are any markers on his file."

Morrison nodded. He seemed to have everything in hand, which was no less than she expected.

"I hear that MacKenzie has started back at work? That's excellent news."

Ryan nodded.

"She's planning to do two or three days per week to begin with and I've agreed to be flexible on that. It's still early days."

"Of course. If there's anything she needs—"

"She'll let us know," Ryan interjected smoothly. "But I'm keeping an eye on her. We all are."

The tone suggested, ever so subtly, that his team looked out for one another. Not being party to that, Morrison was left out in the cold.

Her lips flattened.

"There was another matter I wanted to discuss."

She found herself bristling under his silent scrutiny and came straight to the point.

"I was disappointed by your reaction the other morning, when I told you of the new appointee to the superintendent position," she said, flatly. "While you are naturally—shall we say, *reserved*?—I thought your behaviour was out of character, even for you."

She realised he was not going to help her by volunteering any information, so she needed to be even more blunt.

"I want you to tell me why you have a problem with DCI Lucas. Surely it can't be something as trivial as a brief history together, over a decade ago."

A muscle ticked in his jaw and Ryan looked away for a moment. When he turned back, his eyes were completely veiled.

"I have no grievance on record against DCI Lucas."

"Alright," Morrison said, a bit testily. "You say you don't have a formal grievance but what about an informal one? Don't try and tell me everything is tickety-boo, because I wasn't born yesterday."

Ryan felt the old fear creep back, the worry that he could be wrong or that he would not be believed. He remembered how Lucas had behaved all those years ago and what she had done; the times she had made him doubt his own sanity. Had he magnified those memories over time? Perhaps she had changed; recovered and found inner peace.

Pigs might fly.

Ryan opened his mouth to tell Morrison about the times he had feared for his safety; the times Lucas had threatened suicide if he should ever leave her; the horror at coming home to his flat in London to find her there with a firearm held to her head.

At the time, he hadn't put it on record out of a sense of sympathy and misguided pity, and it had been his single biggest mistake. He had been a much younger man, barely twenty-three to her more worldly thirty-two, and he hadn't the first idea how to manage such a volatile situation. Lucas was his superior and they had been discreet from the start because personal relationships had been discouraged in the ranks. Unfortunately, that meant nobody knew of it and Lucas threatened to deny any intimacy between them if Ryan raised it with the brass.

When he'd overridden her threat and tentatively mentioned it to one of his colleagues, they'd laughed.

Grow a pair of balls, mate.

Man up.

Apparently, it was inconceivable for a man like Ryan to be the subject of unwanted attention. He'd been told he should stop complaining and that other men would kill to have a woman like Jennifer Lucas in their lives. Back then, he'd been young and proud, unwilling to embarrass himself any further by showing them the scars of his short-lived romance.

He wondered whether the response would have been different if he'd been a woman.

But that was then.

Ryan was a different man now, with ten more years of life experience. He knew what it meant to be a partner in a meaningful relationship, where neither party was ever made to feel trapped, or worse. He didn't mind the jokes around the canteen or the banter from his friends because he'd made a new life for himself from the ashes of the old one.

He'd built something good here, something solid that was worth protecting.

Ryan had just made up his mind to tell Morrison the real reason for his concern, when she said something that stopped him.

"I don't know whether it will interest you to know that DCI Lucas will be moving north with her *husband*," Morrison said, and watched relief pass over Ryan's face.

It was like a weight had been lifted from his shoulders. He was delighted to know that Lucas had left her troubles behind her and gone on to find happiness in the years that had passed. He couldn't wait to tell Anna about this development.

"As you can see, there really should be no awkwardness," Morrison continued. "Unless there's something else you feel I should know?"

Ryan thought of Lucas's husband and of the uncomfortable position it may put her in if he were to rake up the past. For all he knew, she had children who could be affected by any repercussions.

"No. No," he said again, more firmly this time. "There's nothing."

Therein, Ryan made his second big mistake.

Ryan found his team gathered around Lowerson's desk, waiting for him. "Everything alright, lad?"

Phillips gave him a sharp look but Ryan nodded and felt relaxed for the first time in days. It might be awkward working with Lucas at first but there was a lot of water under the bridge.

"What are we all looking at?"

He walked around to lean over Lowerson's shoulder and look at an e-mail from one of the investigators in the financial investigation unit, then grabbed a spare chair and wheeled it across to join their little huddle.

"Where's Mac?"

"On her way back," Phillips told him. "Faulkner's still at it but there's no need for her to hang around."

Ryan nodded.

"Alright. Where are we at?"

"I've been focusing on Victor Swann's household documents—mortgage, pensions and so on, while Yates has been liaising with the FIU to peel away the top layer."

Lowerson reached behind him to grasp a sheaf of papers showing Swann's personal current account and handed it to Ryan, who skim-read the figures, paying attention to transactions highlighted in neon yellow and green.

"As you can see from those accounts, Swann had access to considerable funds and spent them freely."

Ryan's eyebrows raised when he noted £1,000 had been spent on a solid silver and 18ct gold cartridge pen.

"There are some weighty cash deposits here," Ryan observed.

"Yes, it confirms what we already suspected. There was more to Victor than met the eye," Lowerson said, then showed him a different set of papers. "These are some of the papers we found scattered on the floor of his house."

Ryan looked down at a set of sale documents for the retirement bungalow, which had been bought with a small mortgage. Flipping the page, he found pensions and life insurance documentation, showing that Victor had invested heavily in both.

"There isn't much out of the ordinary there, nothing that was flagged by the money laundering reporting officer at the bank, anyway," Lowerson said. "But at this point, I'll hand over to Yates, who can tell you the fun stuff."

He gave her an encouraging smile.

"Um, yes. The disparity of income and expenditure seemed suspicious, so I contacted our colleagues in FIU. They tell me that Victor Swann has several markers on their system for separate transactions over the space of at least two years, owing to unusually high cash deposits and outgoings, but he was not being actively investigated."

"Why not?"

"Resources, they tell me. Frankly, sir, they 'have bigger fish to fry than a pensioner splashing the cash'. That's a direct quote from them."

It was the same story they'd heard many times before.

"I explained the potential link between Swann and one or more members of the household at Cragside to the FIU investigator and I've submitted the paperwork for them to go ahead and seek full disclosure of all Swann's records from his bank. We've only been able to find one current account and two savings accounts held with the same bank, both of which contain a moderate sum."

"There might be more accounts but it will take time to find them," Ryan predicted.

"Yes."

"I bet there'll be a timeshare in Marbella hidden somewhere, 'n all," Phillips grumbled, thinking that all he could look forward to in his dotage was an annual trip to Butlins.

"So," Ryan said, moving swiftly on, "they're going to come back to us with Swann's financial records. What about tracing the source of these cash deposits?"

Yates gave him a pained look.

"The only way we can really do that is to seek speculative access to the private accounts of the people on our list, to see if there are withdrawals of a similar amount and date range as the deposits made into Swann's account. We'd need to make a formal application to see those records, which isn't granted lightly."

"We've got a long list," Lowerson agreed. "But we need to whittle that down to a short list otherwise we'll get nowhere with the banks."

Ryan clapped his hands together.

"Let's get whittling."

CHAPTER 22

Just before three o'clock, MacKenzie stepped through the shiny automatic doors of the main entrance to the new police headquarters in Wallsend. The foyer was large and open-plan, without any sign of the mouldy walls and persistent smell of urine and bleach that had been a defining feature of their old workplace. The visitors' chairs were brand new but made of the same cheap plastic so they could be wiped clean. The clientele was just the same as before: a mixture of people who had fallen prey to substance abuse, prostitutes, local thugs, and students seeking a crime reference number for the mobile phone they'd lost during a heavy night out at the weekend.

Everything felt familiar, yet unfamiliar.

"Denise!"

She swung around to see a couple of uniforms heading across to greet her.

"Great to see you back on your feet! How are you feeling?"

She listened to their well-meaning remarks and forced a smile, thanked them for their good wishes, then moved away as a small headache started to pound in the base of her skull. In another moment, the headache would intensify and she'd black out.

MacKenzie made it to the other side of the security doors and was grateful to find she had the corridor to herself.

Her vision was spinning.

"No," she told her treacherous mind. "Not again. Not today."

She leaned back against the wall and closed her eyes, visualising herself in a safe place, with warm sun on her skin and quiet music playing in her ears. Her breathing slowed to an even pace and the headache receded.

"That's better," she muttered and made her way to the first floor.

MacKenzie found the rest of her team holed up in a small meeting room, where Phillips was product-testing a state-of-the-art flat screen television mounted on the wall. "Good to see you're all hard at it," she declared, taking a seat beside Phillips at the oval-shaped conference table.

"Yeah, yeah," he said, fiddling with the buttons.

"It's plain to see I've come back to work just in time. The public don't pay you to watch *Judge Judy*."

"You've arrived in the nick of time," Ryan agreed and confiscated the remote control from Phillips. "We were about to eliminate some suspects from our list of eight."

He ran through a summary of what they'd learned so far about Victor Swann's accounts, as well as their reasons for suspecting that someone at the house might have been financing the old man.

"It goes like this," Ryan said, as he stood at the head of the room and spread his hands. "Victor was accepting cash from a person or persons unknown, who may have killed him. After Victor died, they raided his house and locker to recover something incriminating. The following day, Alice Chapman is found dead at the bottom of the valley. Bearing in mind the odds and ends belonging to Victor we found scattered around her body, it stands to reason that Alice had found or come into possession of them—"

Ryan broke off as an alternative scenario presented itself.

"No," he said. "It's more likely she interrupted somebody who was in possession of Victor's things. Putting two and two together, Alice came up with the correct number and ran towards the bridge, where there was a struggle and Victor's bits and pieces ended up at the bottom of Debdon Burn with her."

"Why would she head for the bridge?" Lowerson asked. "Why not run towards her car?"

"It was raining heavily," Ryan postulated. "If she was running in fear, she might have been disoriented…"

He trailed off as the truth hit him.

"Ah, God…" He ran an angry hand over his neck and then swore viciously. "The pathway over that bridge and through the trees leads to nowhere except the cottage I'm renting with Anna. She was running to tell us what she'd discovered," he said, sadly. "Alice was running for help but we weren't there for her."

"There's no way you could have known," Phillips said, always the voice of reason.

Ryan shoved the guilt to one side for now. He would deal with that later and add Alice to the reel of other victims whose faces crowded his dreams.

"All of this suggests Victor knew something important enough to extort regular payments from our unknown perp."

"But who?" Yates asked, beginning to come out of her shell. "We're still no closer to discovering who was paying these bribes, if that's what they were."

Ryan smiled knowingly.

"That's where a bit of common sense comes in," he said. "If we assume Victor was pushed and, the following day, Alice was chased down and then bodily thrown over the side of the bridge, there's one important characteristic our killer needed."

"Physical strength," MacKenzie murmured.

"Exactly." Ryan pointed his finger to capture the thought. "Turning to our list of suspects, there are several we can cross off straight away."

He shuffled some papers and found copies of their photographs which he laid out in a row on the table.

"We can strike Lionel and Cassandra off the list, and Maggie," Phillips said. "They're all at least seventy and none of them could have chased a girl half their age, let alone forced her over the side of a bridge."

"Agreed. Added to which, Maggie was within my sight throughout Saturday evening when Victor went missing and Cassandra was around for most of it, too."

Ryan removed three of the photographs so they could see who remained.

"Although those two under-gardeners are physically able, they're both well alibied," MacKenzie said.

"If we work on most likely probabilities, I would say that leaves three serious contenders," Ryan murmured. "Dave Quibble, Martin Henderson and Charlotte Shapiro."

He was suddenly reminded of Charlotte Shapiro's scratched hands, and remembered she had been the one to find Alice's body. It was a well-known fact that killers often returned to the scene of their crimes, especially if they were looking for something they'd lost.

There was a short silence, then Ryan turned to address Yates.

"I think that's a short list the FIU can work with, don't you?"

She nodded happily.

"I'll get onto it right away, sir."

As Yates sprang up to alert the finance unit and set the wheels in motion for special account monitoring orders, Ryan looked back down at the three faces staring up at him and wondered.

There was no time. Any moment now, the police could burst in with a warrant to search and seize and that would be the end of everything. All their careful plans would turn to dust, all the years of trying and grasping at every little opportunity would be wasted.

What, then, would they have to show for taking a life?

They shuddered and carried on pulling out papers from the hidden unit at the back of the desk. Once the unit was cleaned out and they'd had a good feel around for any stray papers, they bundled the stack into a plain canvas bag and headed out to stuff it into the boot of their car.

Come nightfall, they would find the perfect spot for a bonfire.

Back at CID Headquarters, Ryan's good mood was vanishing rapidly. "What the hell is this? Amateurs Anonymous?"

He glared at each of them in turn and at least they had the grace to look sheepish.

"I don't know how we missed that one, guv." Lowerson was the first to speak, and the others in the room silently commended his bravery.

"Neither do I, considering you all have two eyes and a brain inside your heads," Ryan shot back.

"We'll get onto it straight away," Phillips assured him, with a nervous glance towards MacKenzie.

"Don't look at me," she said, holding her hands up.

Ryan watched them pass the proverbial parcel among themselves and shook his head.

"Count yourselves lucky I'm not sending you all back to cadet training school for a refresher course," he muttered. "As it is, I'm going to overlook the fact that nobody has contacted Victor's mobile phone company yet, despite it being one of the first and most obvious things we look for."

"I suppose I didn't think an old bloke like him would have a mobile phone," Lowerson confessed, drawing disbelieving glances from around the room.

Ryan told himself to remain calm.

"Jack, I realise that anyone over the age of thirty-five seems 'old' to you. But, to the rest of us, age is just a number. We might have a few more lines but we're mostly the same as we always were, which includes Victor Swann. You need to get the idea out of your head that age equates to incapacity."

"I narf feel the draughts, now, like," Phillips threw in, and Ryan slapped a hand to his face. "And my knees creak a lot more than they used to."

"Fascinating insight," Ryan muttered, and came back to the point.

"Look, if Victor Swann could run a highly successful cottage business in blackmail and extortion, he sure as hell could operate a mobile phone. That's probably what our perp was looking for when they raided his locker."

MacKenzie looked at the inventory of items found scattered around Alice Chapman's body.

"No mention of a mobile phone on the list," she confirmed.

"Yet we know Victor must have had one."

"Somebody took it?"

"It looks that way, doesn't it? I want to know what was on that phone and where it is now."

"I'll get in touch with the phone company," Lowerson offered, and fled the room.

As the door clicked shut, Ryan turned to the others with a private smile.

"Ah, youth."

Anna spent most of the day finalising details for the wedding, which was fast approaching. She grappled with last-minute cancellations and tussled with caterers, spoke to friends who were due to attend and organised for a large donation to be made to the food banks in Newcastle. She thought it only fair that, if they planned to enjoy a hearty wedding breakfast, they should spare a thought for others who were not so fortunate while they stuffed their faces with fruit cake. Her wedding dress was now safely ensconced in the spare bedroom with the door firmly shut. She had never considered herself to be a superstitious person but it was an established tradition that the groom should not see her dress before the big day and she planned to stick to it.

Anna sat down briefly on the bed, looked at the long white protective cover hanging on the back of the door and thought of one thing.

Her mother.

Sara Taylor had been a beautiful woman, taken too young by a man whose obsession had driven him mad. Anna's childhood was riddled with memories of domestic abuse and drunken scenes. She and her sister had grown up with the spectre of shame hanging over their heads and, on a small island community, it had been hard to hide from it. She had felt a terrible sense of relief when her father died, his body smashed against the rocks at the foot of Lindisfarne Castle many years ago.

Inexplicably, she still mourned him; more so in the last couple of years since she'd found out that he hadn't been responsible for her mother's death, or his own, for that matter. Andy Taylor might have been a big man with hard hands, but he hadn't killed her mother and he hadn't killed himself.

Small comfort.

When she walked down the aisle in just over a week, it struck her that she would have no father to cling to for support. There would be no mother to help her to dress and pin her veil, no sister to laugh and drink champagne with beforehand. She had friends, of course, but it wasn't the same.

Anna stood up and smoothed a hand over the dress hanging on the back of the door and, for the first time in a long while, felt utterly alone.

CHAPTER 23

It was just before five o'clock when Ryan excused himself and took an hour's personal time to tend to something very important. He was pleased to see the weather was still holding and fluffy white clouds made their slow journey across an otherwise clear sky. He left Lowerson and Yates in charge of telecommunications while they awaited news from the financial investigation unit, and MacKenzie and Phillips took charge of all other business in his absence. That included forensic updates and wading through the ever-growing pile of paperwork that had been generated over the past few days. They would continue to delve into the history of each person of interest and contact him as soon as there was any development.

With that reassurance, Ryan drove back to the rental cottage at Cragside. It was tempting to stop for a word with Faulkner to check how the groundwork was coming along but he deliberately steered the car away from the main house and took the smaller access road directly to the cottage. If there was any news, Faulkner would get in touch.

Anna looked up in surprise when the front door opened and automatically checked her watch.

"You're home early," she said, searching his face to see if anything was wrong.

Ryan smiled enigmatically.

"Put your shoes on, I'm taking you out," he said.

Anna waved at the piles of books on the kitchen table.

"I'd really love to but I've been tied up with wedding nonsense all morning and I need to get down to some work."

"Well, I've got some more wedding nonsense for you."

"Have we forgotten to book something?"

For the life of her, she couldn't think what. Ryan's mother had been invaluable over the past few months, helping to replace so many of the things that had been lost in the fire at Anna's cottage, as well as dealing with the bureaucracy of planning a large event. Ryan's parents had stayed with them for over a month, primarily so that Eve Finley-Ryan could hold her son close and thank whichever higher power had kept him safe from the Hacker.

"It's nothing like that," Ryan told her but didn't elaborate. "Now, woman, are you going to obey your soon-to-be-husband or do I need to drag you barefoot?"

Anna gave him an eloquent look and he laughed appreciatively.

"Chance would be a fine thing."

Anna rose to find her shoes but took her time about it, on principle.

A few minutes later when they were driving towards Rothbury, she turned to him again.

"Are you going to tell me where we're going?"

Ryan smiled to himself.

"Nope."

She watched his hard profile as he steered the car and folded her arms.

"I don't like surprises," she said, although that was possibly because she'd never had any.

"I hope you'll like this one," he said softly.

Ryan drove through the handsome town of Rothbury and followed the road which ran parallel to the Coquet river. They wound through the valley and through villages with names straight out of Tolkien; they passed Thropton, Flotterton and Caistron, skirting around the Northumberland National Park until they reached the ancient village of Elsdon. It was a favourite place of Anna's to visit, not only because it was chocolate-box pretty but because of its rich local history. They had spent many a happy Sunday afternoon wandering the motte and bailey castle while Anna chattered about fortifications against Border reivers and Ryan looked forward to lunch at the pub. The landscape undulated gently and, when the light fell in a certain way against the hillside, the village looked almost ethereal.

"Oh, this is a nice idea," Anna said happily. "Did you want to have dinner nearby?"

Ryan held his tongue.

Anna gave him a frustrated glare and wondered what he was up to.

Ryan didn't stop and park the car in any of the usual places but carried on a little further past the village until they came to an unmarked turning. He took it and began to climb, the road shielded by tall hedgerows on either side.

"I need to think about getting a more practical car," he said under his breath.

Suddenly they emerged onto a plateau of higher ground and Ryan slowed to watch out for another unmarked turn.

"Need to get some lights up here," he added and was grateful it was summer so there was another hour or two of sunlight left in the day.

Anna barely had time to wonder what had come over him when Ryan let out a small sound of relief and stopped the car to jump out beside a plain wooden gate. He fished out a set of keys and pushed it open before jogging back to the car and turning inside.

Seated beside him, she watched as the scenery came slowly into view. She could see Elsdon nestled in the valley beneath, like a model village with its peel tower and church spire. As Ryan pulled the car to a stop, the clouds shifted and long beams of light fell upon the village, turning its stone into a soft, apricot hue.

"It's beautiful up here," she murmured.

Ryan watched her face soften, then reached over to squeeze her hand.

"Let's go for a walk."

Anna was happy to comply and they began to stroll further along the wide ridge of land with panoramic views across the dale. When they had walked a little further, Ryan slung his arm around her shoulder and tugged her against his body.

"Thank you for bringing me up here," she said. "I always find this area so restful."

"Me too," he said and took a deep breath.

"What do you think about buying a place here?"

Anna twisted and looked up into his earnest face.

"Really? Isn't the commute a bit inconvenient for you?"

"I don't mind the drive," Ryan said. "But it's further away from Durham and your work at the university."

Anna mulled it over.

"I only have three days of teaching; the rest of the time I could work from home. It would certainly be a change from living just across the river from the faculty, though."

She paused.

"Is that why you brought me up here? Is there a house for sale in the area?"

"You could say that. There's a parcel of land."

"Where?"

"You're standing on it," he murmured, and she stepped away to turn around and get a better look.

She faced him again with excited eyes.

"All of *this*?"

Ryan nodded.

"It's almost three acres in total," he told her, pointing towards the gate. "From there, it includes the land reaching to the hedgerows on three sides, and down to the edge of the hill."

Anna pressed her hand to her mouth, already imagining what could be built.

"It's not agricultural land?"

"No, I've already spoken to the planning office," he assured her, and almost added that he already had planning permission approved in principle. "You like it, then?"

She laughed.

"Like it? I *love* it!" But as soon as the words left her lips, her face fell again. "I suppose it's very expensive, though."

Ryan could have kissed her and, in another moment, he would. It was hardly a regular topic of conversation but she was aware of his family history and the privileged childhood he had enjoyed. What she didn't know was the extent of the legacy left to him by his maternal grandmother, which could have allowed him never to work again.

But that wasn't his way.

It was almost embarrassing to admit to that kind of good fortune and he hardly touched it other than to check the status of the various philanthropic ventures he'd set in motion over ten years ago. He'd used the money only three times for his own personal use: once, to fund his police cadet training in London; the second time, to purchase his first and only property on the Quayside in Newcastle, which was now lying vacant; and thirdly, to purchase the parcel of land they now stood on.

He looked across at the woman he loved.

"It's yours," he told her.

Anna thought she had misheard him.

"What do you mean?"

"I found it months ago," he admitted. "Long before the fire in Durham. The sale went through six weeks ago and the title is in your name. I always planned to give it to you as a wedding present and I hoped that we could build something here, together. For ourselves and, one day, maybe, our children."

She felt tears burn the back of her eyes and she looked away, out across the hills. Her breath started to hitch and she put a hand to her stomach to settle it, so she could find the right words.

Her eyes were brilliant when she looked at him again.

"I don't know what to say or how to tell you what I'm feeling."

Her lips trembled and he made as if to step forward but she held him off, just for another moment.

"I want you to know that I don't need anything like this." She swept an arm out to encompass the land. "I love you for everything you are, not everything you have."

He reached out to touch her hair.

"I know that."

"Good. I couldn't stand it if you thought otherwise."

The thought of Anna being a gold-digger was so ridiculous, he almost laughed.

"I can always put it up for sale, if you don't want it?"

She turned on him with horrified eyes and, catching the mirth dancing on his face, launched herself at him.

"Thank you," she said and kissed him.

There on the brow of the hill, they planned the house they would build. It would have floor-to-ceiling windows on three sides so they could enjoy the view of the countryside they both loved. They spoke of the little village community and of the friends they hoped to make and of the walks they could take over the moors and in the National Park.

"I only have one request," Ryan said, as they finally made their way home.

Anna slanted him a look.

"You want a hot tub, don't you?"

"Got it in one."

Their excitement was interrupted not long afterwards by a call from Phillips. "Got a minute?"

"I've got several," Ryan said, using the hands-free function as he drove back to Cragside. "What's up?"

"I reckon we've had a bit of a breakthrough," Phillips said, his voice crackling through the car speakers. "Lowerson's just come off the phone to the telephone company. They checked the records from Victor Swann's mobile phone and they've confirmed it was last transmitting at 18:54 on Saturday night, after which there was nothing."

"How accurate is the radius?"

"There's a mast in the grounds at Cragside so they've been able to triangulate to within fifty metres and we think the phone was last active within the house. But that's not all," Phillips said. "Lowerson's pushing through the paperwork so they can release the text messages they've got recorded on their system."

"How soon until they can get them through to us?"

"You know what these companies are like," Phillips groused. "It's all 'computer says no' and on the dot of five they're off shift. The compliance officer we need to get hold of works flexi-hours and he won't be back on until seven a.m. tomorrow."

"At which time, I want you to be ready and waiting to breathe down his neck."

"More than happy to," his sergeant replied.

"Any word on DNA?"

"They're going as fast as they can."

Ryan slowed the car for the turn into Cragside estate and nearly collided with Henderson's vehicle as it zoomed down the narrow road. He performed an emergency stop, swore volubly and watched the estate manager's tail lights disappear in his rear-view mirror.

"Hello?" At the other end of the line, Phillips winced as the air turned blue.

"Sorry Frank, that wasn't directed at you," Ryan said. "How about finances?"

"Yates has pulled an absolute blinder," Phillips said proudly. "She's been working with the team in FIU all afternoon and they've managed to get the records on Martin Henderson. He's got three SARs marked on the system for suspiciously large purchases made in cash."

"What for?"

"The deposit for his car, for one thing. I don't know what kind of magic that lass has up her sleeve but the compliance officer at Henderson's bank expedited the account monitoring order and it took effect just before six o'clock. We've been waiting for them to feed us some of the data and it's just come through for the past week, to begin with."

"And?" Ryan wasn't one to waste words.

"Henderson made a large withdrawal last week, which roughly matches the amount paid into Victor Swann's current account shortly afterwards."

They had arrived outside the rental cottage but Ryan and Anna remained seated in the car until the conversation ended.

"Frank? Tell the lab to put a rush on testing the DNA sample belonging to Martin Henderson."

"MacKenzie's already told them to do that very thing."

Ryan smiled appreciatively.

"Quick off the mark."

"We're looking at the bloke's paperwork now," Phillips continued. "He's got some company listed as his former employer but, funnily enough, I don't see anything listed on Companies House. The contact details he's given don't match up either."

"You think he's fudged the details on his CV to get the job?"

"Aye, that's what I reckon. Schmoozed his way into it because they're a rich old couple and he wants to get his sticky fingers on some of their dosh. I wonder what he's been fiddling, while their backs have been turned."

Ryan weighed their options as he stared out through the windscreen at the ornamental gardens.

"We'll give it a few more hours to see if anything else comes through from Faulkner or the bank but, first thing tomorrow morning, we're bringing him in."

Phillips gave a satisfied grunt.

"I'll be up with the larks."

"In the meantime, I want eyes on him throughout the night. I saw him tearing out of the estate driveway less than fifteen minutes ago and I don't trust him not to rabbit off the estate and hole himself up on the Costa del Sol."

"Consider it done."

CHAPTER 24

Martin Henderson swerved his car to the side of the road, drawing an angry peal of abuse and a loud honk from the unfortunate driver behind. Ignoring them, he craned his neck to see if Ryan was following him but the road was empty.

He turned back to the wheel and closed his eyes.

It was not supposed to be like this.

When he'd taken the job at Cragside, it had been with only one goal in mind and that was to make money. He didn't care how he did it, although he preferred fast jobs rather than the cons that took months or years. He wasn't a spring chicken and he had plans to retire after one last big flurry.

Henderson was long past feeling guilty about his profession; if you grew up poor enough, hungry enough, you started to feel like you were entitled to the kind of wealth other people had at their fingertips.

Money makes money, his school teacher had said. *Work hard and you'll get there in the end.*

Henderson sneered at the memory.

Spend his life scrimping and saving, begging for chances, working his fingers to the bone? There had to be an easier way.

Eventually, he'd found it.

Or, perhaps, it had found him.

Either way, he'd taken to crime like a duck to water. In the early days, he'd worked alone but he had since learned to appreciate the benefits of having a business partner.

Conscious that he was keeping them waiting, Henderson looked at the clock on the dashboard and checked the rear-view mirror one last time.

Time to plan his exit strategy.

Dusk was falling as Ryan made his way through the trees to pay his last visit of the evening. His shoes crunched lightly against the pathway while he listened to nightjars *churring* in the trees and foxes rustling somewhere in the shadows. As the iron bridge came into view, he could see the police boundary line had been removed and he knew that Faulkner's team had completed their work. He paused for a moment to look down into the burn below, imagining how Alice Chapman must have felt in the moments before she was thrown.

Terrified.

Ryan's knuckles gleamed white against the iron railing as he imagined gripping Henderson's scrawny neck and he thrust away from the edge with a sharp sound of annoyance. In the morning, he would squeeze the estate manager, metaphorically speaking of course, and it was a cheerful thought.

Ryan turned away and carried on towards the main house, looking up at its high walls with a kind of reverence.

What mysteries did those walls conceal?

Cragside had spent over a hundred years hidden among the trees like a mythical elven castle and now it was a living museum for an unconventional old couple with more money than they could spend in one lifetime. At first, he'd wondered why—why live in the past, when the world was striding forward?

During the last four months spent living on the estate, he'd come to appreciate that there was a comforting nostalgia to life at Cragside. Those who lived inside its otherworldly bubble could pretend the horrors and afflictions of modern life did not affect them.

But they were wrong.

A killer walked among them now, bursting the protective bubble and dragging them all brutishly back to reality. He walked among them without conscience and Ryan recognised the type because he had seen it many times before. It was cold-blooded, motivated only by self-interest and not by any of the animalistic urges or psychosexual disorders that had defined a man like the Hacker.

For Martin Henderson, it was purely business.

As Ryan reached up to tug the old brass bell beside the front door, he had to wonder which was worse: a person who killed violently because their victim represented something important to them; or a person who killed coldly and dispassionately because their victim represented nothing at all except a means to an end.

When Cassandra Gilbert opened the door, it looked as if she had aged ten years since he had first met her at the party on Saturday night. Her eyes were tired and, although she had been unwell, he suspected that her insomnia had nothing to do with a flu virus. "Mrs Gilbert, I'm sorry to disturb you but I wonder if I might have a word in private?"

Ryan had been trained to observe body language. Right now, with her shoulders hunched in defeat and her eyes downcast, he knew immediately that Cassandra understood why he had come.

"Do we—do we have to talk about it?"

"Yes, I'm afraid we do."

As he stepped inside the hallway, he made a discreet survey.

"Is your husband at home this evening?"

"Lionel is reading in the library," she told him. "We could sit in one of the other rooms?"

She raised hopeful eyes.

"Yes, that would be fine."

He followed her through to a smaller morning room and waited as she turned on a couple of side lamps, bathing the room in a sepia light.

"Would you like some tea?"

She stood beside the door, fiddling with her wedding ring.

"No, thank you. I don't want to take up too much of your time."

She nodded and closed the door with a soft click.

Ryan waited until she had seated herself in one of the chintzy armchairs and then took one opposite, noticing for the first time how much of an anachronism she looked amid the Victorian décor when dressed in her normal clothing. Today, she wore classy beige linen slacks and a cream silk shirt over comfortable-looking sandals, rather than a heavy taffeta dress and bustle.

There was a short pause during which the mantel clock chimed seven-thirty.

"What did you want to speak to me about?"

Ryan prepared to bite the bullet.

"I suspect you know what I've come to talk about, Cassandra. We found some intimate photographs of you while conducting a search of Victor's home and possessions."

She looked down at her hands and Ryan felt no better than the ungentlemanly cad he'd played in *The Mysterious Case of the Disappearing Duchess*. It was unchivalrous to question a lady's private affairs, especially when the lady in question was old enough to be his grandmother.

Unfortunately, his work was peppered with uncomfortable moments like these.

"Oh?" Her voice quivered. "What kind of photographs?"

"Cassandra…" His voice held a warning, now. "Lying to the police is a serious matter. Remember, I was aware of these photographs two days ago but I'm only asking you about them now because they may have some bearing on our investigation."

She realised she had underestimated him.

"Thank you," she murmured. "I hadn't realised."

"Unless the evidence pertains to an investigation, it isn't any of my business."

"Thank you," she said again. "If I tell you what happened, will you tell my husband?"

Sticky ground, he thought.

"Unless the information you give me will require you to give evidence at trial, I see no need for your husband to become aware of it." He paused and waited until she looked him in the eye. "This is an informal discussion but please understand that whatever you *do* tell me may later be used in evidence."

He recited the standard caution.

"I understand." She nodded, clearly gathering her courage. "You—you know I married Lionel back in 1998. I was a widow after my husband died and left me with two children. It was a struggle for many years," she remembered, looking down at the glistening jewels on her fingers and feeling nauseous.

"I managed to bring the kids up and give them a decent life," she continued. "You're too young to know what it's like when your children leave home and start their own families, but you feel bereft. It's a lonely life, if you haven't anybody to share it with. In my early sixties, it was getting so bad, I took a part-time job at a golf club because I thought it would help to fill the time. That's where I met Lionel."

Ryan said nothing and his face betrayed no emotion but she read his thoughts all the same.

"I know how it looks," she said. "Lionel can be overbearing. He's spent a lifetime being in charge and he finds it difficult to let go, especially now his health is failing. But believe me, inspector, he can be charming when he wants to be."

"But?"

She smiled slightly.

"You're a perceptive one, aren't you? Lionel spoiled me and he's been so good to my children, considering his usual outlook towards people wanting a 'free ride'. I'll always be grateful to him for that. But there's never been any physical chemistry between us; we married for companionship."

"It often happens."

"Yes." She nodded. "We get along very well and always have. I'm used to his moods and, I suppose, he's used to mine. But I'm still a woman and, especially back then, I still had needs."

She looked up, as if she were expecting him to comment, but Ryan merely listened.

"Victor was Lionel's valet long before he met me. Victor had been with him for years. I don't know how it happened, really, but we became friends. Gradually, that developed into…more than friends," she finished, lamely.

"And he took photographs of your, ah, time together?"

"Yes," she nodded miserably. "You must think me a very stupid woman."

"I think nothing of the kind," Ryan assured her.

All he saw seated before him was a nice, lonely woman who had been taken in by a man who made her feel desirable. It happened every day and the roles might just as easily have been reversed.

"Anyway, this was years ago and at one time I was even thinking of leaving Lionel to run away with Victor." She laughed briefly at the folly of her younger self. "Then I found out that Lionel had cancer. It looked very bad—stage three bowel cancer. He needed an operation, chemotherapy, a lot of care and he wears a colostomy bag now. I couldn't leave him, so I called it all off."

"Victor took it badly?"

"At first, but he recovered soon enough," she said bitterly. "Within a couple of months, he was threatening to tell Lionel everything unless I gave him some money. I thought the stress might have killed Lionel, so I paid him off."

"When was this?"

"Over ten years ago," she said. "I've been paying him ever since. Lionel loves me, you see, and it would break his heart."

There were tears in her eyes now and her shoulders began to shake. Without a word, Ryan covered the distance and crouched down beside her chair.

"Did you tell anyone, Cassandra?"

She looked up at him with misery etched into the lines of her face.

"Who would I tell? It would devastate and embarrass everyone concerned. I've carried it all these years, having to see *him* every day and be reminded that he was slowly bleeding me dry."

Ryan took her hand and gave it a quick squeeze.

"Do you think Lionel knows?"

She looked startled.

"I—well, I paid Victor in cash from my own account. Lionel gives me a very generous allowance and never asks where I spend the money. He trusts me," she finished, guiltily. "I don't see how he could have found out, unless Victor told him, but I don't think he ever did."

"I suppose you felt relieved when Victor died."

She thought of telling a polite lie but one look at Ryan's face convinced her otherwise.

"I couldn't help but feel relieved. It felt like I could sleep soundly for the first time in over ten years, without the sword of Damocles hanging over my head."

Ryan nodded. It was natural enough.

"I'd like you to give me copies of your bank accounts, if you have them. I will apply for them through the formal channels but you would save me and the investigation an awful lot of time if you would agree to hand them over."

She gave a small shrug.

"What does it matter now? I've told you everything. Come with me and I'll see what I can do."

They headed upstairs towards one of the smaller studies where she kept her paperwork and Ryan asked another question.

"Cassandra, who handles the finances? I mean, the daily running of the estate."

"Oh, it's quite complicated," she said. "Lionel still keeps a tight rein on everything. Martin manages the estate and he has access to a sort of 'kitty' account to pay for things that crop up, but anything over a certain amount and he has to ask Lionel for approval."

She tapped her finger against her lip as she thought.

"Maggie has access to a separate account for domestic expenses, so she can pay the cleaning company, the window cleaners and laundry services. I used to manage all of that, until it became too much for me and, since we travel quite a bit, it made sense to employ a housekeeper."

"Of course," Ryan agreed, looking meaningfully around the gallery as they made their way to her study. "There must be an awful lot to manage. When did Maggie join you here?"

"Oh, about five years ago," Cassandra replied. "She's been a godsend."

"How about the other staff? Does anybody else have access to ready cash?"

"I suppose you could say all the heads of the estate have access to *some* money because Charlotte is signatory on an account to cover the gardeners' wages and any outsourcing, plant buying and whatnot."

"What about Dave Quibble?"

"No, I don't think he has access to an account but he applies to Lionel for whatever funding he needs for specialist conservation of the house and grounds and he usually gets it. Lionel gave him the money so he could hire Alice to do that painting restoration," she said unhappily.

Ryan listened and thought that it was all fertile ground for an unscrupulous person skimming off the top.

"I suppose you run everything past an accountant?"

"Oh, goodness, yes!" Cassandra laughed as she unlocked one of the desk drawers in her study. "Lionel has a team of accountants he's been using for years."

Ryan made a note of the name she gave him, then quickly wrote out a chit for the personal accounts paperwork she handed to him.

"These are the most recent statements," she told him. "I hope they help you."

Ryan glanced briefly at the columns of numbers and spotted an amount matching one of the deposits in Victor Swann's account. With any luck, he could eliminate all those payments made by Cassandra Gilbert so they could focus on the remaining cash deposits and their source.

"Thank you," he said, turning to leave. "You've done the right thing."

"I feel better already."

As he turned to leave, she called him back.

"Chief inspector? Do you really think somebody is doing this for money?"

He gave a brief nod.

"Be careful, Cassandra, and remember to lock your door."

Ten miles south of Cragside, Martin Henderson pulled off the motorway and drove along a darkened country road leading to one of the many scattered hamlets comprising the landscape of Northumberland. Nothing stirred in the streets; unusually, there was no village pub and people kept themselves to themselves. On the outskirts of the hamlet there was a large set of electric gates with a video monitoring system. Henderson stopped the car and got out to press the buzzer. The disembodied voice of a security guard came through the microphone and he gave his name, glancing nervously behind him as he did so.

"For God's sake, open the gates. I can't hang around out here much longer, someone might see me."

The gates swished open on well-oiled hinges and Henderson accelerated through.

He followed a driveway consisting of a long avenue of conifers, manicured and primped, leading to an impressive manor house at the end. At one time, it had been home to a family of local landowners but now it was the residence of an even bigger magnate.

Henderson was shown into the house by a dead-eyed security guard who patted him down. It was the same procedure every time and he held his arms out like the docile servant he was.

"Through there," the man barked, jerking his thumb in the direction of the kitchen.

It was an enormous, gleaming affair with yards of marble countertop and waxed oak. Six stools were arranged around a central island where Henderson's business partner was perched, chatting to a couple of his minders while he nibbled on a selection of olives. A well-known soap opera played out on the flat screen television mounted to the wall.

"Look what the wind has blown in, lads," he scoffed when he spotted Henderson lurking in the doorway.

"Good to see you, Bob."

Bob Singh was in his early thirties, with the glossy looks of a premier league football player and a broad Teesside accent. He might have looked like the boy next door but his mind was a finely-honed tool that had enabled him to become a multi-millionaire by the time he'd reached his thirtieth birthday. Unfortunately, much of his money had been gained through a series of underhand property and drug deals and therefore required expert laundering. The scale of his ventures made it necessary for him to delegate that important task to a handful of carefully screened and selected individuals who shared his love of money and were pleasingly short on morals.

For the time being, Martin Henderson was one of them.

"D' you want a drink, mate?"

Singh made a big show of making his visitors welcome, even ones he planned to axe the following day.

"No, no, I'm fine," Henderson lied.

"How about an olive?"

Singh held out the tray of olives and waited until Henderson took one, recognising that the offer had been an exercise in power rather than a desire to be hospitable. He watched while Henderson chewed and forced a Kalamata olive down his gullet. Singh gave him a false, shark-like smile.

"I've been a little bit concerned about the state of our venture, Martin, what with the police crawling all over the place. I was very worried when I heard Ryan was the one leading the investigation. Wasn't I, lads?"

The other men gathered around the island made sounds of agreement, staring at Henderson with vacant eyes.

"*Very* worried," Singh emphasized, all pretence of geniality now long gone. "Reassure me, Martin, because I'm thinking seriously about cancelling the terms of our agreement."

Henderson tasted olive-flavoured bile on his tongue.

"The police don't have anything," he said, in the firmest tone he could muster. "I've destroyed all the company paperwork and they won't find anything else."

"Really? A little birdy tells me that the FIU have been called in. Now, why would the financial investigation unit be involved in a case of accidental death, Martin?

And what's this I hear on the news about it being a murder investigation now?"

"I—I don't know," Henderson stammered. "You know what they're like, always looking for a headline…"

"Shall I tell you what I think, mate? I think somebody *did* murder those poor buggers up at Cragside and that *somebody* didn't really think it through. If they had, they would have considered the fact that a famous detective is living on their doorstep, one who isn't known for letting things lie."

"I didn't—" Henderson started to deny any involvement but was interrupted again.

"Don't bullshit me, Martin. What about the old couple? They might change their mind about selling the land, if someone should happen to tell them you're nothing but a little con artist who isn't above a bit of grubby murder."

"I gave them references, certificates, everything when I applied for the job."

"And all of it forged." Singh gave a short laugh and popped another olive in his mouth. "You know, Martin, I've always liked you. The thing is, mate, the art of cleaning dirty money relies on the middle man remaining inconspicuous. You need to be the bloke everybody trusts to manage the estate, so that when you tell them a bit of land needs selling off, they believe you. You need to spend within your legitimate salary, so people don't start asking questions or generating suspicious activity reports. Are you following me, so far?"

"Yes."

"I heard you were a pro, somebody who'd been in the game a while and knew how to operate. That's why I let you in, Martin. That's why I trusted you with my money."

Singh's voice remained at the same maddeningly reasonable tone.

"You think you can make a mug of me, Martin, is that it? Do you think that I wouldn't notice you rocking up to my house driving a top-spec car and shoving a ten-grand watch in my face, like you're the Godfather?"

The room fell ominously silent and Henderson watched Singh chew the last olive in suspended slow motion.

"That's the reason the FIU are looking at you. Because you put yourself on the telly and put yourself in the frame. Because you, with your piss-poor upbringing, just couldn't resist swanning around like King Dick for a day."

Singh wiped his hands on a napkin and then pushed his face so far into Henderson's they were almost touching.

"Is that who you think you are, Martin? King Dick?"

"N-no. I mean, I'm not. No."

"Listen carefully, you little twat. As far as I'm concerned, our relationship ends here. I want every scrap of paper you've ever touched to be ash by the end of the day. I want everything cleared out of that house as if it never existed. I want the companies completely shut down. Do you understand?"

It took a special kind of criminal to command men older than himself but Singh had proved himself more than capable. White collar crime might have been his most lucrative venture but it was not where he had started out.

His reputation preceded him.

"Now bugger off."

Henderson scrambled off the stool and backed towards the door.

"One last thing, mate," Singh called out. "You blab one word to the pigs and it'll be the last thing you ever do."

After he'd gone, Singh turned back to the men around the table.

"He's a liability."

CHAPTER 25

Henderson drove until he reached the border of Scotland, another forty miles north of Cragside. From there, he could drive to Stranraer and catch the first ferry over to Northern Ireland, then drive down to Cork where he had friends who could help him.

That was another lie.

He didn't have friends, he had paid associates.

He needed time to think and, when he saw a sign for a cheap roadside hotel, he pulled in, driving his car around to the back of the car park where it couldn't be seen from the road.

It turned out to be more of a guest house than a hotel, run by a sour-faced woman who barely asked his name, let alone queried why he was paying for a room in cash. She pocketed the money and then retreated into one of the back rooms where a television blared while Henderson locked himself into a squalid little room which held the faint odour of smoke and sex.

He splashed cold water on his face and looked at himself in the cracked mirror above the sink in the corner of the room. There was no en suite bathroom, only a shared toilet and bathtub further down the hall bearing an assortment of stains.

What the hell was he going to do?

The reflection staring back at him was of a man past his prime, desperately trying to cling on to the life he had built on a foundation of sand. Everything from his haircut to his handmade shoes had been the best that money could buy. He didn't care too much about what passed for good taste, so long as he could tell himself it was the best.

It was important that he had the best.

It was even more important for people to *know* it was the best.

He wanted *respect*, damn it, from all the people who'd been born with a silver spoon in their mouths, never having to worry about where the next meal was coming from. He wanted them to stand and admire his shiny car and to ask about its leather seats and gadgets. He wanted them to wonder what he did for a living and to imagine it was something important, and then he wanted to tell them to mind their own business when they asked. He'd golfed with almost every rich man in the county and attended the best parties, so he could see his picture in the society column of the local paper alongside every has-been celebrity in the neighbourhood.

He hated them all.

The way he saw it, he was performing a public service by redistributing their wealth. It might have been going into his own coffers but at least it was better than seeing the fat cats get fatter.

Not that he ever felt inclined to stick his hand in his pocket and help his fellow man, mind you. Those scroungers could get off their arses and find a job, like he had.

He wasn't Robin Hood.

Henderson remembered the old days when he'd been a boy growing up on the docks in Newcastle, when there hadn't been two pennies to rub together. He'd worn hand-me-downs and shoes that were too big for his feet, he'd eaten cheap food and dreamed of having lots of money one day. That dream had sustained him through the hard years, when he'd toed the line alongside all the other lads from school and gone to work with his hands. He'd clawed his way up the ladder until…well, until it all changed and he'd been out in the cold again, back to square one. After that, it had been every man for himself.

Years had passed and he'd lived some real highs, especially back in the eighties and nineties. He'd splashed money about and bought himself companionship from young men who wouldn't look twice at him otherwise. Without a steady income stream, there would be nobody to keep him company at night.

He started to cry big, self-pitying tears that rocked his body.

He needed to get to Ireland. If he stayed, he'd either be arrested or killed. But his passport, his documents, his *things* were all back at the estate manager's cottage and he couldn't leave without them. Besides, Singh was right; he needed to destroy the paper trail—and not just the stack he'd hidden in his car boot.

Now that the first waves of panic had receded, he forced himself to think clearly.

What did the police really have?

Circumstantial evidence, maybe. He imagined they'd found out he'd lied on his CV to get the job at Cragside. Well, that was nothing to do with a murder investigation. He'd talk his way around that with the Gilberts soon enough, especially Cassandra, who would listen to any old sob story. As for his bank accounts, if the FIU had anything serious they'd have arrested him already. As for Victor…he hadn't told Singh about the money he'd paid the blackmailing old bastard. That was private business. If the police matched up any cash withdrawals, he'd tell them it was pure coincidence or play the 'no comment' card.

Then, there was the girl.

He closed his eyes briefly and saw hers, wide and filled with terror as she'd fallen from the bridge. It had given him a sleepless night but, in the end, there'd been no other choice. It was nothing personal. If anything, it was her own damn fault for being such a nosy bitch. If she'd gone home rather than hanging around to wheedle into other people's affairs, she would never have got herself killed.

It had been a hell of a job finding Victor's mobile phone down by the burn and he wasn't sure what information would be logged by the telephone company. That was a worry but he'd always used a throwaway, pay-as-you-go mobile phone when arranging an exchange. Good luck to Ryan and his band of merry men making *that* connection in a hurry. He ran his hands over his head, smoothing down the hair he had left, then straightened his tie. In another minute, he'd put a call through to his solicitor.

It was time to brazen it out.

***

Lowerson and Yates were parked conspicuously on the tarmacked driveway leading up to the main entrance of the house and were ideally placed to see anybody entering or leaving the estate. Another police car was parked beside the farm entrance on the off-chance Henderson would return via that route. The idea was for him to *know* he was being watched. In fact, Ryan had given explicit instructions that he wanted Martin Henderson to be sweating by the time they pulled him in for questioning the following morning. "Hard to believe nobody else was available to do the surveillance," Yates grumbled. "What if we get an update from the FIU?"

"They'll call you," Lowerson said. "Or they'll call Ryan."

They fell silent again, watching the empty driveway for signs of approaching vehicles.

Lowerson let out a long sigh.

"So, why don't you tell me a bit about yourself?"

Yates continued to look ahead, already feeling nervous about what he might ask, or what she might say.

"Why do you want to know?"

Lowerson made an irritable sound.

"Some people call it making friendly conversation," he said, not bothering to keep the sarcasm from his voice. Over three hours had passed since they'd begun their surveillance duty and, since she'd barely spoken a civil word the entire time, it was beginning to feel like a hostage situation—where *he* was the hostage.

"What, ah, what do you want to know? I'm not a very interesting person."

"Gee, I don't know; the usual stuff. How old are you? Where are you from? Why did you join the police force? How long have you had a crush on Ryan?"

Her hands clenched on the wheel.

"What? What makes you say that?"

"Oh, come on"—he flapped a hand in the air—"it's written all over your face."

Melanie almost buried her head in her hands.

"I don't know what you're talking about."

Lowerson shrugged and looked out of the side window but all he saw was the reflection of her pale, anxious face.

"Look, it doesn't matter," he told her. "I'm sure nobody's noticed."

"You did," she muttered.

Lowerson opened his mouth to tell her that it was only because he had a personal interest, then snapped it shut again. There was only so much rejection a man could take in one week.

"Well, I'm not going to sky-write it, am I? We've all had crushes at work. They pass quickly enough," he added, hoping fervently that his would pass sooner rather than later.

"It's embarrassing," she surprised him by saying. "I feel like an idiot."

He could relate.

"You're being too hard on yourself," he said, turning around in his chair to face her. "You'll snap out of it, once you get used to working with him. He's human, like the rest of us."

Yates nodded but didn't seem convinced.

"He's also getting married," he felt bound to point out, and Yates looked down at her hands.

"Why don't you tell me about *yourself*?" she said quickly, desperate to change the subject.

Lowerson gave her an understanding smile and was happy to play along if it helped her to relax. He could almost hear the nerves buzzing inside her head and it was starting to make him edgy.

"I was born and bred in Gateshead. I have an older brother, Mike, who lives in Edinburgh and works as a software engineer. He's married with a couple of kids, which makes me 'Uncle Jack'. *Cool* Uncle Jack," he corrected himself. "I've just bought my first home and I have a cat called Marbles."

"You do?"

Lowerson lifted a self-conscious shoulder.

"I'd introduce you to her but Marbles gets very jealous of other women."

Yates chuckled.

"I'm saving up a deposit for my own place," she confided. "It seems a long way off, though."

"Stick to your goal and you'll get there in the end," he said, casually inspiring her to carry on.

There was a short, comfortable silence before Yates spoke again.

"Do you think Henderson has done a bunk?"

Lowerson shook his head and pointed towards the driveway. Sure enough, the headlights of a car could be seen motoring along the empty road. It slowed as it approached and the driver caught a glimpse of them sitting at the top of the road, then accelerated past them with an angry jerk of gears.

Yates started the engine and they moved slowly after him, repositioning themselves near to the estate manager's cottage so they could keep a closer eye on Henderson for the next hour or so, when a patrol car was due to relieve them.

"Henderson had to come back," Lowerson remarked eventually. "He's got nowhere else to go."

Henderson hurried inside the estate manager's cottage and slammed the door shut behind him, breathing hard.

He hadn't expected to find a surveillance car waiting for him and he began to wonder if the police knew more than he thought. He needed to take care of business.

Galvanised, Henderson went from room to room shutting the curtains and bolting the doors. He needed to check every corner of the house and divest it of incriminating evidence, a task that required utmost privacy.

When he entered the kitchen, his eyes fell on a pair of his shoes sitting on the drying rack next to the sink, their soles sparkling clean from lashings of bleach the previous day. It wasn't enough to clean them, he realised. He needed to get rid of them altogether, like he had done with the clothes he'd worn. They were now a pile of ash along with the papers he'd shoved in his boot earlier, now burnt to cinders on a bonfire near the Scottish border.

But if the police got a search warrant, they'd find those shoes and ask him why they were covered in bleach.

Stupid!

Why would anyone clean their leather shoes with bleach? He might as well stamp 'GUILTY' on his forehead and be done with it.

Henderson was so consumed by his own ineptitude that it was a while before he noticed the simple white envelope lying on the kitchen floor, where someone had slipped it beneath the door. He reached for it with trembling fingers and removed a sheet of paper bearing a typed message:

I KNOW ABOUT THE VALIANT.
MEET ME IN THE ARMSTRONG ROOM
AT 9 P.M. TOMORROW.
DON'T BE LATE.

Henderson felt his stomach heave and thought, at first, that it was a message from the grave. Victor Swann had been the only person to know about *The Valiant* and the role he'd played in its devastation so many years ago. He must have told someone, Henderson thought frantically, or somebody had worked it out the same way Victor had.

Either way, he needed to find out what they knew and negotiate terms to his satisfaction.

He could still hear the screams, even now.

They sounded inhuman, like pigs being slaughtered or foxes mating in the night. The sound of the fire drowned them out eventually but he imagined he still heard them, softer now, as they choked on the smoke fumes that billowed up in black clouds to fill the sky above the river.

He remembered hearing wood splinter as the long ladders leading down into the half-built ship succumbed to the flames and the crackle of metal as it bent against the heat.

Hundreds ran down to the shipyard to watch *The Valiant* go up in flames, to stand by and stare mutely as husbands and fathers died before their eyes, and it seemed as if the world paused. Sounds were drowned out and it was as if he were swimming underwater, cushioned by his own disbelief. The screams of his neighbours grew closer and closer until everything came back into sharp focus.

The lucky ones stumbled out of the shipyard to catch their breath, coughing and spluttering, unable to fight the blaze that continued to burn its way through the ship from the bottom up.

Beside him, a woman turned to clutch his arm, her eyes wild with grief.

"You should be glad you're one of the lucky ones," she told him.

He wanted to shake her off, to thrust her away so he didn't have to see the devastation on her face or hear it in her voice. But then she sat down, right there on the cobblestones at his feet and hugged her arms around her knees. He wanted to shout at her to stand up.

Instead, he ran.

She called after him but he kept on running, his skinny legs pumping faster and faster so he didn't have to see it. If he didn't have to see it, maybe he could convince himself it never happened.

But he could still hear the screams.

CHAPTER 26

Wednesday 17ᵗʰ August

The dawn broke over the hills and glades of Northumberland in one seamless fusion of colour, casting out the darkness to bring forth a new day. It could not come a moment too soon for the people who lived and worked in the small community of Cragside, whose equilibrium had been rudely shattered in the wake of a double tragedy. Theirs had been a charmed existence, filled with beauty and culture, funded by an old couple who had created a living museum to the past. Now, it was beginning to feel more like a mausoleum.

Fully dressed and polishing off his second coffee, Ryan watched the morning awaken and thought philosophically of the human condition. There were two types of people in the world: those who controlled their base urges and those who didn't. Everyone had those urges, to one degree or another, but their visibility varied from one person to the next. He had only to look to his own life experiences to illustrate the point: four months ago, it had been within his power to kill a murderer with his own bare hands. Many would have forgiven him and called it self-defence or public service. Controlling the primal instinct had almost cost Ryan his own life but in taking that decision he had retained a part of himself he held very dear: the part which had a fundamental respect for all human life.

There were other types of urges, ones that could be more easily disguised day-to-day but, when unleashed, could be the most destructive of all. He thought of Martin Henderson as he swilled the last of his coffee, then downed it in one gulp. There was a man who had spent sixty-two years trying to prove himself the alpha in any given scenario, like a rutting stag whose antlers had never fully grown. The thought of it was almost laughable but Ryan didn't break a smile. Henderson's desire to acquire more prestige had already led to the deaths of two people. Ryan had frequently observed that, once a person took a life, they found it considerably easier to take a second or a third, especially where emotion did not come into it.

He was very much afraid that, if they did not act quickly, Henderson would not hesitate to kill a third time, should the occasion arise.

The day beckoned.

Phillips and MacKenzie arrived at the cottage at eight o'clock sharp to brief their senior investigating officer.

Lowerson and Yates had been given the morning off, in recognition of their late night spent in surveillance, but would join them after lunch. Anna had already bidden them farewell and taken herself off to Durham for a day spent inside the university library, which he understood to be code for telling him she missed the old place and was looking forward to the start of a new term when they returned from honeymoon in September. Until then, there was the small business of murder to attend to.

"Mornin' boss," Phillips said as he made himself comfortable in the kitchen and began to make a pot of tea.

"Help yourself, why don't you?"

"Aye, I will, ta very much."

Ryan and MacKenzie settled themselves at the kitchen table, where they were joined by Phillips a moment later. He set three steaming mugs of milky tea in front of them and, while he went in search of sugar, they decided to make a start.

"Alright, let's recap what we know so far." Ryan leaned his forearms on the table and linked his fingers together.

"Got any biscuits?" Phillips called out, his head concealed by a cupboard door.

"Jar next to the toaster," Ryan told him, then continued as if there had been no interruption. "Beginning with Victor Swann, Lowerson tells me that he spoke to the compliance officer at the telecoms company on the dot of seven this morning. They've started to send through the text messages they store remotely from Victor's account, although there's still no sign of the phone itself. I've had a quick glance at the texts recorded from the week before he died and they make for interesting reading."

He handed Phillips and MacKenzie a sheet of paper containing copies of the most pertinent text messages.

"TR at 6," he read aloud, giving the date of the message. "TR at 10."

Ryan looked up.

"I've already checked the dates of these messages against the dates of cash deposits into Victor's current account and they match very closely. Depending on the time of day, cash was deposited into the account on the same day before closing time or the very next morning."

"What a coincidence," MacKenzie observed. "And were there any matching cash withdrawals from Martin Henderson's account on the same day, or possibly the day before?"

"Funnily enough, there were." Ryan smiled wolfishly.

"What does 'TR' stand for?" Phillips queried.

"I've been trying to figure that out and it's no easy task, since there are endless meeting places on the estate. It's also possible they made their exchanges somewhere else altogether."

"Turbine room?" MacKenzie suggested. "Turret room?"

"Could have been either of those," Ryan agreed. "But it doesn't matter so much now. What matters most is that we needed a direct link between Victor Swann and Martin Henderson. Unfortunately, the sender's number in each of these messages seems to change on a weekly basis, even though the form and content remains the same."

"Burner mobile," Phillips said. "Maybe he's not quite as thick as we thought."

"Let's not jump to conclusions," Ryan quipped.

"We've still got the accounts data," MacKenzie steered them deftly back to the point. "That should be enough to bring him in for questioning."

"It is," Ryan confirmed. "But it would make for a stronger case all round if we could throw more at him. Thanks to the accounts monitoring order that's been in place since late yesterday afternoon, we could see he used his debit card at a roadside service station thirty-five miles north of here, close to Jedburgh and the Scottish border."

"Bit late to go for a scenic drive," Phillips remarked.

"That's what I thought, which is why I've e-mailed a request for all available CCTV footage from the roads between here and there. There may not be much if he took the back roads but I want to know where he went and who he saw last night."

MacKenzie nodded and tapped her finger against the file she'd brought along with her.

"I've pulled together everything I could find on Martin Henderson," she said. "It makes for interesting reading, especially when you discover that his name isn't Henderson at all, it's Jennings."

"The plot thickens," Phillips pronounced and took a dramatic slurp of his tea.

"He changed his name legally in 1975 and has been known as Henderson ever since. The work history on the

CV he provided to the Gilberts seems to show a man who's been in steady employment for most of his life, working in various roles to do with estate management."

"But?"

"Half the employers listed on those records don't seem to exist and never have; or, if they did, their company records have since vanished from the digital trail. I've sent to Companies House for copies of any paper records they might have but that's going to take time."

"How about his last employer, before he got the job here at Cragside?"

"It's listed as some wealthy so-and-so in Ireland," she replied. "I took the trouble of checking it out and I can tell you, there's no such place as Longvenney Manor."

"Henderson lied again, you think?"

"Aye, he sounds like he's been in the game a while," Phillips said. "We just have to prove it."

"There's the difficulty." Ryan pushed away from his chair, needing to pace around a bit. "Besides, while fraud is all very interesting, it doesn't provide any direct link to the deaths of Victor Swann and Alice Chapman."

"Unless Victor found out about his tall tales and decided to milk him for pocket money," Phillips suggested.

"It's supposition," Ryan said. "Not enough to charge him with anything, especially with no previous. Tell me there's been some good news on forensics?"

Phillips let out a blustery sigh.

"Faulkner's been up half the night with his team, poring over the stuff he brought in. They're still at it now, poor sods. Anyway, the top and bottom of it is, they've identified the fibres found beneath Alice Chapman's nails and it's a match for black leather, the type you might find on a pair of gloves."

"We'd need to search Henderson's cottage but, without being able to prove reasonable grounds for suspicion, we won't get a warrant."

"Not like the old days, when you could just barge in," Phillips complained.

"We're a police *service* now, not a *force*, remember?" Ryan said.

Phillips snorted.

"What about the DNA testing?" Ryan asked.

"They're trying to match it now but all they've been able to get is tiny particles—low copy number DNA. If there was anything else, it was washed away by the storm or else the river."

"Any match on the DNA database?"

"None so far."

Ryan leaned back against the kitchen counter and tried to remain objective. The CSIs and forensic specialists were doing all they could, he knew that and he trusted it. It was not their fault that there was no convenient hair follicle or clump of skin to lead them directly to their prime suspect. Instead, all they appeared to have was LCN DNA which was notoriously weak evidence in court. The trace particles were so minute that any decent defence barrister would argue that they could have been transferred when Alice Chapman stood too close to somebody or brushed against them earlier in the day.

It was that easy.

"Let me know when they've matched it up, all the same," he told them. "Individually, it may be flimsy but, collectively, we might be able to put something together that'll hold up."

Ryan turned to the next line of enquiry.

"I spoke to Yates this morning, who's been in contact with the investigator in the FIU. They've been scouring their databases to try to follow the money, as it were, but the best they've got is a series of large cash transactions reported by car and antique dealerships, that sort of thing. None of the purchases match up on Henderson's accounts, or at least not on the accounts we've been able to find."

"Surely—?" Phillips began.

But Ryan shook his head.

"If I worked in the FIU, I'd be looking forward to a nice juicy case of fraud, identity and financial. Given his age and apparent means, they might find a nice bit of boiler room fraud thrown in there."

"Retro," Phillips commented.

"Sadly, we're interested in whether the man has gone further than dishonesty offences and has dabbled in murder as well."

"Can't you work together with the FIU and pull him in for an interview on their turf, sweat him out a bit?"

They looked among themselves and Ryan snatched up his phone to make the call.

CHAPTER 27

Martin Henderson took his time getting ready, grooming himself until he was fully satisfied with the result. His vanity routine took almost an hour, factoring in the time spent blow-drying what was left of his hair and twenty minutes using his new ultrasonic 'lifting and firming' device that was designed to keep jowls at bay.

It wasn't working.

He had a good mind to make a complaint to the charlatans who'd sold it to him down at the salon in Newcastle.

His routine was interrupted by a knock at the door and a quick glance at the time told him it was almost nine o'clock. He patted his tie and told himself to remain calm, then moved downstairs to answer the door.

But it was not Ryan standing on his doorstep, as he might have expected.

A good-looking woman of diminutive height stood before him, dressed in what he would have described as smart-casual wear, with a blazer over well-cut jeans.

Beside her was an older man, also dressed down. They removed their warrant cards and held them out.

"Martin Henderson?"

He squinted at the little plastic cards.

"Yes?"

"Good morning, Mr Henderson," she said, politely. "My name is Detective Inspector Anika Salam and this is my partner, Detective Sergeant Henry Tomlinson."

"What do you want?"

"We would like to ask you some questions under caution regarding certain financial transactions of yours. Would you be willing to attend an interview with us?"

"Now?"

"If you wouldn't mind."

Henderson looked down his nose at her.

"I'm not one of the plebs you're probably used to dealing with," he sneered. "If you want an interview, you're supposed to send me an invitation in writing. I know my rights."

Salam and Tomlinson looked at each other with mock embarrassment.

"Oh, darn. In that case, I guess we'll just have to arrest you on suspicion of fraud, conspiracy to defraud and false accounting. Don't even get me started on the money laundering offences," she said cheerfully.

Henderson broke out in a cold sweat.

"I bet that interview under caution is looking pretty good right now, son," Tomlinson said, man-to-man. "If I were you, I'd reconsider."

"I'm calling my lawyer," Henderson stuttered and almost ran to the phone.

As he disappeared into the hallway, Salam and Tomlinson took a good survey of the space they could see inside the house and shrugged.

"I think this one's going to be fun," she said.

———

After a hasty phone call to his solicitor and a fabricated story to his employer about needing to go into the city, Henderson followed Salam and Tomlinson to the police station in his own car. Thanks to round-the-clock surveillance of his home and vehicle, he still hadn't been able to get rid of the shoes he'd worn on the day Alice Chapman died. He'd tried to light a fire in the living room grate, hoping to burn the offending articles, but unfortunately there was no kindling or firelighters. If he had left the house to get some, he would have risked being seen by the surveillance team and being asked some extremely awkward questions about why he was seen buying firewood and lighters in high summer. He only hoped they wouldn't procure a search warrant before he'd had time to think of a plan. When he arrived at police headquarters in Newcastle, Henderson was met by the same solicitor who had been present on the day of DNA testing at Cragside. They were shown into a small meeting room inside the interview suite where they held a lengthy consultation, following which they were taken to an interview room where they were left for a further fifteen minutes to stew in their own juices.

At quarter-past ten, the door opened and Henderson's face registered shock.

"DI Anika Salam entering interview room 1 with DCI Maxwell Finley-Ryan, the time is sixteen minutes past ten on Wednesday the seventeenth of August," she stated clearly, for the record.

The two detectives took their seats at a table for four, with Ryan sitting directly opposite Henderson.

"If you could please state your names for the recording," Salam instructed them.

"Melissa Kettering of Kettering, Quinlan and Associates."

There was a pause until Henderson realised it was his turn.

"Martin Henderson," he snapped, unable to meet Ryan's eye.

Salam recited the standard police caution, making sure they went by the book.

"Do you understand all that, Mr Henderson?"

"Of course, I do. I'm not an idiot. I want to know what *he's* doing here." He jabbed a bony finger towards Ryan's face and his solicitor gave him a warning look.

Ryan smiled lazily and leaned back comfortably in his chair.

"During the course of DCI Ryan's investigation into the deaths of two people on the Cragside estate, of which you are manager, he sought the assistance of the financial investigation unit. Certain matters came to light which have led us to open our own investigation, which is why you're here today. DCI Ryan will therefore be note-taking during this interview."

"Well, I want it *noted* for the record that my client has been extremely cooperative in agreeing to attend voluntarily today," Kettering began, with a hauteur that must have taken years to perfect. "You acted in clear breach of the Police and Criminal Evidence Act when you failed to give my client proper written notice of this interview."

"A requirement which your client was happy to waive, since he was feeling so cooperative," Salam put in.

"Under threat of arrest," the other woman hissed.

"There was no threat at all," Salam said, with a smile for Henderson. "I would have been very happy to arrest Mr Henderson."

Ryan's lips twitched.

"Now, let's get down to business." Salam clasped her hands together on the table top. "Please could you tell us your age and current profession, Mr Henderson, as well as your residential address?"

He answered in a grudging monotone.

"And I understand you do not own the estate manager's cottage but live there as part of the compensation package from your employers, Lionel and Cassandra Gilbert?"

"Yes," he muttered.

"I hope there's a point to these questions, detective inspector," Kettering spoke out again. "We were afforded no pre-interview briefing or any indication of what you intend to ask my client, which is another breach for the record."

"Actually, there's no obligation for us to brief you ahead of an interview. Normally, we do, but what can I say? We just didn't feel like it today."

The solicitor's mouth snapped shut.

"We understand you are an experienced estate manager, Mr Henderson. Can you tell us where you have worked previously?"

Henderson swallowed.

"It's all listed on my work record, isn't it?"

"Where is the relevance, detective? Perhaps we should be asking to see *your* CV?"

The solicitor exchanged a smirk with her client.

"Oh, it's quite simple, Ms Kettering. None of the companies Mr Henderson claims to have worked for actually exist." She turned to the sixty-something man and watched him wipe perspiration from his lip.

"Can you explain that?"

"No comment."

His Adam's apple bobbed as he swallowed and he could feel Ryan's eyes boring into him.

"You are aware that, should this interview be used as evidence in court proceedings, adverse inferences may be drawn from your refusal to answer?"

Henderson folded his arms across his chest while Salam listed his entire work history, or at least the version he'd included on the CV he provided to the Gilberts.

"None of these stately homes exist, nor do the companies who are listed as your previous employers. Can you explain that, Mr Henderson?"

"No comment."

And so it went on.

Eventually, Salam came around to the next line of questioning concerning Henderson's transactional history.

"In January of this year, you purchased a BMW i8 hybrid sports car, is that correct?"

"Yes."

He could hardly deny it, since the car was parked in the car park outside.

"The money laundering officer at the car dealership registered a suspicious report following your purchase, Mr Henderson. Do you know why?"

"No comment."

"Can you tell us the recommended retail price of a BMW i8?"

"No idea," he lied.

"A steal at £105,000, depending on the specifications," Ryan spoke up for the first time.

"I'm told you paid a deposit of nearly twenty-five per cent of the retail price in cash, Mr Henderson. That's a lot of money to have lying around the house."

Salam removed a scanned copy of the contract he had signed at the dealership and handed it to his solicitor before reciting its contents for the audio record.

"No comment."

Henderson cleared his throat and trained his eyes on the ceiling, then looked away quickly when he realised the room was equipped with four cameras to capture his anxious face from every angle.

"There's been a string of large cash transactions dating back over at least three years." She reeled off a few more. "Can you tell me how you managed to fund these purchases, Mr Henderson?"

"No comment."

Ryan watched the estate manager with mounting dislike. They had expected him to fall back on a 'no comment' interview but having to listen to it was frustrating nonetheless.

"Coming around to more recent events, we'd like to ask you about some cash withdrawals made from your current account last week."

Henderson sent his solicitor a panicked look.

"Ah, just a moment, detective. How is it that you have access to my client's personal account records?"

Ryan licked the tip of his index finger and rifled through a sheaf of papers until he found what he was looking for.

"Let the record show I am handing a scanned copy of the account monitoring order to Ms Kettering, which was executed yesterday evening through the proper channels."

"I want a moment to confer with my client."

"By all means," Ryan said, affably. "We'll leave you to talk it over."

Ryan and DI Anika Salam wandered through to the observation room next door, where they joined their respective sergeants. The two men appeared to be getting on like a house on fire and Phillips was presently regaling Henry Tomlinson with some tale or other concerning Newcastle United's footballing glory days.

"Any word from Faulkner?" Ryan asked.

Phillips pulled a face.

"Sorry, guv, I had a call from him while you were interviewing. He's having to re-test the samples because there was some cross-contamination, which wouldn't do us much good in court. He's working as quickly as he can but essentially he has to start from scratch."

Ryan stuck his hands in his pockets and jiggled the car keys he found there.

"Without that DNA, we've got nothing to hold him," he muttered.

He stared through the window to where Henderson and his solicitor sat with their heads together, plotting, no doubt.

Ryan turned back to DI Salam.

"Have you got enough to hold him for twenty-four hours?"

She shook her head.

"You know as well as I do, fraud is a tough nut to crack. I need much longer to put my case together; it could take months to trace the source of the money. I only brought him in as a favour to you," she said.

"I know, and it's appreciated."

Ryan nodded towards the window.

"Let me predict what's about to happen. We're going to spend another hour going through every suspicious transaction going in and out of his current account, particularly over the last two months he's been resident at Cragside, and he's going to tell us 'no comment' or disclaim any connection with Victor Swann. Then, his solicitor will start mouthing off about supposition and circumstantial evidence and demand to leave. We're going to have to let them, because he's giving us nothing to work with."

"You never know," Phillips said hopefully. "He looks the type to crack."

"He's a cockroach," Ryan muttered. "Unfortunately, they're very resilient."

An hour later, Ryan walked out of Interview Room 1 and Phillips fell into step beside him. Not long afterwards, they watched Martin Henderson sweep out of the police car park with a deliberate flourish.

"Told you so," was all he said.

CHAPTER 28

The rest of the day passed in a haze of frenzied activity. The men and women attached to Operation Lightbulb redoubled their efforts to catch a killer who had figuratively stuck two fingers up and waltzed out of police headquarters as if he hadn't a care in the world.

Ryan was hunched over his desk re-reading the witness statements taken after both incidents when there was a tap on his shoulder.

"Boss? You've got visitors downstairs," Lowerson said.

Ryan knew immediately who they were and reached inside one of his desk drawers for the spare necktie he kept there for occasions requiring a greater degree of formality, such as meeting the parents of a recently murdered young woman.

His legs felt heavy as he walked along the carpeted hallway towards the stairwell that would lead him downstairs to one of the 'family rooms' earmarked for these occasions. He prepared what he would say to them and checked he had a spare business card containing the details of a bereavement counselling service they could contact.

As he reached the ground floor, he made his way along another corridor and then took a breath before pushing open a door marked 'OCCUPIED.'

Planned speeches and business cards flew out of his mind.

Ryan's first thought was that Alice Chapman's parents seemed so small in the large room, huddled together on the foamy blue visitors' chairs arranged around a central coffee table. A dying peace lily stood in the corner next to an assortment of leaflets touting meditation, funeral services and solicitors' firms and he made a mental note to have them removed. Families of the deceased didn't need ambulance chasers adding to their woes.

He cleared his throat discreetly.

"Mr and Mrs Chapman?"

They both looked up and focused their attention on the tall, dark-haired stranger filling the doorway.

"DCI Ryan?" Carol Chapman looked at him with unfocused eyes while her husband rose from his chair and put a steadying hand on her shoulder.

Ryan closed the door behind him and made his way across the room.

They seemed incapable of speech, both wearing the kind of dazed expression he'd seen many times before. It was the shock. Some families harboured a false, unrealistic hope that there had been a dreadful mistake until they met the officer in charge of investigating their loved one's murder. He could see that hope dying before his very eyes and it twisted like a knife in his belly.

"I'm very sorry for your loss," he murmured.

They were trite words he'd uttered hundreds of times before but they remained true. He was more sorry than he could say, looking at this couple who had brought a baby into the world and watched it grow into an accomplished woman, only to see her destroyed.

It was unthinkable, unspeakable, but it was the reality he dealt with every day.

"Why don't we sit down?" He urged Simon Chapman into the chair beside his wife, before the man keeled over. "Can I offer you anything? Tea? Coffee?"

"She's really gone, isn't she?" Carol whispered, ignoring the question while tears fell silently down her face.

Ryan looked her in the eye.

"Yes, I'm afraid she is. I'm sorry."

Carole let out a low, agonised moan unlike anything he'd heard before. She crumpled against her husband, who wrapped his arms around her and began to rock them both.

Ryan reached for a nearby box of tissues and placed it on the table in front of them.

"I saw—I saw on the news, some people are saying she killed herself," Simon stammered, with sudden anger. "My daughter would never have done that. *Never.*"

"I know that," Ryan told him quietly, and it opened another floodgate.

"I—I can't…I can't believe somebody has taken my daughter," he choked out, sobbing openly now. "What kind of animal did this to her?"

His eyes were wild now, almost mad.

"I'm working hard to find them, Mr Chapman."

"What's taking you so long?" Simon burst out, his voice cracking on the last word. "Surely, you must know who?"

Ryan felt his throat working and bore down hard.

"We're investigating a number of leads…" he trailed off, unable to bring himself to tell a lie, however well-intentioned. He looked up and his eyes burned silver. "We have a suspect, Mr Chapman. We are working around the clock to find the evidence to charge him and, as soon as we do, you will be the first to know."

Carol Chapman raised shaking fingers to brush the tears from her face while she gathered the strength to ask him something she needed to know, for the sake of her own sanity.

"Was she—was my baby hurt, *like that*?"

Ryan understood immediately and, on this occasion, could take small comfort in telling her that there had been no sexual assault.

"There's no sign that your daughter's murder was sexually motivated, Mrs Chapman," he answered in a carefully neutral tone, designed to cushion the blow.

"Then—then, why?" she asked brokenly.

Ryan faltered. How could he tell this woman that her child had died because of something so paltry as money, or greed?

How could he tell her that the person who had considered his own entitlement to be greater than Alice Chapman's life had walked free from the very building where they sat, earlier that same day?

"We are doing absolutely everything in our power to bring her killer to justice," was all he could tell them.

They looked at him mutely, faces ravaged by grief.

"I trust you," her father said.

After Ryan requisitioned a squad car to take Simon and Carol Chapman back to their hotel, he watched them leave and felt that heavy burden weighing against his heart.

Martin Henderson felt invincible. Since arriving back at Cragside just after the lunchtime rush, he made a point of going back to work as usual. The estate had returned to full capacity, with staff and visitors being allowed to return now that the CSIs had completed their work with only the pathways near the burn remaining closed pending further enquiries, whatever that meant. He watched families roaming the forest and gardeners pruning the rhododendron bushes and could almost believe nothing had ever happened.

Life went on as normal and people would forget, eventually.

He strolled beneath the stone archway leading to the courtyard where Victor had been found and stood for a moment looking down at the ground, which was spotless after a thorough clean-up.

Rest in peace, he thought nastily.

As he rounded the edge of the house, he saw Cassandra Gilbert chatting with her housekeeper and she waved him across.

"Hello, Martin," she said and he was delighted to hear genuine pleasure at his return. It would make his job all the simpler, when the time came. "How did your errands go in town?"

"Oh, fine, fine," he said vaguely.

"Was it the opticians or the dentist?"

"The, ah, the dentist. Have to keep these teeth pearly white," he said, lying through them. "It looks like everything's running smoothly here?"

"Oh, yes, everyone's really pulled together these last few days," Cassandra said. "It's been an awful time but Maggie and I were just saying, the police *might* have it wrong, mightn't they? Alice's death could have been an accident, after all?"

"I just don't know anyone who could have hurt that lovely girl," the other woman chimed in, her lips quivering. "It doesn't make any sense."

Henderson made noises of sympathy and agreement but felt his stomach rumble and wondered what was on the dinner menu at the tea room.

"I'm going to speak to Ryan the moment he gets back today," Cassandra said. "I'm sure he'll be able to give us an update on their investigation. Surely, they must be getting close."

Henderson felt a shiver, despite the warm weather.

"Why don't you leave that to me?" he offered, magnanimously. "I'll have a word with him and see what progress has been made."

"Would you? You're so kind."

"Don't mention it."

As they turned to leave, his mask slipped just for a moment as he wondered whether either of the two old women might have been responsible for sending him that note. If they had, they needn't think age would be any barrier to the kind of punishment he had in mind. He would protect himself against anybody who posed a threat, young or old.

It could be any of them, he thought.

He watched Dave Quibble step outside the house with one of his student conservationists, who had returned to work. His eyes narrowed as the man paused to give him a civil smile that held no real warmth. They'd never liked one another, Henderson had known that from the start, and the man was intelligent enough to dig into his past and look in all the right places.

He spent the next hour greasing his way around the other staff in the house and grounds before making a perfunctory appearance in his office on the ground floor. Henderson watched people closely, looking for signs that they might be the mysterious sender, but eventually he gave up and settled down to wait.

He'd find out at nine o'clock.

CHAPTER 29

The call came through at precisely eight thirty-six p.m.

Ryan and his team continued to work solidly in one of the smaller conference rooms at police headquarters, where they had barely risen from their seats other than to cater for life's basic needs, when Faulkner rang.

Ryan snatched up the phone.

"Tom? Give me some good news."

"The LCN DNA is a match for Martin Henderson. It was a complex job, because the sample was so small and we had to extract it from Alice Chapman's own cells, then amplify it so we could do a proper analysis. Even then, it was only a fraction of the size of a grain of salt."

"But you're sure?" Ryan pressed.

"As sure as modern science allows us to be," Faulkner replied. "But yes, I'm confident."

"That's good enough. Thanks Tom, I owe you a pint."

Ryan rang off and was out of his chair in one smooth movement. The other members of his team looked up with curious, computer-dazed eyes.

"We've got a green light," he told them. "We're bringing the bastard in for good this time."

Lowerson *whooped* and did a funny little dance in his chair, while Yates looked on in amusement.

"Lowerson, Yates? I want you in position beside the service entrance to the estate, in case Henderson decides to make things difficult," Ryan told them. "Phillips? You're with me. MacKenzie? Do you want in on this?"

She gave him a look that would have terrified a weaker man.

"Ask a stupid question," she muttered, grabbing her coat.

Ryan grinned and clapped his hands together.

"Let's go."

Oblivious to the convoy of police cars that were speeding towards him, Martin Henderson checked his watch again. *Ten to nine.*

In a few minutes, he was due to meet with an unknown person but it had to be someone who was already inside the house or who had access to it. Unfortunately, that didn't narrow down the pool of suspects or give him any hint as to their identity, since the house was still brimming with people.

The Gilberts were enjoying dinner with some friends at a small dining table in the library downstairs and, as far as he knew, they were on to coffee and truffles. He'd seen Maggie and one of the other catering staff bustling in and out of the kitchen serving food but now their footsteps had fallen quiet.

He left his office and poked his head into the staff room, where he was irritated to find Charlotte Shapiro chatting to Dave Quibble about their plans to restore the Victorian irrigation canals through some of the land and he decided to leave them to it before he was drawn into conversation.

The main hallway was quiet, infused with lamplight.

He didn't feel threatened, now he knew there were so many people in the house, but their presence made his plans much riskier than before.

He checked his watch again.

Five to nine.

Time to go.

Phillips slammed his foot against an imaginary brake in the passenger foot well of Ryan's car as they swerved past a white van, which was a clear indication of just how low they had stooped in the driving stakes. Ryan appeared nonplussed and continued to manoeuvre between late evening traffic with all the speed and precision that came with advanced police driving certification. "There's a squad car already up there keeping an eye on the house," Phillips reminded him. "Henderson won't be able to run off anytime in the next fifteen minutes."

"We've said that before," Ryan muttered, flicking on his siren to get past a stream of slow-moving cars.

Phillips shifted in his seat.

"Can't wait to see his face when we slap him in handcuffs," he couldn't help adding. "Do you think we should do it quietly, so as not to upset the old couple?"

Ryan looked away from the road long enough to bestow a disbelieving glance.

"Lionel Gilbert is as strong as an ox and his wife is just the same," he said. "Honestly, you're as bad as Lowerson. If I went around with the same kind of attitude towards anyone over a certain age, I'd have put you out to pasture long ago."

Phillips bristled.

"Watch it, lad. There's plenty life in this old dog yet."

Ryan laughed and flicked his indicator to take the slip road off the dual carriageway.

Henderson checked the hallway downstairs to make sure nobody was around, then slipped up the main flight of oak stairs next to the front door. Lamps fizzed atop the wide newel posts to guide his way inside the darkened house. He moved softly, with the gait of a much younger man thanks to a regular diet and exercise regime he'd implemented since giving up vodka and cocaine in the late nineties. It had been fun for a while, he supposed, but he needed to be in possession of all his faculties to act on the many small opportunities that life presented.

He moved cautiously along a long corridor towards the Armstrong room, which was tucked in the furthermost wing on the first floor of the house. He approved of the choice of venue, at least. The room was used as an exhibition space telling the story of William Armstrong's illustrious history and its impact on the North East but it was seldom used by the family or staff except when showing visitors around the house—it was bound to be empty at that time of day.

He heard the faint sound of laughter trickling through the house from the library downstairs and reminded himself to leave via the front door, for the benefit of the surveillance officers who continued to lurk beside the gates.

His eyes scanned the doorways as he passed, half expecting someone to step out.

Nobody did.

As he reached the end of the corridor, he entered a small hallway with several doors leading off it. To his left, there was a bedroom, the morning room and a second bedroom. To his right, there was another small hallway and a set of metal doors housing the old lift shaft, which was no longer in use. He knew Dave Quibble had ideas about bringing it back to life but it was a delicate project, spanning all three floors of the house, and for now the project was shelved. Just beside the lift doors, there was another oak panelled door leading to the Armstrong room.

Henderson looked over his shoulder one last time before pushing open the door.

After an awkward stand-off over whose turn it was to drive, Lowerson had bowed to the old adage about ladies going first and found himself riding shotgun while Yates floored it all the way to Cragside. He had to admit, he was impressed.

He was less impressed by the collection of CDs he'd found rattling in her glove compartment, consisting mostly of *Andrew Lloyd Webber's Greatest Musical Hits* and what he would have called 'angsty' indie music from the early millennium.

Where were the dance floor hits? A token summer anthem, at least?

"So, ah, what do you like to do in your downtime, Yates?"

Her eyes didn't leave the road ahead but she frowned.

"What do you mean?"

Lowerson rolled his eyes.

"When you're not working, what do you do? Apart from listening to *The Phantom of the Opera*, that is."

"I like to read."

Lowerson scratched the stubble on his chin and wondered what it was about this moody, uncommunicative woman he liked so damn much.

"What do you read? Crime fiction?"

Yates blushed and was glad it was too dark for him to see it. She had a penchant for sweet romance novels but she wasn't about to tell him that.

"Ah, you know, this and that."

Lowerson watched the lights of passing traffic as they zoomed along the fast lane.

"I quite like romance novels," he said, nonchalantly. "I get enough of the gritty stuff in my day job."

In the near darkness, he couldn't see her smile.

Henderson pushed open the door to the Armstrong room and found it empty. He reached for the light switch on the wall then decided against it, not wishing to draw attention to himself in case anyone else should pass by. The light from the hallway was weak but sufficient for present purposes.

He prowled around the room, which was a basic square with several wall-mounted placards and some exhibits inside a central unit with Perspex casing to protect it from damage. He held his watch up to the light and tried to read the dial.

One minute to nine.

Any second now, he would find out who they were and what they wanted.

And then, he would find a way to get rid of them.

Henderson positioned himself just behind the door, so that he would see them entering the room before they saw him. He stood there in silence, feeling the wall against his back, then frowned as he heard a creaking sound coming from somewhere close by.

He was about to investigate, when the house was plunged into darkness once again.

Ryan swung his car through the gates and was forced to reduce his speed along the narrow driveway, for which Phillips was eternally grateful. They followed the road over the little stone bridge next to the Archimedes screw and heard the water bubbling furiously through its crushing blades as they passed. They rounded a bend and the house materialised through the trees, its windows flaming brightly against the inky blue-black sky. "It doesn't look real, does it?" Phillips said, his eyes trained on the perfect backdrop.

"It's not going to disappear before your eyes," Ryan muttered.

Then, in a moment of extreme irony, that is exactly what happened.

The two men looked on in shock as the house seemed to disappear, its walls blending with the colour of the night sky and the trees surrounding it.

CHAPTER 30

"What the *hell*?"

Martin Henderson swore beneath his breath as the lights went out. He stepped away from the wall to begin feeling his way towards the doorway but the house was pitch black and he could barely see his own hand in front of his face. The circuit had blown again, he thought, which was hardly surprising when a couple of old crackpots insisted on living like Victorian throwbacks rather than relying on the National Grid like the rest of the known world.

The sooner he could get away from here, the better.

His fingers brushed against the architrave on the doorway and he began to retrace his steps using the wall as a guide, no longer concerned about keeping his meeting at nine o'clock. He only hoped the other person was having as much trouble as he was, finding their way through the maze of rooms in the old house.

When his fingers touched nothing but air, he realised he'd reached the turning to lead him back into the small hallway outside the bedrooms and the morning room, and the lift shaft was somewhere over his left shoulder.

Blind without any light source, Henderson's other senses were heightened considerably. He shivered as he stepped in front of the doors to the lift shaft, feeling an icy breath of wind brush against his cheeks. His brain was slow to compute the fact and he did not realise the implication until it was too late.

The doors were open.

The figure stepped out in front of him, barely making a creak against the floorboards but it was enough to alert him to the presence of another.

"For *The Valiant*," they whispered.

Two firm hands came up to thrust against his chest and Henderson stumbled in the darkness, a strangled gasp escaping his throat as he fell backward into the empty lift shaft. Down and down he fell, landing with a nauseating thud in the basement three flights below.

Ryan and Phillips pulled up outside the main entrance to the house just as the lighting was restored. The front door was open and they hurried inside, where they found a small crowd of people gathered in the hallway. Ryan made a mental note of who was present and added Dave Quibble to the list when he joined them from the direction of the fuse box in the servants' corridor next to the kitchen. "I definitely need to call in a specialist," he declared, cheerfully. "I'm damned if I know why the power keeps failing; there isn't any shortage of hydroelectricity."

Ryan counted the faces he could see and found a very important one to be missing.

"Where's Martin Henderson?" he demanded.

Only just registering his arrival, the crowd turned to look at him in surprise.

"Hello, Ryan." Cassandra Gilbert stepped forward, sliding easily into her role as hostess. "I think Martin was working in his office until recently. Maggie? Would you be a dear and ask him to join us?"

The housekeeper headed off down the hallway to seek him out.

"What happened here?" Ryan asked.

This time, it was Lionel's turn to respond.

"What the devil do you think happened? The blasted lights went out again and I spilled port all over the ruddy place!"

Ryan didn't bother to comment because he had spotted Maggie returning to them and she was alone.

"I'm sorry, he isn't in his office," she said, worriedly. "I had a quick look down the hall but I can't see him anywhere."

"He's not in the staff room," Charlotte Shapiro put in. "I've just been in there."

Ryan slipped his mobile phone from his jacket pocket and put an immediate call through to the surveillance team outside the estate manager's cottage, exchanged a few brief words and then slipped it into his pocket again.

He turned to Phillips, keeping his voice lowered.

"Henderson's car is still parked in the staff car park and the surveillance team say he's been in here all day."

"I'll check in with Lowerson and Yates, just to be sure he hasn't legged it," Phillips said, then added, "I get a bad feeling about this."

"You and me both, Frank."

With that, Ryan turned back to the crowd. Other than the Gilberts, there were four people he didn't recognise but assumed were friends given their evening attire. Dave Quibble stood in his anorak as if he'd been about to go home and Charlotte Shapiro stood beside him dressed in her favourite dark green gilet. Maggie stood beside a couple of women he recognised as part-time catering staff who sometimes worked shifts in the tea room or at the house.

"If I could ask you all to stay seated in the library for the time being—"

"Why?" Lionel demanded. "What gives you the right to order me about in my own house?"

Ryan simply flipped out his warrant card.

"*This* gives me the right," he explained, in a flat voice. "We are about to conduct a search of the house but, before we do, I would like to issue a friendly warning. We are here this evening to arrest Martin Henderson on charges of murder. If any of you are aware of his whereabouts or have information that could help lead us to him, you should tell us now."

He paused but nobody was forthcoming.

"I'm sure I don't need to remind any of you that obstruction of justice is a serious offence," he said.

Looking among their faces, all he saw was stunned shock.

"Alright, we'll search the place from top to bottom."

They agreed to separate, with Ryan taking the ground and basement levels of the house while Phillips concentrated on the upper floors, telling himself the stairs were good for his constitution. They searched with a single-minded intensity, leaving no door unopened and making a note of any that were locked. In the end, there was no need to trouble the housekeeper or the Gilberts for a key, because Ryan found the body almost as soon as he descended from the kitchen into the cellar. The lift shaft was located directly to the left of the stairs, in the chilly depths of the basement. There was no lift, since it had been removed to a specialist restoration company for refurbishment, leaving the shaft empty from the basement all the way up to the second floor. At first glance, there was no way of knowing how far Henderson had fallen, or from which floor, but his skull had smashed against the stone like an eggshell and he lay in a rapidly congealing pool of his own blood.

Ryan stared at Henderson's corpse, hardly believing his eyes.

What the hell was happening?

He felt a sudden chill and glanced over his shoulder, half expecting to find someone standing beside him, but the basement was empty.

A few minutes later, Phillips joined him. "Lowerson and Yates are upstairs taking statements," he said. "Faulkner's on his way."

Ryan nodded, moving to look at the body from a different angle.

"He must've jumped," Phillips declared. "It's the only explanation."

"Is it?" Ryan wondered.

"It has to be!" Phillips burst out, gesticulating towards Henderson's lifeless body. "Because I'm damned if I know who's going around popping people off like flies if it wasn't him."

Ryan continued to take photographs for his file while they waited for the local doctor to pay her third visit of the week.

"The fact Henderson is now dead doesn't make him any less of a killer," he said quietly.

Phillips grunted.

"All the more reason for him to jump, if you ask me. The bloke knew we were onto him and couldn't stand the thought of going to prison."

"It doesn't fit his personality," Ryan said.

"He was a coward," Phillips argued.

"Yes, but too much a coward to take his own life. He valued himself too much and was arrogant enough to think he'd walk away from his crimes."

Ryan took another careful step, leaving a wide berth around the body. He studied the placement of the limbs and torso, the pattern of the injuries that he could see, and swore softly.

"Henderson fell face-up."

Phillips frowned and edged forward until the full effect of blunt force trauma came into view.

"Aye, it looks that way," he admitted, swallowing hard.

"The coroner will have the final say but in every case of suicide by falling I've seen in the past fifteen years, the body was found face-down, not face-up like this."

Phillips nodded slowly.

"The jumper normally steps out, or leaps off whatever they're standing on, so they land feet first or face-first," he agreed thoughtfully, craning his neck to look up the dark lift shaft. "It's a straight drop, too."

They heard a sound echoing around the walls of the basement and then the tread of footsteps, signalling the arrival of the doctor. Before she joined them, Phillips spoke in an urgent undertone.

"If he was pushed, then we've missed someone or something along the way."

"Oh, yes." Ryan let out a short, mirthless laugh. "We've been fools, Frank."

Killing had been so terribly easy. It had been a surprise to find just how easy it had been. They'd worried whether it would play on their conscience or deprive them of a portion of their own soul in exchange for the taking of another. Was 'an eye for an eye' really the best way to avenge the deaths of all those who were lost so long ago?

But they needn't have worried.

Their eyes had locked with Henderson's in the darkness, just as he'd fallen backward into the abyss of his own making, and it had been beautiful. To see his fear, his comprehension—too little, too late but an awareness all the same—would surely be worth every momentary regret they might feel for the rest of their lives.

He was gone, obliterated, destroyed, as he'd once destroyed so many others.

They felt no guilt, only a deep and abiding sense of peace they hadn't known in over forty years.

"Do you think it's all over now? Martin killed Victor and Alice and now he's killed himself. Surely that'll be an end to it?"

They turned to look at the frightened face of the person seated beside them.

"I hope so," they murmured. "I really hope so."

And it was true.

They hoped Ryan would leave it to rest now, to move on with his happy life. He had so many years ahead of him, untarnished by tragedy of the kind they'd been forced to live with each day. How could he understand the kind of pain they'd suffered, that their whole family had suffered? It was right and proper for him to step back and leave it be.

But as Ryan re-entered the room, they recognised the fierce expression he wore. It spoke of incorruptibility and an unyielding, uncompromising search for the truth, however unpalatable.

Their eyes closed briefly and when they re-opened, they were resigned.

So be it.

CHAPTER 31

Thursday 18th August

"I want you to forget everything you thought you knew about this case."

Ryan's bald statement was addressed to his team, who had assembled for what he had unsmilingly termed a 'crisis briefing'. Each of them had worked long past midnight and showed signs of fatigue but they'd arrived at his cottage promptly at eight o'clock just the same.

"I've had some news from Jeff Pinter already this morning," Ryan told them. "He's finished Victor Swann's post-mortem and his findings put a very different complexion on matters."

Ryan stood with his back to the wall, where he'd tacked up a line of five photographs, consisting of the Gilberts, Maggie, Charlotte Shapiro and Dave Quibble, beside images of Victor Swann, Alice Chapman and Martin Henderson. Beneath that, he'd created a list of secondary suspects, including the serving staff and guests who had been present in the house the previous evening.

He moved across to tap a finger against Victor's face.

"Pinter believes the evidence points to an accidental fall. There were no marks of aggression on Victor's body and no indications of forced impact. Added to which, Pinter found something Victor didn't even know himself: his brain showed all the classic signs that he was developing Parkinson's Disease, which often leads to a disordered gait and regular trips or falls."

There were murmurs around the kitchen table.

"Lionel Gilbert mentioned something like that in one of his statements," Lowerson remembered. "He said Victor had been in good health but he was getting on a bit because he was 'tripping all over the place'. He didn't mention anything about Parkinson's, though."

"Yes, there's no record of it in his medical notes, which means Victor was probably unaware of it himself. The official cause of death was cardiac arrest brought on by severe head trauma, as we thought."

"He still might have been pushed," Phillips persisted. "It fits everything we know about his character...the fact he was blackmailing Henderson and Cassandra Gilbert. There may be even more we don't know about because we still haven't accounted for all the cash payments."

"All that remains true," Ryan nodded. "Added to which, it's notoriously difficult to determine whether a death by falling was accidental, suicide or murder."

He took a chair at the head of the kitchen table and leaned forward to convey his next message.

"After this latest development with Henderson, I've been asking myself whether we've been led down the garden path. We assumed Victor Swann's death was suspicious because somebody took the opportunity to ransack his locker and his home."

"Aye, well that's a suspicious thing to do," Phillips defended.

Ryan held up a hand.

"Bear with me, for a second, while I propose an alternative scenario."

The table fell quiet as four pairs of inquisitive eyes turned towards him.

"If Pinter is right and Victor Swann's death was pure accident, we have to assume Henderson ransacked the man's locker and home simply because the opportunity presented itself. Whatever Swann was using to blackmail him was important enough to extort regular payments and important enough to send him rushing off on the same night the man died, risking exposure to get hold of what we assumed was Victor's phone."

"It must be to do with the Gilberts," MacKenzie said. "They're rich and we know how much Henderson liked money."

"But what was he planning?" Yates asked.

"We don't know yet," Ryan answered. "I'll be speaking to the FIU shortly to see if they've made any headway on finding the answer. But let's say Henderson cleaned out Swann's locker in the early hours of Sunday morning, while we were on site. He needed to find somewhere to stash it inside the house because he couldn't risk being seen taking it back to his cottage."

Ryan picked up a stray paperclip and began to fiddle with it as he transported himself inside the mind of a killer.

"I think Alice Chapman died because she found Henderson in the act of reclaiming his stolen goods on Sunday night. He thought he was alone but she'd lost track of time—as she often did—and worked after hours. She found him and connected the dots."

"He might not have killed Swann but he still killed that girl," Phillips said obstinately. "We've got his DNA."

Ryan nodded.

"I agree that Henderson is still the most likely candidate for Alice Chapman's murder and I wouldn't be surprised to find more evidence coming to light once Faulkner's had a chance to go over his home and car, not to mention his clothes."

Phillips folded his arms and Ryan knew what was going through his sergeant's mind because he was thinking the same thing.

"I'm disappointed too, Frank. Henderson's death has deprived Carol and Simon Chapman of a proper trial and justice for their daughter."

"Can't they do it posthumously?" Yates asked.

"No." Ryan was firm. "Trials in absentia are extremely rare; it's almost impossible to have a fair trial if the accused isn't there to defend himself."

"But if the evidence is overwhelming?"

Ryan sighed.

"I understand how you feel and, believe me, if the man were still alive, I'd be doing everything in my power to see him convicted for his crimes. But the rules are in place for a reason, much as they might frustrate us."

Ryan thought of Alice Chapman's parents and of how he would tell them that, although he'd found her killer, they'd never be able to look him in the eye. It was easy to talk in terms of black and white but what about all the shades of grey in between? He understood very well the heartache of losing a loved one and of the desire for retribution, but it would not bring them back to life.

He pushed the thought to one side because if he allowed himself to think too long or too hard about the wheels of justice, he'd pack it all in and never come to work again.

Irritated, he flung the paperclip back onto the desk.

"If Henderson didn't fall but was *pushed*, I have to ask myself why." He looked at each of his team in turn, eyes blazing. "Why kill a man who was already under suspicion for murder? It doesn't make sense because it has nothing to do with what happened to Alice or Victor."

"It might have been an accident, if somebody left the lift doors open?"

Ryan turned to Yates and was glad to see she was asking the right questions.

"The Gilberts keep the lift doors shut and a safety barrier is put across each of the entrances as an added precaution," he told her. "Even without it, you could fall against the closed doors and they'd stay shut, so it's perfectly safe. Last night, Faulkner checked the doors on each level and there were scratches against the lift doors on the first floor, which suggests they were forced open. The CSIs are searching for something long and relatively thin, hard enough to force the doors, like a fire poker, to see if they can match traces of the metal from the lift doors."

"You're saying we've got a second killer on our hands?" Phillips asked. "But, Henderson—?"

"If we stop thinking of Victor Swann's death as being anything other than an accident and we assume that Alice Chapman's murder was not planned, I find myself wondering whether Martin Henderson's death was the only premeditated event in all of this."

Ryan sat back and watched the penny drop.

"If somebody planned to kill Henderson all along, how could they know he'd be there at that time?" Phillips asked.

"They couldn't, but maybe they orchestrated a chain of events so that he would be," Ryan said.

"How could they know Victor and Alice would die?"

"They didn't—don't you see?" Ryan tried to be patient. "If they only ever planned to kill Henderson, they must have been as shocked as we were to find out that Victor had died. When Alice followed shortly after, they were as much in the dark as we were—no pun intended."

"If what you're saying is true, the other two deaths have given our killer a bit of cover," Phillips pointed out. "So long as we were looking elsewhere, they could carry on with their plan."

"This is all conjecture," MacKenzie said. "What makes you think this is the right line to follow?"

Ryan steepled his index fingers and rested them against his lips.

"It's the power failures," he said. "Two deaths happened during those power failures. What if the first one was just a rehearsal and the one last night was the real thing?"

Phillips slowly began to nod.

"I can see it," he said. "Bloody hell, I can see it now. But how do we prove it?"

Ryan inclined his head.

"At this precise moment, we haven't got a scrap of evidence to prove any of that theory. Whoever pushed Martin Henderson to his death probably went home and slept like a baby last night because there isn't a damn thing to connect them. So far, at least."

"I like a challenge," MacKenzie said, with a wicked grin.

"Good, because that's what we've got. We need to find out what Henderson did, to whom, and why it was so bad someone killed him for it."

Phillips scratched the side of his face.

"Don't ask for much, do you?"

A moment later, Anna stepped into the kitchen and found them huddled around the table with their heads together.

"You're as thick as thieves," she said. "What are you plotting?"

"A killer's downfall," Ryan said, shortly.

Anna pulled a face and left them to it, feeling sorry for whoever would be on the receiving end.

The working theory that Martin Henderson died because of a past misdeed was not particularly helpful, considering the mounting body of evidence being accumulated by the financial investigation unit alone. Their separate enquiry had already established that the man's history had been entirely falsified and they were working closely with various government bodies to unravel the lies. Ryan had a lengthy telephone conversation with DI Anika Salam, whose team resources were stretched to the limit and who found herself in the uncomfortable position of having to abandon the investigation now that their prime suspect was dead.

"I want to help you but we're snowed under with enquiries," she said, apologetically. "We could spend weeks on this but, in the end, we'd have nobody to charge."

"People like Martin Henderson never work alone," Ryan argued. "Odds are, you'd find his network and haul in some of the bigger fish."

That gave her pause for thought.

"That's a lot riding on 'ifs' and 'maybes,'" she said.

"You know he was dirty." Ryan pulled out every persuasive skill he had and didn't feel a moment's guilt about it. "Don't you want to chase down the bad guys? Don't you want to see them brought to heel, to pay their debt to society? There are too many people living off the fat of the land—"

His spiel came to an abrupt stop, as a thought struck him.

"*Land*," he repeated. "It's been staring us in the face. Why else would Henderson pretend to have a history of estate management? Why come and work at Cragside?"

At the other end of the line, Salam sat up a bit straighter in her chair.

"You think he wanted to spin something with the land up there?"

"Speak to Lionel Gilbert and ask him if he was planning to sell off any parcels of land on Henderson's recommendation. Then ask him if he'd received an offer from anyone to buy it. I'm betting an offer will have come from a newly formed company, which we will find has closed down its operations in the last few days. Follow that company all the way back and you'll find your big fish, Anika."

There was a short pause on the line.

"Are you interested in a transfer to the FIU?"

Ryan laughed.

"I'll leave financial crime to the experts. Wouldn't hurt to take a closer look at some of the local estate agents, while you're at it," he tagged on.

Salam chuckled.

"Alright, you've convinced me. We'll speak to Lionel Gilbert to see if your theory's right and take it from there."

"One last thing," Ryan said. "Before he was Martin Henderson, he was Martin Jennings. What have you been able to find from that period of his life?"

"It seems to have been the only time he *wasn't* involved in anything untoward. Until the age of twenty-one, when he changed his name and started to go by Henderson, Martin Jennings was just a lad who worked down at the dockyards in Newcastle."

"Why did he change his name around then?"

"Who knows?" she said. "I can't see any obvious reason from the files."

"Can you send across everything you have?"

"Consider it done."

After he ended the call, Ryan sat back in his chair and considered the type of person Martin Henderson had been. It hadn't surprised him to learn that Henderson had walked away from a life of honest hard work in favour of one where he was willing to lie, cheat and steal to make a quick buck. It was a question of weak character and, unfortunately, it made their work all the harder. If Martin Henderson had spent over forty years casually trampling over the lives of others in his quest for personal gain, who could say how many enemies he had made in the process? Added to which, his crimes were impersonal; all the deals he had been party to, all the back-handers, had a human cost but they were faceless, nameless people whose pensions or livelihoods had been affected.

Then again, he had not been too squeamish to kill Alice Chapman in cold blood.

Who else had Martin Henderson hurt?

The possibilities were endless.

CHAPTER 32

The key to everything came unexpectedly from his fiancée.

Having dispatched his team on a mission to uncover everything there was to know about Martin Henderson and the five people who remained on his suspect list, Ryan was seated quietly at the kitchen table trawling through background checks. He was disappointed to find there was hardly a speeding ticket among them and was about to harangue the CSIs for any further news when Anna wandered into the kitchen, intending to grab a snack and then leave him to it.

"Making any progress?"

She began rooting around in the fridge for ham and cheese.

Behind her, Ryan made a disgruntled noise.

"They're all squeaky clean," he complained. "I was hoping to see a drunk and disorderly, maybe a few pops for assault."

Anna smiled into the fridge.

"Just too law-abiding, eh?"

"One of them killed Martin Henderson, I know it," he muttered. "But until I can find the reason *why*, they're wandering around hiding in plain sight."

Anna reached for a knife and began to lather butter on four slices of bread, not bothering to ask if Ryan wanted a sandwich.

He always wanted a sandwich.

"Why don't you tell me what you know about Martin Henderson so far? Whenever I think of him, I just picture an obnoxious sixty-two-year-old with an ego the size of a small planet."

Ryan grinned, despite himself. As summaries went, it was pretty accurate.

"He was born in Wallsend, not far from our new police headquarters, actually. He used to be Martin Jennings until he changed his name when he was twenty-one."

Anna slapped some ham on the bread.

"Why'd he change his name?"

"That's one of the questions I'd like to answer, but I can't figure it out. There was no death in the family, no trauma on record. In 1975, he was just some lad who worked down at the shipyard—"

"Bad year to be working at the shipyard," Anna said, as she began to cut thin slices of cheese.

Ryan looked up with interest.

"Why?"

Anna paused and turned to face him, butter knife still in hand.

"That was the year *The Valiant* went up in flames. It was a terrible tragedy, not just for the men working on the ship but for their families and the whole community. We learned about it at school."

Ryan felt something *click*.

"Tell me what happened."

Anna set the knife down and cast her mind back.

"It was before I was born, so I only remember bits and pieces about it from school or from what people have told me."

"That's alright, I'll look up the detail later. I just want to know the general gist."

"Well, you already know shipbuilding was a major industry on Tyneside. Hundreds of men used to work on the ships—it wasn't really women's work, back then. Most of them lived locally, in the streets leading down to the docks or just across the river."

Ryan knew the area well.

"The industry was changing in the seventies and it wasn't as prolific as it had been in years gone by, but they were still building ships and *The Valiant* was one of them. Halfway through its completion, it went up in flames when the welders started work on the lower decks one morning."

"Why?" he asked softly, thinking of the sad loss of life.

"The official report said there was too much oxygen in the air, which made it highly flammable. They had a big oxygen tank on the top deck, with pipes to supply the decks below. Turns out one of the pipes had been left to leak during the night but nobody ever figured out how it happened. The men responsible for checking the pipes were adamant they had done the proper checks and the logs were up to date."

Ryan looked at the paperwork strewn across the table and began sifting through it until he found the information sent through from the FIU.

He skim-read the detail and then turned back to Anna.

"A young Martin Jennings worked for a shipbuilding company at that time."

"Then he probably worked it," Anna said. "He was lucky to survive."

Perhaps luck hadn't come into it, Ryan thought.

Anna turned back to her sandwiches and a moment later his arms came around her in a tight embrace.

"Thank you," he said. "Without meaning to, you might have just put your finger on what's at the heart of this case."

Anna smiled and stuck a sandwich wedge in his mouth.

"Anything to help the boys in blue."

Not for the first time in the past twelve hours, Tom Faulkner was asking himself why he didn't apply for a nice desk job. There would be no blood and gore to contend with, no unsociable working hours and, if the pay was going to be average, at least he wouldn't need to spend it on endless cartons of washing detergent to remove the scent of chemicals that seemed to follow him wherever he went. He stepped out of the estate manager's cottage in his plastic overalls and untucked the hood, breathing deeply of the fresh air. Bees buzzed in the rhododendron bushes and the sun blazed at its highest point in the sky, defying the air of gloom that had fallen upon the estate. He wondered what it would be like to work in a place like this, to enjoy its beauty and see the lighter side to nature rather than the darker side he was exposed to each day.

Just then, he spotted her.

Charlotte Shapiro was riding astride a quad bike, motoring along one of the access roads that took her past the cottage where he stood. The breeze ruffled her hair and gave colour to her cheeks but she wore a determined expression and exuded an air of extreme capability he found both attractive and fearsome.

"Hello!"

Spotting him, she slowed the bike and cut its loud engine to a purr.

"No rest for the wicked, eh?" She nodded towards the cottage and the group of CSIs moving in and out.

Faulkner made a non-committal sound and felt himself growing hot under her scrutiny.

"You must be due a day off, after this is all over?"

Charlotte gave him a winsome smile.

Faulkner opened his mouth and shut it again, like a fish.

"Um, yes. I think so."

She turned the engine off completely and swivelled in her chair so that she was perched on the edge of the quad bike.

"Just tell me to get lost, if you're too busy to chat," she said, but made no move to drive away.

"Ah, no, it's alright. I can take five minutes."

She nodded, watching the CSIs moving around.

"I saw a mechanic arrive earlier to take Henderson's car away," she said. "I guess you have to check that for evidence, too?"

Faulkner nodded.

"Hard to believe all this is happening," she said, pulling out a packet of mints from the pocket of her gilet. She offered him one but he shook his head. "I've worked here for years and we've never seen anything worse than a couple of broken arms. Usually kids trying to climb the trees," she added with a smile.

"It can happen anywhere," Faulkner replied.

"Well, I know, but…I only hope Cassandra and Lionel won't be too upset by it all. It really isn't their fault any of this happened."

"It's a pity nobody saw Henderson just before he died," Faulkner said.

"Well, he was just hanging around," she said. "Dave told me he'd been up at the house all day, as if he'd been waiting for something. Of course, none of us knew he was planning to jump."

Faulkner didn't bother to correct her.

"It seems like everyone was working late, last night," he said instead.

"It's like that up here," she said. "We don't tend to worry about strict hours and it's easy to lose track of the time. I was supposed to meet Dave at six-thirty for a chat about some irrigation work we want to do, but we ended up having drinks and canapés with the Gilberts and their friends. They're such lovely people."

Her last words were tinged with regret.

"So everybody was in the same room when the lights went out at nine o'clock?"

"Oh, no," she said, shaking her head. "We were all over the place. I was in the bathroom, Dave was in his office, I think, and the Gilberts were in the library entertaining. I think Cassandra stepped out for a moment because I ran into her in the hallway and she was coming from the direction of the stairs."

She looked across the rock gardens to the trees beyond, thinking of the previous evening.

"It's amazing how darkness can be disorientating. I hate the dark," she muttered.

Suddenly, she seemed to brighten.

"I'm going to do something very forward and give you my number."

He turned beetroot red.

"Now, there's no need to have a heart attack," she chuckled. "Hasn't a woman ever given you her number before?"

"Ah, not recently, no."

"Their loss." She gave him an impish smile and started searching for a pen. Her hand fell on something heavy and silver in one of her pockets and, unthinkingly, she drew it out and began to scribble on the back of a business card.

She handed it to him and Faulkner drew off his gloves, wondering what to say, fighting the urge to kneel down and kiss her feet.

"Give me a call if you're ever off duty," she told him, and fired up the engine.

She gave a brisk wave and Faulkner watched her bright blonde head disappear around the bend. He looked down at the card in his hand and wondered whether his luck had finally changed.

CHAPTER 33

After a short search of the house, Ryan found Dave Quibble in the turret room.

He stood beside the window looking out across the valley, surrounded by pots and brushes left over from its use as a studio by Alice Chapman. The portrait she had so painstakingly begun to restore had been removed to another firm of specialists, for fear that exposure to air and light might cause harm if left for too long.

It was a timely reminder that Quibble's first loyalty was to inanimate artefacts and not the things that lived and breathed around them.

Ryan made a swift assessment of the man's demeanour, which seemed somehow defeated. Quibble's shoulders were hunched and his face downcast. He rested a hand against the wall as he continued to look out across the trees.

"Dave?"

His shoulders straightened immediately and he seemed to gather himself before turning to greet Ryan.

"Hello, Ryan. Just taking a break." He lifted a hand towards the window. "It's the best view in the house from up here."

Ryan took a step closer but didn't move to stand beside him.

"It's been a difficult time," he offered, sincerely.

Quibble ran an agitated hand through his hair and looked around the room, at all the objects and antiques, then back at Ryan.

"I spend my life thinking about the past, about *things*," he said. "Even when Victor died…well, I'm ashamed to admit, I didn't feel too upset. He was an old man, it somehow seemed like he'd lived a full life."

There was the difference between them, Ryan realised. His own approach did not differ whether a victim was young or old, rich or poor, black or white, male or female, gay or straight. As far as he was concerned, they were all victims and deserved his full attention.

"But when Alice died, it really hit me," Quibble said. "A young woman like that, with so much talent…"

Ryan read a flicker of something else beneath the grief.

"You liked her?"

Quibble shifted his feet.

"I never told her," he said defensively. "I was her boss, for one thing, and almost old enough to be her father."

Ryan knew the value of silence in drawing people out, so he said nothing.

"You're sure it was Henderson who killed her?" Quibble asked, after a moment.

"We're almost certain, yes."

Quibble's face hardened into something almost unrecognisable.

"Murderous bastard," he spat. "It's no secret I never liked the man, but to kill—"

He broke off and swiped a hand across his mouth, as if it would help to clear the nasty taste on his tongue.

"I underestimated him," he finished bleakly.

"It seems nobody liked Henderson very much."

Quibble didn't answer directly.

"He's gone now. He'll never hurt anyone again."

Ryan took another step into the room and idly picked up one of the paintbrushes sitting in a porcelain cup.

"We still haven't got to the bottom of why these power cuts keep happening, have we?"

Quibble rubbed a hand across the back of his neck, feeling warm.

"I've looked at everything I can think of," he explained. "I can't work it out."

Ryan looked up with flat grey eyes.

"Can't you?"

The words hung on the air like the dust motes that danced in the beams of light shining through the window. Then Ryan nodded and turned to leave.

Before he reached the door, Quibble called out.

"Ryan? Have you found out why Henderson fell?"

Not 'jumped', Ryan thought. *Not 'pushed', either.*
Interesting.

"You'll be the first to know when I do."

MacKenzie found the housekeeper in her sitting room, which formed part of a small apartment in one of the upper wings of the house. Maggie answered the door with a tired smile and immediately offered to make tea, which was politely declined.

"I was hoping to have a quick chat?" MacKenzie asked.

"Of course, pet. Come in and have a seat."

The room was arranged around a small fireplace with an elaborate Victorian frieze and there were lace doilies as far as the eye could see. Framed pictures of family and friends were arranged across every polished surface and a small knitting bag rested beside one of the armchairs.

"My eldest is having her second child," Maggie said proudly, picking up a pair of tiny woollen booties.

"I didn't realise you had any children?" MacKenzie sank into one of the proffered chairs.

Maggie smiled and pointed to a framed photograph with a man and a woman standing either side of her. Also in the picture were Cassandra and Lionel Gilbert with another man and woman she didn't recognise.

"Who are the others?"

"Oh, those are Cassie's children," Maggie said, lowering her voice. "Ellie and James. They live down south and don't tend to visit much—to be honest, they've never been big fans of Lionel."

"I understand Mrs Gilbert's first husband died?"

"Yes, poor thing. It was years ago and Cassie never talks about it much."

She reached across to a box of chocolates and offered one to Denise, who shook her head. Maggie popped a truffle in her mouth and settled in for a good chat.

"I'm still reeling from what happened last night," she said between bites. "I can hardly believe that Martin would kill himself; he seemed so, well—"

She made a rolling motion with her fingers and tried to find a delicate way of saying 'full of himself'.

"Confident," she decided.

"We are investigating Mr Henderson's death as a suspicious incident. Anything you can remember around nine o'clock last night would be very helpful."

The housekeeper sank back in her chair, lost for words.

"I don't understand," she said and her face crumpled into sad lines. "Cragside is a beautiful, peaceful place. Murders just don't happen here."

MacKenzie didn't bother to point out the obvious fact that murders could and had happened there.

"I understand Cragside is important to you," she said gently.

"It's been my life these past few years, since the children don't need me around so much. I have a place, here," she said, tearfully. "I can keep the house looking beautiful and feel…useful, I suppose."

MacKenzie held out the box of chocolates with a smile and Maggie laughed.

"Go on then."

While chewing, she pulled herself together.

"You were asking me about last night," she said firmly. "Let me think about this. I told that nice constable about what I saw but if you need me to go over it again?"

"If you don't mind," MacKenzie prodded.

"Well, Lionel and Cassie had friends over for dinner, to cheer themselves up a bit. They arrived just after six and I had canapés ready for them."

"Prepared on site or catered?"

"Oh, these were easy to do on site. I had a couple of catering staff to take care of the cooking and the serving, I just fiddled with things here and there and directed them where to go," she laughed.

"They arrived at six?"

"Yes. At around six-thirty, Cassie came through to the kitchen and invited us to have a drink with them. She asked Charlotte and Dave to join us too, and we all went into the library. It turned into more of a soirée. Cassie's never been one for too much pomp and circumstance; it doesn't suit her."

"How long did the, ah, soirée last?" MacKenzie wasn't overly familiar with the usual running time of a soirée.

"They chatted for a good long while," Maggie said. "You know what Lionel can be like once he gets going. And Dave, for that matter. Get him started on all the little things that need doing in this house and you're in for a long night."

MacKenzie smiled politely.

"I popped in and out with the serving staff, so the dinner wouldn't be ruined. When the main courses came, we left the Gilberts to their guests. Charlotte and Dave went off to the staff room for a chat, I think."

"Do you remember where you were when the lights went out?"

"Oh yes," Maggie said. "I was clearing some of the dirty dishes from the table in the library and everything just went black. I panicked a bit and dropped one of the plates on the floor in the hallway outside, which left a bit of a mark," she said worriedly.

"Did you see anyone else?"

"I couldn't see much, love, but I could hear the serving staff shrieking in the kitchen and I think I heard somebody's footsteps heading down to the fuse box. The flooring in the servants' corridor is stone, so you can hear everything."

"You didn't see anybody going upstairs?"

Maggie shook her head.

"I didn't see a soul."

While MacKenzie listened to the housekeeper extol the benefits of knitting for relieving stress in the workplace, Lowerson and Yates were being educated about 'the good old days' by the master of Cragside house. They were seated in the morning room on the first floor, which was a replica of the library beneath it and enjoyed views of the woodland leading down to the burn from a huge bay window spanning one wall.

"Always knew Henderson was fishy," Lionel surprised them all by saying.

"You were telling me just last week how good it was to have him here to help manage the estate," Cassandra argued.

"Doesn't mean I wasn't keeping my beady eye on him," he snapped, while the two detectives listened with interest. "Why d' you think I never signed those papers he kept pushing at me? I wanted to look at it myself. I wasn't about to sign away acres of land just on his say-so!"

Lionel let out a booming laugh.

"Wasn't surprised at all when your colleague called me earlier," he said as he turned back to Lowerson and Yates. "Turns out Martin was cooking the books, eh? Some men just can't help themselves."

"Or women," Cassandra put in, for the sake of equality.

Lionel made a dismissive sound.

"Fact is, if the little blighter had swindled me, I'd have been tempted to throw him down the lift shaft myself."

"*Lionel!*"

"Oh, stop flapping, woman. They want the truth, don't they?" He gestured an imperious hand to where Lowerson and Yates sat with their hands in their laps.

"All the same, he's dead, and at our house…"

"That's another blasted liberty, if you ask me," Lionel bellowed, very much back to his former self now his flu had cleared up. "Sullying my house with death so that you can barely move without tripping over the fuzz."

He eyed Lowerson with obvious dislike.

"That's another thing," Lionel blustered, thinking of the younger generation. "In my day, we didn't have things like *selfies*—whoever heard of such a thing!—or *onesies*, whatever the hell they are."

"Ellie bought you one in the shape of a banana last Christmas," Cassandra muttered.

Lionel scowled and turned back to Lowerson.

"Well? Don't just stand there looking sheepish, tell us who's been going around turning my house into a bleedin' mortuary!"

Lowerson was finally given a chance to speak and he decided to use it wisely, since the opportunity might not come around again.

"Mr Gilbert, it would help us to know your precise movements last night, particularly between five to and ten past nine."

Lionel turned a slow shade of red.

"I hope you're not having the impertinence to suggest I'd do off with somebody in my own home?"

Yates raised an eyebrow and wondered if that meant he would happily 'do off' with somebody elsewhere.

"They have to ask, Lionel," Cassandra told him.

He drew in a laboured breath and gave them a look of extreme sufferance.

"Well, I was in the library the whole time. The lights went out and we all wondered what had happened *this* time. Cassie went off to investigate."

Lowerson and Yates turned their mild gaze onto the mistress of Cragside, who looked startled.

"Well, yes, I told you in my statement, I went off to see what had happened."

"And you were gone a bloody long time, too!"

Cassandra sent him a frustrated glare, while Yates calmly brought up a digital copy of her statement from the previous evening.

"Mrs Gilbert, last night you said you were in the library throughout the blackout, until everyone went out into the hallway together."

There was an awkward silence.

"I—I must have made a mistake."

"Would you like to amend your statement now?"

"I—yes, I think I'd better."

Phillips made his way through the myriad terraced streets running parallel to the River Tyne on the eastern edges of Newcastle. He felt an odd sense of homecoming, having grown up on the city's western edge in a working-class area that was a mirror image of the one he drove through now. It had none of the gloss of the city centre; there were no chic wine bars, upmarket restaurants or expensive shops. There was an aura of disillusionment that permeated the walls of the cheap pre-fab houses that had been built temporarily following the Second World War and had never been replaced by anything better, despite the promises of successive governments. *One day*, they said.

No amount of new brickwork or community centres could replace the loss of an industry that had been the lifeblood of almost every family in the neighbourhood. Though nearly forty years had passed since the old shipyards closed their doors, the sense of abandonment still felt fresh. As Phillips drove further into the industry's old heartland, it was impossible to suppress a feeling of grief when the sight of a single crane suddenly came into view, and impossible not to remember a time when there had been dozens.

Yet there was hope beneath it all.

Northerners were from hardy, fighting stock and it took more than a few knocks to crush their spirit. Phillips could see that in the fresh coats of paint on the walls, the neatly tended gardens and the new businesses popping up in the old shop fronts on the high street. A group of women stood chatting and laughing outside a local supermarket and, to Phillips, they represented everything that was good about his city; they were getting on with life and living it, not harkening back to the past.

He came to a stop at a set of traffic lights and glanced at the building to his left, which bore a sign saying, 'ST. PETER'S CLUB'. He smiled and shook his head, thinking back to his younger days and the times he'd driven his father down here for a pint with his mates and a sing-song around the bar. Nobody had called it by its true name for years; it had always been known as 'The Bottom Club' and had been a meeting place for local men for at least fifty years. Its doors were closed now and he wondered whether the locals still gathered there, and whether the community spirit lived on despite the hardships it had faced.

He hoped so.

The lights changed and Phillips put the car in gear, hardening his heart so that he could focus on the reason he was here. Half a mile north lay the new police headquarters but he had been given a different mission, one which might provide the final answer they were searching for.

As he passed the site where tall ships and destroyers had once been raised onto the water, Phillips slowed his car, watching for the building that still housed the records from the old days. He almost didn't notice the beginning of Hadrian's Wall jutting from the ground, its ancient stonework seeming out of place among the industrial surrounds but, on reflection, very fitting. Here, within footsteps of each other, were the remnants of two magnificent empires.

Phillips spotted the place he was looking for and, a few minutes later, he shook hands with a young man who had agreed to help him search for the records they needed.

As he stepped over the threshold, he cast his gaze upward to the sky and to the sun which was already beginning its slow descent.

The clock was ticking.

Ryan set aside the papers he had now read a dozen times and set off through the forest to complete a final, vital task that would resolve the question that had been puzzling him since the beginning. What had caused the power failures at such precise times? First, eleven o'clock on Saturday evening and then nine o'clock last night. He refused to believe it was a coincidence.

Ryan paused as he always did on the iron bridge spanning the burn to look down into the gorge where Alice Chapman had fallen. Although her killer was now a victim himself, it made no difference to his approach. He would seek justice for Henderson, just as he had for Alice Chapman, for the principle was the same. It was not for anybody to play God or to judge who should live and who should die.

Only the law could balance the scales.

He continued across the bridge and let himself into the house, careful not to make his presence known. He'd deliberately chosen a time when most people would be busy with work but he paused to listen out for any sounds of footfall, just in case. Then he moved quickly to begin an intensive search of some of the rooms, stopping to check he was alone before shifting large items of furniture.

It only took ten minutes to find what he was looking for.

Ryan smiled grimly and then turned to retrace his steps, leaving just as quietly as he had come.

CHAPTER 34

By four o'clock, there was still no word from Phillips.

Ryan's team assembled once again in the rental cottage, with Faulkner in attendance and Jeff Pinter on speakerphone.

"I've done the post-mortem on Henderson." His upper-crusty voice rang out into the kitchen and Ryan hastily adjusted the volume.

"What did you find?"

"Well, firstly, he couldn't have been dead more than half an hour when you found him in the basement," Pinter said. "His core body temperature was still thirty-seven degrees and his skin was warm to the touch."

"What about the rest of him?" Ryan asked.

Pinter gave a theatrical sigh.

"In cases of rapid deceleration such as we see in victims of falling, there are all the usual arterial lacerations, haemorrhage...almost every organ in Henderson's body was torn apart by extreme impact."

Yates swallowed a gulp of tea and felt it slosh around her stomach, settling uneasily as she listened to the pathologist.

"One of his nails was badly torn on his right hand and Faulkner tells me the corresponding fragment was found during their search. After some testing today, they were able to match the metal compound beneath the nail fragment to the type found on the lift doors on the first floor of the house."

"Defensive wound, you think?"

"Not for me to say," Pinter was quick to point out. "I can only tell you what shape he was in but, if you want my opinion, I'd say he was making a grab for something to hold on to as he fell."

"Anything in his blood?" Ryan enquired. "Anything that would point to accident or suicide?"

"I put a rush on the toxicology report, as requested. His bloodwork came back nil of alcohol or drugs, other than a small quantity of propanoic acid, otherwise known as ibuprofen. That certainly wouldn't have impaired his judgment. As for any pathological indications of suicide, there were no historic contusions or lacerations on his arms or wrists that might support a psychiatric history of suicidal tendencies."

Ryan nodded, glad to have his own suspicions confirmed.

"Anything else we need to know?"

"Just a lot of medical bumf," Pinter said honestly. "I'll send my report through to you now."

"Thanks, Jeff."

Ryan stabbed the red button on his phone to end the call and looked up at his team, who were half-seated, half-standing around the kitchen in a state of agitation. He knew the feeling; it came when an investigation was taking too long, when they had worked solidly for days and there were no fruits to show for it.

All that would change very soon.

"So"—he clapped his hands to get their attention—"Pinter has more or less confirmed that Henderson was pushed. Faulkner? What can you tell us from the forensic side?"

The senior CSI had shed his plastic suit and was now wearing a pair of crumpled, straight-leg jeans and a t-shirt with a faded motif of *Sgt Pepper's Lonely Hearts Club Band* on the front. A pair of wire-rimmed glasses sat on the end of his nose.

"We spent all of last night and most of today going over the basement and Henderson's personal items. Firstly, I should mention that we found large quantities of bleach sloshed on his kitchen floor and concentrated in one area. When will they *ever* learn that bleach doesn't mask blood residue?" Faulkner wondered aloud. "There were specks of it beneath the bleach and we sent the samples to the lab, who tested it immediately against Alice Chapman's blood type. There was an initial match."

Ryan nodded. It was just as he had expected.

"Henderson's shoes?"

"Yes," Faulkner nodded. "The shoes he was wearing when he died were also covered in bleach, which still hadn't managed to cover up traces of blood which was, incidentally, another match for Alice Chapman's type A-positive. It seems likely he trudged around her body looking for Victor Swann's phone and then came home with bits of her still clinging to his shoes."

"Charming," MacKenzie muttered.

"Sorry, Mac. Force of habit," Faulkner said. It was easy to talk of bodies as inanimate objects, no longer invested with thoughts or feelings, but they'd all been people once.

"That adds weight to what we already know, which is that Henderson killed Alice Chapman," Ryan said. "But what about the person who killed *him*? Did they leave anything of themselves behind?"

"There's always a trace," Faulkner agreed. "Unfortunately, that trace was well covered by somebody who clearly thought ahead. We swabbed Henderson's clothing for skin cell or sweat impression marks, where they might have used their hands to push him. Unfortunately, all we found were fibres of the kind you might find on thick gardening gloves or something of that ilk. We'd need to seize clothing to find a match."

Ryan nodded.

"What else?"

Faulkner reached inside a cardboard box file and retrieved a plastic evidence bag containing a few torn fragments of paper.

"We found these bits of paper behind the fire grate at Henderson's cottage. They're too small to decipher any words but we'll get around to testing them for prints and DNA."

"You're thinking it could have been a note torn up by Henderson and the rest was burned?"

Faulkner shrugged as he shuffled the bag, then put it back inside the box.

"One of the fragments reads 'p.m.', which suggests a time was mentioned. It would explain why Henderson was up at the house at that specific hour, if someone had left him a note with a designated time and place."

Ryan smiled.

"They were sloppy, there, and perhaps a little desperate."

"If it's like you say and the first two deaths weren't meant to happen, there was a police presence at Cragside that might have been completely absent if Henderson had been the only person to die in a tragic fall," MacKenzie said. "The killer knew we were closing in on Henderson and their chance to kill him would disappear as soon as we took him into custody."

"They had to act quickly," Ryan agreed. "As do we."

He stood up and paced around the floor to work off some adrenaline.

"Martin Henderson—previously Jennings—changed his name in the summer of 1975 at a time when he was working as a fitter on *The Valiant*. That ship went up in smoke thanks to somebody's negligence and, though we can't yet prove it, my hunch is that young Martin Jennings was involved in some way or another. That inferno killed nearly a hundred men whose families were left behind to pick up the pieces."

Ryan paused to think of it and found he could hardly imagine the devastation.

"Wives who were left widowed, children who were left fatherless, siblings who lost a brother," he said. "Any one of them could have found out about Henderson's involvement and harboured a grudge all these years, waiting to even the score."

They all turned to look at the faces of the remaining suspects on the wall and Ryan studied each of them in turn.

"Imagine finding out that your worst enemy was coming to work with you, here at Cragside. Or imagine deliberately hiring him, to have him within your net. Any one of these people could be the right age and, now that physicality is less of an issue, even Lionel himself could have trotted upstairs like a mountain goat to see off his estate manager. Problem is, we can't prove which of them it was."

Just then, they heard the click of the front door opening and closing. Phillips ambled into the room looking hot and bothered.

"Stuck in traffic for half hour," he grumbled.

"Did you have any luck?" Ryan asked, eyeing the plastic wallet in Phillips' hand.

His sergeant waggled it enticingly.

"Aye, I've brought home the bacon, as usual."

MacKenzie rolled her eyes but gave him a peck on the cheek as he took a seat beside her and rolled up his shirtsleeves.

There was a pregnant silence as they waited for Ryan to cast his eye over the list of those who had died the day *The Valiant* had gone up in flames. They watched him drag a finger down the columns, his face softening as he thought of all those who were lost, until he found a name he recognised.

"Bingo," he murmured.

Ryan wasted no time feeling surprised, or even upset, but instead splayed his palms on the table top and thought of how they could set a trap.

"Everything we have is circumstantial," he said. "Even this name. There isn't a jury in the land that would convict 'beyond all reasonable doubt', so we need to find a way to prove it."

He surprised them all by flashing a smile.

"I think I know how to do it but we need to move quickly. This person is volatile and unpredictable now they've taken a life. It creates a sense of invincibility in the minds of some killers and, if they suspect that another person saw them or might know something, they could kill again to protect themselves or their family."

There were nods around the table.

"So what are we going to do?" Lowerson asked.

"We're going to beat them at their own game, Jack."

Sunset over Cragside was an almost religious experience. For a short while, the sky seemed to ignite and spread amber flame over the treetops, dazzling the person who looked out from the uppermost turret and remembered a day many years ago when fire had filled the sky.

There was no smell of burning flesh here, and no ghostly screams of those long dead, only the quiet sound of a carriage clock on the mantelpiece.

Its incessant *tick, tick, ticking* seemed to grow louder and louder, as if to remind them that time waited for no man and there was still work to be done. There were loose ends to tie up, it seemed, and the prospect gave them no joy.

But there were others to think of, those who needed to be protected.

It was all for the greater good.

Darkness had fallen by the time Maggie finished clearing the dinner plates and the house was bathed in gentle lamplight, which she much preferred to the brash sunlight that showed up every line and wrinkle in the old mercury-coated mirrors dotted around the house. Every time she stopped to polish them, she came face to face with the effects of time and gravity and, though she told herself it was the natural course of things, she remembered when she'd seen a very different reflection staring back at her. She let out a little sigh and leaned against the big old ceramic Butler sink so she could slip her foot out of its comfortable rubber-soled shoe and roll her ankle around. Joint pain was just another thing to get used to, she supposed, and she slipped her foot back into the shoe to give her other foot the same treatment.

Maggie checked the time on the wall, which told her it was a few minutes before nine, and she wondered whether it would be another long night. The Gilberts were entertaining again and, though she shouldn't grumble, it would have been nice to have an evening off duty considering all the recent drama. It set her nerves on edge.

She wondered where the catering staff had gone, then clucked her tongue and began to rummage around for a tea towel, humming an old northern folk song beneath her breath.

On the stroke of nine, the room fell into darkness.

Maggie let out a yelp and spun around, clutching the tea towel to her chest. The kitchen was completely dark but for the glow of a solar-powered light from the courtyard outside.

"Hello! Is anybody there?"

She waited to hear the patter of footsteps against the stone corridor but there was nothing to be heard except the drip of the tap. Drawing a shaky breath, she told herself not to panic. She could sort this out, if need be.

She began to make her way towards the light switch on the wall beside the basement stairs, careful not to step too far. Her hand crept up the wall and she flicked the little switch, to no avail.

"Hello?"

Her voice echoed around the empty room.

Everyone had retired to one of the smaller reception rooms upstairs and probably couldn't hear her. In another moment, somebody would come along, she thought.

But the darkness was intense and she felt her chest constricting with anxiety.

She couldn't wait for somebody to come.

Maggie began to lower herself downstairs into the basement, feeling her way from memory rather than anything else. She was grateful for the thick-soled shoes which gripped the uneven stone and let out a breath of relief when she regained firm ground.

The basement was black as night and she prayed she wouldn't trip over an errant box or piece of debris left over by the CSI team earlier in the day. She moved across the room with careful steps until her bad hip caught painfully against the edge of something large and metal.

Maggie let out a sharp sound of pain and clutched a hand to her side, thinking there would be an almighty bruise tomorrow. She crouched down and began to feel along the wall, then she heard a movement behind her.

Her heart leapt into her throat as a blinding torchlight shone into her eyes.

"Hello, Maggie."

She raised a shaking hand to her eyes, trying to see who it was.

"Who's there?" she whispered.

"Don't you recognise me?"

Her eyes were frantic, searching the darkness for a means to escape. The back door leading to the courtyard wasn't far. If she could push past them and run...

"It's over, Maggie."

She recognised the voice and knew then that it was over.

CHAPTER 35

"Ryan."

The housekeeper said his name and he lowered the spotlight to her hand, which still rested on the little timer device plugged in to the power socket of the washing machine in the very depths of the basement.

"What have you got in your hand, Maggie?"

Her fist clutched the clever little piece of plastic and she thought of coming up with some excuse, some reason why she'd known to come here when the lights went out, but there was none.

She was the only person who had known it was there.

"How did you know?" she asked as she stood up slowly, the timer still clutched in her hand.

"Your name," he said simply. "It's Ramshaw."

Ryan saw her nod in the light of his torch.

"Joe's name."

"You set the timer on the plug beside the washing machine so it would turn on for a few minutes at eleven o'clock last

Saturday night, then you set it again for nine o'clock last night. You knew the surge of power would be too much for the circuit to handle. It was so easy."

She didn't bother to deny it and looked down at the timer in her hand.

"I was sure I had put the timer on the single setting but it's set for a daily repeat at nine o'clock. I thought I had better come down and get rid of it. I must be getting old..." She trailed off, understanding spreading across her face. "You set this up, didn't you?"

Ryan shrugged his shoulders, his half-smile not quite reaching his eyes.

"What are you going to do now, lad?" She said the last word as a kind of endearment, as if she were speaking to her own child. "What do you think is the right thing to do?"

"I think you know the answer to that," he said flatly.

"Is it really that simple?" she demanded. "Think of all the lives lost aboard that ship, all the children who grew up without fathers because of that snivelling little *bastard*!"

Gone was the softly-spoken grandmother now, he thought. Her tone was hard and filled with hatred.

"You blame him for *The Valiant*?"

"Yes, I blame him," she snarled. "Who else was responsible? I searched for answers for years afterwards because I believed those poor men who checked the oxygen valves. I spoke to them and I believed them, so there had to be another cause."

"The inquest ruled it accidental."

"The inquest was a cover up," she spat, her eyes flashing at him in the darkness. "They didn't know then what I only found out years later. Martin Jennings, as he was, had been siphoning oxygen from the tanks to re-sell, so he could make himself some pocket money. It was a commodity and, as we all know, Martin loved nothing more than buying and selling. His single, self-centred action cost a hundred and eight lives but he never lost a moment's sleep."

"You told Victor this?"

Maggie gave a short nod.

"That was a mistake," she admitted. "I trusted him and I needed somebody else to know. Still, I was sorry he died."

"Big of you," Ryan said and she looked at him with venom.

"You think you're so clever, don't you?" she said, moving towards him. "You think you're doing the right thing and that society will give you a big slap on the back and say, 'well done'. But they won't. They'll say you locked up a fragile old woman who lost her husband in one of the region's biggest tragedies. They'll say *I* was the real victim here, not that evil, rabid creature I put down last night. He hadn't changed; you're the one who said he killed Alice as well. He'd have kept going too, if I hadn't stopped him."

Ryan could feel her breath hitting the bottom of his chin and thought back to the grief-stricken faces of Alice's parents.

"You're forgetting something, Maggie," he said quietly. "I don't answer to the popular press, I answer to the laws of England. I answer to the common standards of decency that society expects, not some base urge to exact revenge."

"He got what was coming to him!" she shouted, and a fine spray of saliva connected with his face.

"It is not for you to play God," he said.

"You don't understand what it feels like, to have lost someone—"

"I understand," he snapped.

They stood almost nose to nose and didn't even notice when the lights were turned on again and Phillips and MacKenzie joined them, standing a few paces further back.

"He took my husband—the father of my children!"

Ryan nodded.

"And now you've let him take something more important," he said in a low voice. "You let him take your soul."

She flew at him then, scratching and clawing.

Weary now, Ryan held her off, then stepped away and motioned the other two detectives forward to make the arrest. After they led her away amid a stream of obscenities, he let himself out the back door and into the courtyard outside. He didn't bother to look at the ground where Victor had lain but kept walking around the side of the house until he was on higher ground and could rest against one of the craggy rocks and look up at the sky in momentary solitude.

The moon trickled glorious white light onto the slate roof of the house and washed away the darkness, cleansing it of the maleficent force that had, for a while, taken hold of the people who lived there. Ryan leaned back against the rough bark of a tree, wrestling with his conscience.

Should personal vengeance ever be allowed to take precedence over society's laws?

He understood the terrible temptation to take an eye for an eye. He understood the pain of loss, the kind that gnawed at your spirit until there was little left but an embittered shell.

But there had to be something greater, something that was worth fighting for.

He watched a squad car make its journey along the driveway towards the city and resolved to keep fighting.

EPILOGUE

Anna stood in a long column of simple ivory tulle, clutching a bouquet of wild flowers as she stared into the mirror, hardly recognising herself.

Neither her mother nor her sister stood beside her, but another woman did.

"Bend your head a little," MacKenzie told her, carefully securing a veil onto the top of Anna's hair, which fell in long waves down her back.

She stepped aside and surveyed the effect in the mirror.

"You're a vision," she said, gently fluffing the yards of silk. "Are you ready to go and face the music, or should I order a couple of fast horses?"

Anna managed a nervous laugh.

Unlike herself, Ryan had a large and expansive family of aunts, uncles, cousins and second-cousins-twice-removed, all of whom would be joining them for the reception later. Thankfully, at his insistence, the numbers had been kept small for the ceremony so that the disparity would not be quite so obvious and she would not feel so nervous walking down a packed aisle of guests who looked as if they'd wandered off the pages of *Tatler* or *Country Life*.

Ryan had assured her they could drink the average Geordie sailor under the table, which was some small comfort.

Still, it might have been nice to have somebody to cling to.

Just then, there was a soft tap on the bedroom door.

"That'll be the driver," MacKenzie said, rushing about to scoop up her bridesmaid's bouquet and other essential items, such as tissues.

But it was Phillips who stepped cautiously into the room, looking dapper in a navy-blue three-piece suit and a tie in a conservative shade of red.

He looked at Anna in a kind of wonder.

"You're a beauty," he said, then shuffled awkwardly, looking to MacKenzie for encouragement.

From her position over Anna's shoulder, she gave him a nod and a 'hurry up' motion.

"Ah, there's a favour I wanted to ask," he said gruffly, working hard to keep the emotion from his voice. "I, ah, well, I know I'm not your Da and you might not want…that is to say, I don't have any daughters and I wondered if you'd let me have the honour of walking you down the aisle."

Anna couldn't speak for a moment. She stood looking at the short, ruddy-faced man with twinkling brown eyes and realised she had been very wrong to think she had no family.

Here was her family.

"It would make me very happy, Frank," she managed, blinking furiously against the tears that threatened to ruin her mascara. "There's just one small thing I need to change."

Phillips gave her a curious look and watched as Anna began rooting around one of the wardrobes. She came back holding a canary yellow tie with a pattern of tiny red love hearts and miniature cupids.

"I think this would suit you a lot better than the one you're wearing—wouldn't you say?"

Phillips' smile was wide and genuine.

"Now you're talking."

––––––––

They were married on a sunlit afternoon, on a swathe of sandy white beach beneath Bamburgh Castle. The mighty fortress burned a rusty gold as it soaked up the sun's rays and, for once, the North Sea was gentle as it lapped against the shoreline. Anna made her way across the sand dunes and stopped to look out across the water where, further to the north, she could see the tower of Lindisfarne Castle on the island where she had been born. It was fitting, she thought, to be married within sight of her past but not overshadowed by it.

Phillips gave her a quick, comforting squeeze.

"Ready, lass?"

"Let's not keep him waiting too long," she smiled. "He doesn't have you with him to crack any corny jokes."

They made their way down the dunes, pausing to kick off their shoes like all the other guests who stood up from their chairs to meet her in bare feet. Beside a simple arch decorated in wild flowers with the sea as its backdrop, Ryan stood waiting for her in a matching navy-blue suit, his toes curling in the sand.

There was a sea of familiar faces, Anna realised, and every one of them wished her well.

Alex Walker, her childhood friend from the island, stood next to his new boyfriend and winked as she passed. Her good friends from university, making silly, ecstatic faces. Tom Faulkner and Jeff Pinter, both welling up. Jack Lowerson, wearing a brand new shiny grey suit that caught the glare of the sun, and then Ryan's parents, who smiled at her as if she already belonged.

Then, Ryan.

He stood looking out across the water but then he turned to look at her. In that moment, there might have been nobody but the two of them in the world. She would never forget the quiet love in his eyes that were fathoms deep and filled with promise.

While Anna and Ryan stood hand in hand, a woman watched them from the sand dunes. "Lovely day for a wedding, isn't it?" An old man with a cocker spaniel stood beside her, taking in the charming scene. "Looks like they're having a reception on the village green," he added, looking over his shoulder at an impressive marquee. "Local wedding, I reckon."

"He's not local."

"Well, they're a good-looking couple," he commented cheerfully.

"Yes. They are, aren't they?"

There was a note in her voice he didn't like, and the dog let out a bark.

"Well, I best be getting on," he said, but there was no friendly rejoinder and he moved on across the dunes, leaving the woman to her quiet thoughts.

AUTHOR'S NOTE

Some readers may already be aware that Cragside house is a real place, bought and improved upon by the industrialist William Armstrong (later Lord Armstrong) in the 1800s. Nowadays, it is looked after wonderfully well by the National Trust and, should anybody wish to visit, it is open to the public and you may see for yourself the fabulous scenery and ethereal house nestled among the trees that provided the inspiration for this story. As a child, I remember falling in love with its perfect setting and I hope I have been able to convey its spirit on these pages. For the purposes of the story, the 'Gilbert' family and a number of other fictional staff members provided the list of characters (and suspects!) in a closed community setting. In reality, a large and highly skilled staff is on hand to run the house and grounds, none of whom were used as the basis for any of the characters herein.

The true inspiration for this story came from my own family history. My grandparents both herald from the eastern edge of the city of Newcastle and grew up on the streets I have described. Despite moving to a different part of the city, my late grandfather used to return time and again to the 'Bottom Club' to revisit his roots and his friends, to play the drums and sing songs. Both families were affected by the decline of the shipbuilding industry in years gone by, but it is also fair to say they picked themselves up and adopted a stoical attitude toward the vagaries of life. It is this pride and 'can do' attitude I see time and again when I return to my home region and it is important to mention it here.

LJ ROSS
June 2017

ACKNOWLEDGEMENTS

Cragside is the sixth novel in the DCI Ryan series and, much to my surprise and delight, it became a UK number one bestseller on the Amazon Kindle chart as a "pre-order" even before it was released in July 2017. This is undoubtedly thanks to all those lovely readers who have shown such kindness in supporting my books from the very outset, when I released *Holy Island* and wondered whether a few of my family and friends might like to read it! Now, almost a million people in the UK and around the world have read about DCI Ryan's adventures and I am so grateful to every one of them.

A number of special people have contributed to the making of this book, most importantly my husband, James. He has his own busy career and yet always finds the time to offer encouragement and insight, not to mention emergency bars of chocolate when a tricky scene presents itself. My parents and sister have been unstinting in their love and support, as have all my wonderful friends. I am so grateful to the many book bloggers and beta readers who have invested their time reading my books (too numerous to name here) but special mention must be made of: Neats, Bev, Amanda, Kate, Shell, Noelle, Jo, Joseph, Michelle, Kelly, Nadine, Alexina, Emma, Caroline, David, Craig, Dave, Claire, Fiona, Maxine, Netta, Sarah, Susan, Tina and Victoria who have all given up their valuable time to read my books!

In no particular order, my thanks go to all the team at Cragside House and Gardens, who do such a wonderful job of preserving an important piece of local and national history; Mike, a tour guide whose knowledge of the house and its history was unrivalled; Paul Goom, whose electrical expertise was very helpful; Jon Elek and Millie Hoskins; and, all the team at Amazon KDP whose ground-breaking publishing platform has allowed my books to connect with hundreds of thousands of people.

Finally, a big "thank you" to Michelle Shapiro and Jen Lucas, whose incredibly generous charitable donation to The National Autistic Society entitled them to a character in the book—I hope you enjoy reading about your respective alter-egos!

ABOUT THE AUTHOR

LJ Ross is an international bestselling author, best known for creating atmospheric mystery and thriller novels, including the DCI Ryan series of Northumbrian murder mysteries which have sold over five million copies worldwide.

Her debut, *Holy Island*, was released in January 2015 and reached number one in the UK and Australian charts. Since then, she has released a further eighteen novels, all of which have been top three global bestsellers and fifteen of which have been UK #1 bestsellers. Louise has garnered an army of loyal readers through her storytelling and, thanks to them, several of her books reached the coveted #1 spot whilst only available to pre-order ahead of release.

Louise was born in Northumberland, England. She studied undergraduate and postgraduate Law at King's College, University of London and then abroad in Paris and Florence. She spent much of her working life in London, where she was a lawyer for a number of years until taking the decision to change career and pursue her dream to write. Now, she writes full time and lives with her husband and son in Northumberland. She enjoys reading all manner of books, travelling and spending time with family and friends.

If you enjoyed reading *Cragside*, please consider leaving a review online.

DCI Ryan will return in

DARK SKIES

A DCI RYAN MYSTERY (Book #7)

Beware what lies beneath…

One fateful, starry night, three friends embark on a secret camping trip but only two return home. Thirty years later, the body of a teenage boy rises from the depths of England's biggest reservoir and threatens to expose a killer who has lain dormant…until now.

Detective Chief Inspector Ryan returns from honeymoon to face danger from all sides. In the depths of Kielder Forest, a murderer has escaped justice before and will do anything to protect the secrets of the past. Meanwhile, back at Northumbria CID, an old foe has taken the helm as Superintendent and is determined to destroy Ryan at any cost.

Who will prevail in Ryan's most dangerous case yet?

Murder and mystery are peppered with romance and humour in this fast-paced crime whodunit set amidst the spectacular Northumbrian landscape.

DARK SKIES will be available in all good bookshops in August 2020!

If you like DCI Ryan, why not try the bestselling
Alexander Gregory Thrillers by LJ Ross?

IMPOSTOR

AN ALEXANDER GREGORY THRILLER (Book #1)

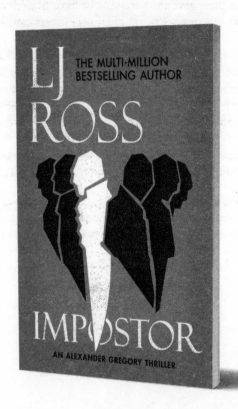

There's a killer inside all of us...

After an elite criminal profiling unit is shut down amidst
a storm of scandal and mismanagement, only one
person emerges unscathed. Forensic psychologist Doctor
Alexander Gregory has a reputation for being able to step
inside the darkest minds to uncover whatever secrets lie
hidden there and, soon enough, he finds himself drawn
into the murky world of murder investigation.

In the beautiful hills of County Mayo, Ireland, a killer is on
the loose. Panic has a stranglehold on its rural community
and the Garda are running out of time. Gregory has
sworn to follow a quiet life but, when the call comes, can
he refuse to help their desperate search for justice?

Murder and mystery are peppered with dark humour in this
fast-paced thriller set amidst the spectacular Irish landscape.

IMPOSTOR is available now in all good bookshops!

LOVE READING?

JOIN THE CLUB...

Join the LJ Ross Book Club to connect with a thriving community of fellow book lovers! To receive a free monthly newsletter with exclusive author interviews and giveaways, sign up at www.ljrossauthor.com or follow the LJ Ross Book Club on social media:

 #LJBookClubTweet

@LJRossAuthor

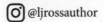 @ljrossauthor